OF VISIONS & SECRETS
TENEBRIS: AN OCCULT ROMANCE, BOOK ONE

KATHRYN ANN KINGSLEY

Copyright © 2022 by Kathryn Ann Kingsley

ASIN: B09VY59XZD

ISBN: 9798824517309

All rights reserved.

No part of this book may be reproduced in any form or by any electronic or mechanical means, including information storage and retrieval systems, without written permission from the author, except for the use of brief quotations in a book review.

This is a work of fiction. Names, characters, places, and incidents either are the product of the author's imagination or are used fictitiously, and any resemblance to locales, events, business establishments, or actual persons—living or dead—is entirely coincidental.

ACKNOWLEDGMENTS

To all my wonderful readers, thank you for inspiring me to keep going. It's your presence, your discourse, and your emails & messages, that fill the tank to keep me going.

(No, not just your tears as has been implied, although those *are* tasty.)

To Lori, my tireless editor, who keeps me on my toes and is always there to cheer me on. It's been three years since our first book series together, and it amazes me how much I've learned and continue to learn. Even if I do fall into word ruts and try to use "little" approximately eighty-three times on a page.

To Kristin, who started the game of "teach Kat to actually write, since she's too stubborn to stop" about fifteen years ago and is still trying to get me to use lay/lie correctly. It'll happen someday; today is not that day.

To my pets, who are just as disruptive as they are helpful.

To my husband, who is just as disruptive as he is helpful.

I couldn't do it without all of you.

A WARNING

Dear wonderful readers,

This series touches on subjects including psychosis, the instability of our realities, and murder. It has a happy ending at the end of the series, but it may be a bumpy ride getting there. All sexual content is consensual.

But as this series is heavily influenced by Lovecraftian styles of horror, I must warn you that there *will* be tentacles. I promise I'll keep it classy.

Y'know. Classy tentacles.

You've been warned.

CHAPTER ONE

Emma would like to have told anyone who had stopped her, as she dangled from the bottom of the rusty iron fire escape, that this was the first time she'd ever broken into someone's home.

She'd like to have said that.

It'd have been a lie.

To be fair, this was all the doorman's fault. If he had just believed her and let her into the building, she wouldn't be stuck outside in the back alley in a cold April drizzle. She kicked her foot, trying to get it up over her head.

It was harder than she thought it'd be.

She kicked again, trying to hook her toe on the bar over her. Swing and a miss. She sighed through the strap of her bag that she held clenched between her teeth. Swing and a miss. She hung there limply for a moment, shutting her eyes.

Emma was having a night. The ride on the streetcar to the hotel had been crowded as everyone was eager to either go home or to one of the jazz clubs in the city, or to crawl into whatever local speakeasy they preferred. She had talked to the doorman hours ago, and when he had turned her down, she knew she had to wait a while until she could try to sneak in.

And so she waited. For hours. Outside. In the rain. Watching the streetcars go by.

This was entirely the doorman's fault. If he hadn't argued with her, everything would be fine! But *no*. Of course not. Blah-blah-blah, "you don't look like a twin," and here she was. The metal dug into her hand, and she shifted her grip only to find the rusty bits were pointy just about everywhere.

She could have pulled down the fire escape ladder and gone up that way, but she was trying to be as quiet as possible. And the sound of that whole thing coming down would be certain to wake up everyone in all the surrounding buildings.

So, here she was.

Dangling.

From a fire escape.

Like a total moron.

This time, she decided to swing, hoping the momentum would help her kick up and over the rung she was hanging from, and allow her to squeeze between the gap in the bars of the railing. That was her hope, anyway. If she failed, she'd probably fall and smash her head on the cobblestones some ten feet beneath her.

No, I'll hit the garbage can I used to jump up here, first. Then *I'll smash my head on the cobblestones.*

What a way to die.

Anyway.

Back, forth, back, forth, back—she kicked as hard as she could. This time, she managed to get her feet onto the bars. It took a lot of wriggling, a lot of squirming, and a lot of muffled swears into the strap in her mouth, but she finally, *finally* got there!

Pulling the bag from her mouth, she let out a puff of air

and looked down at her poor, red palms. They were going to hurt later. But hey, she was lying on her back on the fire escape, and not splattered all over the cobblestones or nursing a broken ankle, so she'd take it.

She was one step closer to finding Elliot. "If you aren't dead, I'm going to murder you," she murmured as she wiped her palms off on her riding pants. She had changed from her far-less-taboo skirt into her trousers in the alley, having absolutely zero desire to deal with the extra fabric wrapping around her face as she tried to flip upside down. The last thing she needed at two in the morning was to get arrested for cross-dressing. Not that she didn't understand the appeal. Truth be told, she much preferred pants to skirts and dresses, but society dictated she wore otherwise. *Stupid men, always getting the rational options.*

It was much easier to get away with wearing pants while she was overseas. Everybody cared less as to whether or not she was adhering to *social norms* when she was riding a camel through the desert or a horse through the jungle.

Stupid men, getting to wear pants.

Oh, well.

Hefting herself up to her feet, she let out a sigh and slung her bag over her shoulder. She only felt a little proud of herself for making it up onto the fire escape. Step one had been to get into the building, so she hadn't even completed that much yet.

Step One—get into the building.

Step Two—break into Elliot's apartment.

Step Three—beat his drugged-up ass halfway to Kingdom Come for disappearing and scaring the shit out of her and the rest of their family.

Step One had proven to be a bit more difficult than anticipated, which gave her little hope for the next phase of the operation. Looking up at the iron fire escape stairs, she pondered her next step. Find someone who had an open window who either wasn't home or was asleep. Hopefully. Maybe. It was a drizzly April night, and although the air was warm-ish, it still had a chill to it that probably meant nobody was sleeping with their window open.

Then she'd have to go to the roof and hope the roof stairs were unlocked.

But she was getting ahead of herself.

She started up the winding scaffolding of the stairs, walking as quietly as possible. It was easy to make noise on the metal structure, and the last thing she wanted was the police to show up and question her.

The first few floors had proven useless. No open windows. She had zero interest in trying to jimmy any of them open or shattering any glass. That was a step too far. Entering was one thing, breaking was another. It was on the sixth floor—of course it had to be the *sixth*—when she finally saw it.

An open window.

Ten feet away from the fire escape.

Shit.

She went all the way up to the last floor, the tenth, to see if she had any other options. No. And no, the roof stairs weren't unlocked.

Double shit.

With a heavy sigh, she shut her eyes and braced herself for what she had to do. She put her hand over her face. "I'm going to murder you, Elliot."

Heading back to the sixth floor, she eyed the open window with wary distrust. No, it wasn't an illusion. It was, in fact, open. The lights were all off inside, hopefully meaning the renters were asleep or not home. The decorative pattern of the brick wall would give her some handholds along the way. There was a ledge that ran to the window from the fire escape. It was deep—probably a foot or more—but it was still *a fucking ledge*.

Looking down the six stories, she let out a small whine. She really, really didn't want to have to do this. But she didn't know as she had a choice.

Taking off her shoes and stockings, she tucked them into her bag and slung it over her shoulder so that it was behind her. She wanted as much grip on the stone as she possibly could. The air was moist, and it left a thin sheen of water on everything. And water meant slippery. Cautiously, she slung a leg over the railing, then the other. She was on the ledge. Next came the harder part—letting go of the railing.

Pressing herself to the wall, she grabbed one of the protruding decorative bricks that was just slightly over her head. Letting out a breath, she used it to swear at her brother, and she began to shuffle along the ledge.

One foot at a time.

Don't look down.

One foot at a time.

Don't look down.

One foot at a—

Her foot slipped on the damp ledge, and she gripped the brick surface as hard as she could. It had only slid an inch, nowhere near the edge of the building, but it still sent her heart racing, pounding in her ears and drowning out the sound of the wind rushing through the alley.

She swore at her brother some more.

Once she could breathe again, she opened her eyes and resumed her sad, slow, pathetic shuffle along the ledge.

One foot at a time.

Don't look down.

This was just like that time in the tropics when she had to cross that rotted-out rope bridge. Totally the same thing.

That had ended great, hadn't it? So this would be great. Everything was *great*.

One foot at a time.

Don't look down.

"I hate you, Elliot."

Finally, after what felt like an eternity, she reached the open window. Suddenly, she realized that the shuffle along the ledge was only half the scary problem. Even though the window was inset, and she could use the jamb to wedge herself there…she still had to wiggle the window all the way open and slip inside.

"I hate you so much." She pressed her shoulder to one side of the jamb, using it as a balance point, and began to carefully lift the window, trying very, *very* hard not to let her weight shift backward.

The mental image of the window popping out in her hands, sending her falling into the alley, played through her head so viscerally that she had to stop for a moment. She pressed her forehead against the top pane of glass and struggled to slow her breathing.

Not now.

Not now.

Please, not now.

The images cleared after a moment, and she could focus again. The window was up high enough that she could squeeze through, but she still had to…lie down, or get her legs in there, or something.

Maybe if she sat or knelt, she could just roll in there?

This was a physics problem she hadn't anticipated. The shuffle on the ledge was supposed to be the challenge, not figuring out how to get *in* the damn window without falling once she had reached it.

Holding on to the window as tightly as she could without risking making her vision a reality, she slowly knelt on the ledge, one knee at a time. Grabbing hold of the bottom of the frame on the inside of the apartment, Emma carefully, very carefully, one inch at a time, slung her legs into the dark abode within.

She slid, far less gracefully than she'd like to admit to anyone who asked, into the room and crumpled quietly to the ground. The fear caught up with her. It surged through her, lighting every nerve of her body on fire. She took a slow, deep breath.

She had done a lot of stupid things in her life. Squeezing into tiny caves, traversing ancient tombs, crossing raging rivers with jagged rocks on rotted-out bridges, sailed through storms, hunted dangerous and wild animals. But that had been up there with the dumbest choices of her life.

So far.

She was only twenty-two, she supposed. Plenty of time to make dumber choices. *Until one kills me.* Poppa had always lectured her about how she needed to stop putting herself in dangerous situations for the thrill of it. And to be fair, this time it hadn't been *just* for the rush and the way it made her body feel electric. She was on a mission this time.

Even if the feeling of the fear leaving her made her shudder. And she was just a little disappointed. But now wasn't the time to debate whether or not she had enjoyed that a little more than she should have.

Namely, because she was sitting on the floor in someone's apartment, having snuck in through an open window. The place was tastefully decorated—actually, lavishly, with all the new trends in furniture and decor. The wallpaper was patterned in geometric, straight lines and shapes, all foiled in shiny metallic silver. It glinted, even in the dim ambient light that came from the city outside. Arnsmouth never was truly dark, even at two in the morning.

Silently, she stood and shuffled out of her riding pants and back into her skirt. Finding a woman standing in their living room in the middle of the night was one thing. Finding a woman who was cross-dressing in the middle of their living room was another. Both would wind up with a telephone call to the police, but one was decidedly weirder than the other. Tugging her stockings back up her legs, she clipped them onto her garters.

She kept her shoes off, however. She wanted to be as quiet as she could. It felt exceedingly stupid, having to re-dress while having illegally entered someone's home, but...standards.

Padding through the apartment, she was glad for their carpets and relatively new constructed floors. Nothing squeaked or creaked as she made her way toward the front door. It didn't seem like anyone was home, but she certainly wasn't going to go peering into the bedrooms to find out.

Reaching the door, she slowly turned the lock. Wincing as it *clicked* open, she waited for a noise from behind her. Nothing. She let out the breath she was holding. They would hopefully just believe they had forgotten to lock the door that night. Opening the door, she peeked out into the hallway.

Empty. The overhead lights were burning dimly in their geometric lighting fixtures. The building wasn't a cheap place to live. She wouldn't expect anything else from Elliot. Looking up and down the hallway once more, she slipped out the door and silently shut it behind her.

Step One—get inside the building. Check.

Putting her shoes back on—just in case she passed someone in the hallway—she set about her next mission.

Step Two—break into Elliot's apartment.

Hopefully, that'd be a lot easier than step one. Straightening her clothes and smoothing out her chin-length, curly hair as best as it *ever* smoothed out, she grinned to herself in triumph as she strode down the hallway, her bag over her shoulder, ready to take on whatever came next.

I'm going to find you, and then I'm going to murder you myself, Elliot Mather.

HE WATCHED as the blood dripped from his knife. In the dim light of the city streets, it glinted in crimson and deep shades of vermillion. But where it didn't shine, the viscous liquid looked almost black in the darkness. And the darkness hungered for it.

The body that had fallen at his feet was already gone. Vanished before it even hit the ground. He hoped it kept his infestation fed...for a little while. The blood on his pocketknife was fascinating to watch as it formed a droplet and fell to the cobblestones whose mortar had just run with the substance. But it was gone now.

Gone without a trace.

With a sigh, he wiped the blade with his handkerchief. The pale cotton fabric turned mottled with blood. He only purchased the cheapest pocket squares that he could find for this exact reason. He went through far too many to keep nice ones.

I suppose I should have some quality ones in reserve.

Now was not the time to debate the merits of keeping silk handkerchiefs for special occasions, yet the errant thought entered his mind, regardless. Once the blade was suitably clean, he flicked it shut and slipped it back into his coat pocket.

Pinching the handkerchief between his pointer and thumb, he held it out in front of him. The darkness at his feet seethed, bubbling and roiling. For within shadows cast by the lamps upon the streets were living things that reached, that wanted, that *hungered.*

An incessant, desperate starvation. Forever left unsated, only tempered.

He grimaced. He despised *them.*

Dropping the handkerchief, he watched it drift to the ground. And the moment it touched the shadow cast by a crate by the wall near him…it was gone.

Consumed.

Turning on his heel, he walked away, pulling the brim of his hat lower over his face. He did not worry about being seen, yet he felt the need to hide all the same. Perhaps because it seemed to him as though the corpse he had created was not the only thing that had been taken, though he could not say precisely what else had been removed. Only that every time he fed the things that hungered in his shadows, a piece of himself disappeared with it.

Pausing at the entrance to the alleyway, he lit the lantern he carried and turned to go back toward his home. The amber light chased away the shadows that writhed around him, though calmer than before.

It didn't matter. They'd return, soon enough. The gaps between the driving need to see them fed were growing shorter and becoming harder to ignore. He kept them at bay as best he could, but the constant urge like a ringing in his head was threatening to drive him insane.

But he could not give in. He could not surrender to their wishes.

For if he did?

His life would be forfeit. And Arnsmouth would be doomed.

CHAPTER TWO

All right, on to Step Two.

Emma looked left, looked right, and ensured that nobody was in the hallway with her. Reaching down the front of her shirt, she stuck her fingers into the edge of her underbust corselette. In a pocket in the fabric she had made, she pulled out what she needed. Her lock-picking tools.

Couldn't hide those anywhere the police might find them.

Putting the thin pick between her teeth for a moment, she slipped the torsion wrench into the slot. Luckily, even though the building was very new and fancy, their cylinder locks on the doors only had a few pins. This was an older style setup and shouldn't take more than a few seconds to pop. Some of the cylinder locks she'd seen were now getting silly, with six or more pins! Really, what was so important that it needed six pins in a spinning cylinder lock to keep out?

Whatever.

She could still pick those. It just took more time.

It was like Poppa always said—*locks only keep out the honest.*

Slipping the pick into the slot, she shut her eyes. It was something that had to be done by feel, and shutting everything else out let her focus on the slight vibrations from the pick. Three pins.

Easy-peasy.

She twisted the cylinder just enough for it to apply pressure, then using the tip of the pick, pushed up the one that was sticking more than its friends. The wrench turned the lock just a little as the offending pin was lifted. Then, the second. Then, the third.

Click.

Lemon-squeezy.

She smiled to herself in triumph as she opened the door and slipped inside, quickly shutting it behind her before re-locking it. Because why not?

As a small upside, Elliot hadn't engaged the deadbolt or thrown the chain. Ugh. Those were the worst to deal with. But her twin was careless with security and safety.

"Why'm I gonna lock my door when I know you can just pick it?"

She smiled to herself. He'd quickly given up on having privacy from her when they were little. She looked at every door and lockbox as a challenge. Pretty soon, Poppa just stopped bothering with them.

She would've stopped in a heartbeat, honestly, if she didn't live for the prideful smile he'd give her each time she managed to sneak into somewhere she wasn't supposed to be. Sure, he tried to play the stern father from time to time, but he failed miserably. No, he took just as much joy in watching her open a locked trunk or learn how to "hotwire" their automobile when he had lost the key to it in a poker game.

"I gambled away the key, not the auto. And keys are only useful if you have the lock it goes to."

The voices of her past played through her head as if they were standing right next to her. Her father, her brother, people living and dead, didn't matter. When she remembered a moment, she could hear their voices as if they were standing beside her.

It'd taken her a long, *long* time to realize that wasn't how other people experienced memories. But it was all right. Her style of memories made her smile and were always a little bit of a source of comfort. Like she wasn't ever *really* alone, if she could recall a conversation with someone she loved.

She turned her attention back to the apartment, shaking her head. This wasn't the time to get stuck in her head. "Elliot?" She frowned when nobody answered. It was a new building, so the lights were all electric. She found the button on the wall and pressed it on, not caring if she woke her brother up from whatever drug-or-alcohol-induced coma he'd put himself in.

"Elliot," she called again, louder than the first time. The apartment she was in was almost a duplicate of the one she had snuck into to get into the building. Geometric wallpaper, pointy, overly modern furniture. It was all trying too hard to be the new form of elegance, in her opinion. Whatever. At least she didn't have to wear bustles or hobble skirts like her mom did. All hail the Suffragettes.

He wasn't in the living room; he wasn't in the bathroom. She was glad she didn't find his corpse moldering away in some corner of the flat. She could smell something rotting, but it wasn't a body.

She knew what that smelled like, and it was something she'd never forget. It wasn't anybody she had known, but still. Not easily dismissed. She wrinkled her nose, the visceral scent coming over her so quickly that she almost retched right then and there. She pushed it away. *Not now, please.* It obediently faded. Rubbing her nose with the back of her hand, she went into the kitchen and found the source of the smell. All of the food in the—*oh, look, he has an electric refrigerator!*

She opened the fridge and wrinkled her nose again. The food was all spoiled, even with the help of the invention's automatic cooling. The contents in the breadbox on the counter were all moldy.

Not being able to help herself, she started throwing out the disgusting and offensive items. She'd scold Elliot for being the slob that he was, but it was clear he hadn't been home in a long time.

It was both a relief and a disappointment. It was a relief that he wasn't rotting away in the apartment. It was a relief that he wasn't drugged out on opium, sitting in a pile of his own filth like last time. But it was a disappointment because she still didn't know where he was or what had happened to him.

With a sigh, she finished filling the trash can with all the rotted food and, hefting it up, walked out of the kitchen toward the front door. She had passed a trash chute on the way to Elliot's apartment, and damn it all if she wasn't going to use it.

Yes, fine, it was two in the morning—three, now—but she wasn't going to sit in her brother's abandoned apartment smelling rotted food.

She disposed of it all as quietly as possible and headed back inside. Good. Now that was done, she could focus on trying to find any clues as to where Elliot might be. She'd ask the front desk if there were any messages left for him, but… the doorman would probably tip them off that she was an interloper. Nope. She was best left to pry on her own.

There were no suitcases and no obvious signs that he had

left in a hurry. Nothing was tipped over or out of place. No signs of violence, or anything being stolen. Heading into his bedroom, she sighed. The bed wasn't made, but that didn't say anything. He had, as far as she was aware, never made a bed once in his life. The fact that their maids growing up always did it for him did nothing to help the pattern.

She pulled the sheets and the quilt up, grumbling under her breath about how much of a slob he was. She tossed the few pieces of abandoned clothing into the hamper and went back to snooping.

Finally, she found his desk, tucked into the corner of the spare bedroom that had clearly just been used for storage. She sat at the chair and stared down at the pile of papers. It was total chaos. She sighed and began sifting through them. Phone bill, electric bill, rent bill, water bill, tuition bill. Each one was marked as *paid on account* or something to that effect.

Poppa paid for everything. He always did, and likely always would. She was in a similar boat, being able to live her life without a job or a worry in the world because Poppa would always have a checkbook out if she needed anything. Or even when she didn't.

She set aside all of the mundane bills or notices and turned them into a tidy little pile on one side of his desk. That gave her some space to look through what was left. A letter to Poppa, asking for him to "smooth over some issues with his marks at University."

Emma rolled her eyes. "You're such an asshole, Elliot." All of the letters to Poppa asking for favors went into another small pile atop the bills but arranged perpendicularly. That left her with another series of letters. She frowned, propping her elbow on the table and looking at them in closer detail.

There was an unopened letter in an envelope marked *return to sender* in tight, efficient script. Whoever her brother had been writing to had no interest in receiving it. It was addressed to one Professor Raphael Saltonstall, 78 Myrtle Street, Arnsmouth. She'd never heard of him before. Ripping the envelope open, she pulled out the letter and unfolded it.

"Dear Professor Saltonstall,

I know you said our last conversation was final, but I have to press you for more details. The organization who is interested in having me join their ranks is adamant that I am perfect for what they're looking for in a new member. They wish to meet me again this week about initiation.

I understand your concerns. I do. But I need your help. I need to understand what they want from me, and you're the only one who has expressed any knowledge of their organization, let alone their intentions.

I need someone to save me from the voices, Professor. It can't go on any longer. Please. And if you won't stop them, the voices say these people will. But I am worried about their Deeper motivations.

Help me. I'm begging you.
Yours in Need,
Elliot Mather"

Emma sighed and shut her eyes. "What the fuck have you gotten yourself into now, El?"

What was with the capitalization on Deeper? It meant something, but she had no clue what. In fact, the whole thing seemed like an amazing clue, if only she had any idea about any of it.

She tucked the letter, including the envelope, into her bag. She knew nothing about Professor Saltonstall, and she knew nothing about whatever so-called organization Elliot was referencing, but she had a lead. And a lead was a victory that made breaking into his apartment worthwhile.

Even if shuffling along the ledge had been an amazing thrill. That had almost been worth it alone.

It was clear from the returned envelope that the professor wasn't interested in talking to Elliot. Marching up to his house and knocking on the door probably wasn't going to get her any answers. No, she'd have to find another way to approach him.

Underneath a list of groceries, she found a small business card, printed on bright red cardstock. It touted the name of an establishment called the "Flesh & Bone." Beneath it, in tidy type, was the phrase "Where everyone is free."

A jazz club, maybe? She turned it over. Written on the back was a woman's first name and a phone number, scrawled in whirly handwriting that definitely was not Elliot's. *Gigi, 0255.* She frowned and tapped the edge of the card on the desk. What was Elliot doing, getting numbers from a woman? They weren't his type, to put it lightly.

But another lead was another lead. She put it into her bag with the letter. She was starting to feel rather good about her prospects of finding her idiot brother. It was very likely that he had wound up falling into some drug den at a club, and he was likely crashing in their back room in lieu of staggering back to his apartment.

That was the most likely scenario, but the letter Elliot had sent the professor worried her. With a long sigh, she shut her eyes for a moment. He had always struggled with the illness that plagued them both. Seeing things that weren't there. Hearing things that didn't exist. Shadow people lurking in the corners of the room, staring at them, whispering about them.

Her voices were linked to her memories, playing out beside her like someone had turned a radio on. But his? His voices...weren't so kind. Constantly telling him to do terrible things, or telling him he was worthless. She'd wake up to find him weeping in the hallway, too hoarse from screaming to even tell them to go away anymore.

It ran in their family, her mother had said. Her sister had suffered the same delusions—the same warped reality—and had spent most of her life in an institution. Suicide had followed. When Emma and Elliot had started displaying the same problems in their early teenage years, her mother had panicked. She had refused to send them to a doctor, and after Emma had learned what they had *done* to her aunt in those asylums, she was very, very glad for it.

So, they had found their own ways to cope.

Elliot had found it in the bottom of a bottle or in opium smoke.

Emma had been far more fortunate.

She had hoped that Elliot was okay, that going to University might help ground him—give him meaning, and purpose, and help drive away the darkness that lingered in his mind. But it seemed that wasn't the case.

Rubbing her hands over her face with another sigh, she went back to the notes on the table. She had more to dig through. It was at the very bottom of the pile that she found something else. Something that ruined every sense of triumph she had earned since she came in through that window. Something that sent a chill coursing down her spine as though someone had dumped ice water down the back of her blouse.

It was a single piece of paper, white parchment, with nothing unique to it.

Nothing, except the shape drawn on the top of the paper. It was geometric in nature. All straight lines, intersecting with each other. One line bisected a triangle, which sat within a square, which sat within a pentagon, which sat within a hexagon. But that wasn't the worrying thing. She would have just assumed her brother was taking a class in geometry.

It was drawn in what she was certain was dried blood. It had ceased to be red, and now was a rusty shade of orange-brown.

And beneath it, in Elliot's hand, drawn as if with the tip of a bloody finger, was a single phrase. *"Momma, help me."* Their mother was dead.

She put the paper down and shut her eyes tight, trying to force away everything that rushed over her all at once. The weeping of the maids was so loud it was as though it were right next to her, and she was back standing in the hallway of their home, watching her father step out of the room, his face drawn in grief, his eyes red and bloodshot.

Illness ran in her mother's family. Some mental, some physical. And it was the latter that had taken her from them a few years ago. It made her eyes sting with tears. The wound was still fresh, even if it was relatively old. She remembered running into Poppa's arms and holding him for as long as she could as he wept onto her shoulder.

Taking in a slow, wavering breath, she forced the memory away. She folded up the bloodstained note and, with a trembling hand, slipped it into her bag with the rest. She looked up and cringed as she saw someone standing in the corner of the room. Someone who wasn't there. They were staring at her, and she could feel their gaze burning into her.

"Stop it, please."

They remained.

She took another deep breath and, shutting her eyes again, placed her palms on her legs and focused on herself. On where she was. On what the chair felt like below her. The air in the room around her was warm, and just a little humid. She could hear the early morning streetcar trundle by as the very first people began to get up and go to work before everyone else.

She was here, she was now, she was all right. "Please, not now. I'm very tired, and you're not helping me right now. Please come back later." Opening her eyes, she looked over to the corner of the room. The person was gone. She smiled. "Thank you."

Being polite seemed to work for her, so she never really argued with the idea. Standing, she rubbed her hand over her eyes again. She was actually exhausted; that much was true. The idea of walking back to her hotel made her want to yack. And Elliot certainly wouldn't mind if she crashed here for the night—one, he wasn't using it, and two, he'd slept on her sofa or spare bed more times than she could count. She headed back to his bedroom and slung her bag onto the foot of the bed.

Stripping down to her underwear, she left her bloomers and brassiere on, but ditched her stockings and corselette. The bones were bendy and hardly like the steel ones her mother used to wear, but she still didn't need them digging into her sides while she slept. She flopped down on the comforter, pulling up a blanket over her. She'd sleep *on* Elliot's bed, but she wasn't going to sleep *in* it.

She knew his lifestyle.

She just hoped she didn't get fleas.

Tomorrow, I'll come up with a plan.

A plan that would start with finding one Professor Raphael Saltonstall.

CHAPTER THREE

It was amazing where you could go, and what you could do, if you did it with enough determination. She had no business being at Arnsmouth University, but she *looked* like she did, and that was enough for everybody she passed.

"Confidence is the best key you can have."

It was another phrase her Poppa liked to say. And it worked. It really, really did.

She playfully blamed him for all the nonsense in her life, not that she didn't enjoy it. And not like he didn't encourage it. Well…within limits. He asked her a while back to keep her "domestic mischief" to a minimum since he did have a reputation to uphold, after all.

Dr. Eustis Mather had a great deal of wealth and influence to wield, but he did ask her kindly to keep herself out of the papers, and away from the prying eyes of the Investigators or the police.

Elliot was a big enough headache for both of them.

It was funny, how it went when you had a troubled sibling. She could get away with anything, as long as she wasn't as problematic as Elliot. He was always getting arrested for drugs, alcohol, and…well, his choice in romantic relationships. Poppa's money and influence always kept him out of the papers, always got him out of the slammer fast enough that nobody knew who he was. And it always lined the pockets of the police who had done the arrest to ensure their silence.

Poppa loved Elliot, just as much as he loved her. But oh, Elliot was such a pain in the *ass*. To Poppa's credit, he only ever wanted Elliot to stop with the drugs and the alcohol—or so much of both—and never once mentioned the fact that Elliot preferred men over women. There were places in the world where such relationships weren't frowned upon. Her father was nothing if not worldly.

You would love the eastern tropics, if you'd ever get on a boat with us. She spoke to Elliot in her mind, as she couldn't talk to him in person. Yet. Once she was done kicking his ribs sore, and screaming at him for terrifying the whole family, she'd finally drag him up the gangway and take him away from Arnsmouth.

Elliot had no desire to travel or see the world, preferring to sit at home and read or go out and party. And, though he'd never said it, Emma was convinced he was afraid of the ocean.

Problematic, that, when there was a boat involved.

Although the last thing she wanted was to misplace Elliot in some opium den somewhere, so maybe it was for the best. Her brother was a good man. A fiercely loyal friend. He just had…darkness. And who didn't have shadows that followed them around? *It's just more literal for some of us, that's all.*

She hugged the stack of books to her chest as she held her head high and walked down the brick walkway of Arnsmouth University. It was a theological school, paid for and owned by the Church of the Benevolent God. They had snuffed and ruffled their feathers about admitting women about twenty years ago, and had threatened to create a female "annex" to their institution, but had finally been won over with the promise of new converts and, more importantly, their family connections and money. They ensured that was the case when they locked any women out from receiving grants or loans.

She wrinkled her nose. Both at the so-called Church that ran the place, and the sexism involved. But old white men were, well, old white men. And they ran the world for the moment. She shouldn't be too judgmental. Her old white father was the reason she got to live the life she led. And the other men in his adventurer's lodge who accepted her into their fold like a son were all...well-meaning. Mostly. She was the exception, not the rule. And the fact that there was a rule at all was her problem.

But she supposed it was one step at a time in the right direction.

After waking up in Elliot's apartment late in the morning, she had searched for his books and notes from his classes. It was pretty easy to find, as he had left it all in his satchel by his coffee table. It didn't look like he had opened a single one of his textbooks, which also wasn't a surprise. Money could buy you everything—including passing grades. Not *good* grades, mind you. Elliot wasn't going to make the honor roll by any stretch of the imagination, if the grade reports she had seen on his desk were any indication. But passing.

All except one.

"Advanced Theoretical Theology" with Professor Raphael Saltonstall. Elliot was failing it spectacularly, which Emma found deeply entertaining, as "Theoretical Theology" sounded entirely made up. What did that even *mean*, anyway? It was clear Elliot didn't know, either. But it gave her a second clue as to what was going on with her twin.

He's failing the class. Poppa can't buy out whatever ancient, withered, old coot is teaching it, probably because the geezer is clinging to how "noble" his profession is. So, Elliot did the next best thing—he blamed his shit grades on his shadows and was trying to play the broken little boy card for sympathy.

She rolled her eyes and sighed, shaking her head. Her heels clicked on the bricks as she walked. The morning was gray and drizzly, continuing the theme from the previous night. But she didn't mind. It was a typical April morning in Arnsmouth. It wasn't literally freezing, so she'd take that as a win. She wore clothing that was both loud yet perfectly suited to a young woman at University. Her skirt reached past her knees, her blouse wasn't revealing, her hair was tucked neatly underneath her finest cloche hat, and her makeup said *I know I look good* without saying *I want you to tell me*.

A few boys stopped to stare at her as she walked by. She smiled and kept going with the amount of confidence a jazz singer would have, stepping out on stage to a packed house. She knew she was pretty. She still fussed in the mirror over every single flaw she had—wishing she was a little skinnier, or a little fuller. Wishing her lips weren't quite the way they were. But that was called being a woman in modern society. Wear this, wear that, look like this, look like that. She tried to shrug it all off as best she could and wear her own body with whatever pride she could muster. Not that it was easy.

But it did feel nice when she caught someone watching her. She would admit that. Being a woman was a double-edged sword—she couldn't hate fashion and reap its benefits at the same time, could she? She didn't want to be a *total* hypocrite.

Idly, she wondered if being a woman made it easier or harder to walk the campus of Arnsmouth University without being questioned by any of the Investigators that were stationed around the campus.

Emma hated the Investigators. She didn't really have much reason to—it wasn't like they ever did anything. They were relics of a bygone age, a reminder of the legends of the city of Arnsmouth, more than anything else. A religious sect who believed they were "fighting the darkness," though as far as she could tell, all they did was just stand there and *stare* at people. They were eerie, with their creepy, pale, unmarked robes and white, featureless masks that obscured their faces.

They were like the police. Only…not.

Servants of the Benevolent God, men and women dedicated to the "purity and safety" of all those within Arnsmouth. Or so they said.

The problem was that the Investigators were everywhere —in every building, on every corner, and always *staring*. Waiting to see something or someone that they suspected was involved in dark magic. The kind of dark magic that had once owned Arnsmouth some three hundred years ago, if anybody actually believed the old wives' tales.

Well, somebody does. They certainly do.

They weren't after the same things as the police. She had seen men kiss in front of them and receive no response. Drunkards, people who were clearly strung out on drugs— she had even seen someone get mugged right in front of one, once. And still the Investigators just *stared*. Watched. And did nothing.

They might just be a silly group of people pretending they were fighting the darkness, but she still got the sense that she was not, under any circumstances, supposed to get in their way. So, when she walked by one standing by a lamppost, seemingly staring at nothing from behind that white, featureless, empty mask, she just held her head high and kept going. Even if something did shiver up her spine as she passed.

She was just a rich girl going to class, nothing out of the ordinary. Nothing suspicious. *I could hide a lot better if I knew what I was hiding from, but it's fine. I'll manage. I've stuck out worse in my life.* Like the time she and Poppa "rescued" that golden statue from the marketplace in that desert city they had wound up in.

They hadn't stolen the statue, they had just liberated it to a museum, that was all. Better it be on display for everybody to see than sitting in someone's private parlor, right? The heist had gone off without a hitch, but oh *boy*, had she stuck out like a sore thumb in that city for a whole lot of reasons. Her gender and the color of her skin had only been the first two, if the most significant.

Fascinating religion there, though. Worshiping gods who had animal heads glued onto human bodies. And that one poor creature that looked like all the leftover animal bits from the other gods, all stitched together. She forgot his name. But he ate the hearts of the damned like a pet dog at a table, begging for scraps. She felt kind of bad for it. She had threatened to hug it, if she ever met it.

Focus, Emma. Focus.

The Investigator she passed seemed to take no notice of her. Good. She was here on a mission—find the silly old man teaching "Advanced Theoretical Theology," and harass him into telling her what he knew about Elliot.

She was very good at talking to silly old men. She had years of practice with it, hanging out in the lodge that her father was a member of. "The Right and Honorable League of Antiquities" found itself embroiled in a lot more excitement than the name would imply.

She'd been granted an "honorary status" with them a few years back, though she couldn't be an *official* member, since she was, well, y'know, a girl. But they all doted on her like a daughter—correction, like a son. She had heard "if only James was more like you" or the like a dozen times in her life, if not more. She didn't mind it. It meant she could ride, drink, shoot, drive, pick locks, and sail to amazing places. A few "if only you were a man" comments a year was worth it to be free.

She knew she lived a good life, shadows and voices notwithstanding. Her family had enough money to ensure she would never have to work a day in her life, and enough influence to keep her from the mental institutions. Her father was training her to be a philanthropist and carry on the family legacy once he was gone. She was going to be Lady Emma Mather someday, a thought that made her snort in laughter every time.

It could be worse. Far, far worse.

Like Elliot.

Her poor brother. She frowned, clutching his stack of books to her chest as though it were him she was hugging instead. While she knew what it was like to hear and see things that weren't there, and to try to cope with living in a reality that was just slightly *off* from everyone else—her voices weren't aggressive. Hers didn't tell her to do things. To hurt herself.

To kill herself.

Please, Elliot...don't be dead. Please don't be dead. She glowered at the pathway ahead of her. *And if you aren't, I'm going to fucking kill you myself.*

The college was beautiful, with its lanes of intersecting pathways through groves of trees and flowers. The world was starting to bloom as it came out of spring, the tulips and daylilies beginning to sprout, their green shoots poking up through the packed winter dirt.

Don't be dead.

She finally reached her destination. She stared up at the imposing building with its enormous, utterly useless columns. She never understood why people decided that buildings had to be so imposing. All the buildings on campus just screamed "look at me, I don't even need my columns to *do* anything, I'm so rich and important."

There was a sign of wealth—superfluous columns.

She sighed. Sometimes she really preferred the simplicity of canvas tents in a desert. The sun, water that tasted a little like the leather skin it came from, and the bleating camels. All the pretense just got on her nerves, sometimes. She could feel the blistering heat on her back as she rode over the dunes, the grit in her teeth from the sandstorm. It was so sudden, it overwhelmed her. Shutting her eyes, she took a moment to process it and let it pass.

Focus, Emma. Focus.

The toll of a bell startled her out of her thoughts, effectively ridding her of the visceral memory. She jumped, nearly dropping all her books. She clutched them tighter to her chest and didn't miss the quiet chuckle of a few of the other students as they walked past. It was the toll of the hour, and the signal that the classes were now switching.

She had to hurry. Didn't want to be late, after all. It was her very first time attending a college lecture! Smirking at the silliness of it all, she headed into the building, her shoes clicking on the stone floor. The sound was almost lost in the rabble and chaos of a hundred students pouring into the same vestibule at once, all heading to their next destinations.

Suddenly, she had to laugh, as she realized something. She had no clue where she was going. She grabbed the arm of another student as they walked by her. "Excuse me. I'm looking for Advanced—" She forgot the name of the class for a moment, as it meant absolutely nothing. "Advanced Theoretical Theology. Do you know what room it's in?"

The student stammered, then narrowed his eyes at her, his brow furrowed. "It's almost the end of the semester. You don't know where your class is?"

Emma shrugged. "I fell out a window while trying to rob the central bank and hit my head. Can't remember. Short term memory loss. The doctors say I'll be right as rain in a few weeks. Or maybe that was a year ago." She grinned. "I honestly don't remember."

The student stammered, stared, then with a nervous gesture, pointed down a hallway. "Room 401."

"Thanks, peach!" She went up on her tiptoes and kissed the young man's cheek. She ran off, waving over her shoulder at him. His face was beet red, and he looked for all the world like she had hit him with an automobile.

She laughed. This was going to be fun, one way or the other. Even if it was because she made it that way in the end.

Because there was mischief to be had, and as Poppa liked to say, *"Where there's trouble, there's Emma Mather."*

CHAPTER FOUR

Emma was rather excited to attend her first—and probably only—college lecture. She wasn't stupid by any means, enjoying reading and studying as much as the next person. But she preferred to learn by experience. Why read about foreign lands when she could go see them herself?

Much better to cut out the middleman.

The room was sparsely populated, which made her plan far riskier than she would have liked. The idea was to slip into the crowd, sit near the back, and get her first read on this "Professor Raphael Saltonstall." Once she had him figured out, she could decide how best to approach him and pry what he knew of Elliot out of him.

But with only fifteen people seated in the stands of the lecture hall?

She was going to *stand out*.

Her confidence faltered as she smiled at the students who turned to look at her, all of them wearing the same expression, which simply asked "what the *fuck* are you doing here?" They were almost all young men, save for one girl who was seated near the back row. Emma walked up to her with a smile. "Mind if I join you?"

The girl blinked at her, just as confused as everyone else. "S—sure."

Emma sat down and plopped her stack of books on the long straight desk in front of them. She held out her hand. "Emma."

The other girl took it shyly. She was a pretty thing, with blonde hair hiding under her own hat, and large green eyes. "S—Sasha." It was clear she wasn't used to being spoken to by random strangers.

"Nice to meet you." She smiled as warmly as she could at the mousy young girl. "I'll tell you a secret…" She cupped her hand near her mouth to direct her voice and dropped her volume to a whisper. "I'm not really in this class. Do you think anybody noticed? I don't think anybody noticed."

Sasha giggled, covering her own mouth with both her hands to stifle the noise. Emma grinned in victory at having made the other girl laugh. Sasha scooted a little closer to her and ducked her head. "What *are* you doing here? Professor Saltonstall is going to be mad."

"I rightly don't care what some old man thinks, to be blunt." Emma shrugged. "And I'm here because of my brother. You wouldn't happen to know Elliot Mather, would you? He was in this class, though…knowing him, he probably never showed up to a lecture. Elliot looks kind of like me. He's gone and misplaced himself, and I'm trying to find him."

Sasha thought about it for a moment, then shook her head. "Sorry."

Emma sighed. "It's all right." She settled back on the bench and picked up one of the books in front of her. She hadn't actually opened it. It was a hardcover copy of a book titled *The Complete Categorizations of Religious Theorems, Second Edition*. By, of course, Professor Raphael Saltonstall.

The *complete* categorization? She scoffed and rolled her eyes. Oh, she couldn't wait to meet this pompous asshole. Probably some stuffy, egotistical, eighty-year-old, I-Know-Everything-Because-I-Said-So type. Old white men had a way of carrying themselves that seemed to always demand respect just because of who and what they were. Add *Academic* on top of that, and it could be positively infuriating. She was going to have a grand old time bickering with some ancient, grizzled, bent-backed—

The door opened. Everyone sat up straight as a man entered the room. He wore a houndstooth suit and carried a mug of what looked like coffee, though it was four in the afternoon. He walked to the desk in front of the blackboard with the exact kind of confidence she had wielded when she had walked in.

The kind of easy familiarity and determination of someone who had every right to be right where they were.

Is that the professor?

And Emma's mouth fell open.

It can't be. No. Gotta be his assistant.

The man who walked in was not grizzled, bent-backed, and gnarled with age and self-importance. Oh, his expression was stern enough. But it was etched on features that looked sharp enough to cut glass. He couldn't be much older than thirty. The hair that was parted and swept back from his face wasn't gray, but so dark it was nearly black. He wore a pair of thin-framed eyeglasses that flashed in the daylight streaming in through the windows on one wall.

He was, without a shadow of a doubt...absolutely gorgeous.

"Is that—" she whispered to Sasha. "Is that Saltonstall?"

"Uh-huh." The young woman shifted and pulled a notebook out from her stack of books and papers.

When Emma glanced at her, she noticed that a slight pink

color stained Sasha's cheeks. Oh. Yes, she could understand that reaction. She could understand that reaction entirely. She might be sharing it, actually. Her own cheeks felt a little warmer than usual. She couldn't help but stare at him.

"Just enjoy the view, trust me," Sasha murmured to her. "He's not...very friendly."

Emma tilted her head thoughtfully as she watched the man as he arranged his papers meticulously on the table before him, barely even casting a glance up at the students who were waiting for him to speak. Sasha was right—he did look quite intense.

She pondered what he was so angry about. *Unless he always wanders around glaring at everything. It does suit him, though, doesn't it?* Speaking of suiting, she found her mouth watering a little at the sight of him. He was tall, his shoulders broad, and he was perfectly trim. There was a smoothness to his movements that was captivating to watch, and she wondered if he had muscles beneath the layers of fabric he wore.

She leaned toward Sasha and whispered, "He's awfully young for a professor."

"Graduated with honors from an ivy league when he was sixteen," she whispered back. "He's been teaching here for almost a decade. They say he's a genius."

"Well, lah-tee-dah."

Sasha giggled, a little louder than she should have, and that finally made the professor's head lift. Emma froze.

Intense was right.

Even from across the room and down a flight of stairs, dark eyes behind thin glasses pinned her right to the spot. She felt as though the man was somehow managing to look *through* her.

One eyebrow arched in incredulous annoyance. "The window for auditing is over." Professor Saltonstall's voice was deep, carrying easily without trying. She shivered at the sound of it and fought the urge to shrink back against the wooden bench. He might be young, but he had all the sense of authority she would have expected from someone in his position.

She swallowed. "I'm not auditing."

"Then leave." He turned his attention back to his papers.

"I'm—" This wasn't how this was supposed to go. She was supposed to sit quietly and listen to the lecture before cornering some doddery old man after the class was over. "I'm writing an article for the Arnsmouth Times."

That earned her another incredulous glare.

She smiled. "Y'know. About geniuses." She paused. "And how underappreciated they are in our society."

His eyes narrowed slightly, but he said nothing. He turned on his heel and headed to the blackboard, picking up a piece of chalk. "The topic for today's discussion is—"

Emma let out a breath and finally let herself relax a little. She smiled at Sasha, who was looking at her as though she were an elephant coming out of the brush at her. She blinked and mouthed *"what?"* to the other young lady.

Sasha shook her head and, picking up her own pencil, began to take notes.

Emma shrugged and, crossing her legs, sat back and folded her arms. She didn't take a single note. It seemed Saltonstall's interest in her had vanished now that he was embroiled in his lecture. She paid halfhearted attention to it, honestly becoming more distracted by simply watching and listening to him more than what he was actually saying.

He was *gorgeous.*

And the way his voice rumbled through the room was doing wonderful things to her. *Maybe Elliot did come to this lecture after all. I don't think I'd be able to stay away.* It was hard to track what the man was talking about, as she was clearly coming in close to the end of a semester with a class that was labeled "advanced." He was talking about the differences between pandeism and panentheism, whatever those were.

The man knew what he was talking about. Or he sounded like he did. And that was half the battle, wasn't it? She certainly didn't know enough to start correcting him on any of it. The way he spoke of it all was with a coldness and an exactness that struck her as odd. It was clear the topic didn't interest him in any way. *Then why teach it? Although I suppose a job's a job.* But something did strike her as curious—he spoke about everything as though it was clearly false, and more of an anthropological study than anything else.

Oh. Right. This was Advanced *Theoretical* Theology. What did she expect? She almost wanted to slap her forehead at how stupid she was. Of course he would have to teach other religions as *theoretical* at Arnsmouth University. There was only one approved religion in Arnsmouth, and practicing anything else would get you arrested. It was something she always thought was rather ridiculous. But laws were laws, and she didn't write any of them. But she practiced no religion, and *that* was apparently fine.

Yet another reason she preferred to explore other countries. The world was just so much bigger than this one dreary coastal city. Honestly, she had spent more of her adult life outside of Arnsmouth than in it. And every time she came back, she was reminded of why.

Professor Saltonstall had moved on to discuss a kind of religion that appeared polytheistic on the surface, but where that wasn't precisely true. Like the far east, where each of the gods was an aspect of one, greater deity.

"Each of the deities performs a necessary duty in those cultures, like the organ of a body performing an important and indelible function that serves to glorify the single, greater deity." He drew a line under the word he had just written, the chalk making a loud *srish* against the blackboard. "Indeed, all theoretical religions could be viewed through this lens with efficacy. It is usually due to the lack of critical intelligence on the part of the practitioner that deems this observation too obtuse to grasp."

Emma chuckled.

Saltonstall turned to stare at her.

She froze. Her laugh must have been louder than she intended it to be. *Whoops.* She smiled faintly and, lifting her hand, wiggled her fingers at him in a slight wave.

"Do you have something to say, Miss…?" Saltonstall lifted his head and straightened his shoulders. Oh, goodness—he really was tall.

"Emma." She sniffed dismissively. "And no. I just found it funny that you were candidly calling everyone else in the entire world idiots, that's all."

Another arch of an eyebrow. He took a moment before he spoke, clearly planning his words. "If you were a legitimate student and had been here for…any of the requirements for this class, or perhaps had attended any class at all"—the room snickered quietly at his jab—"you would understand that when I reference *critical intelligence,* I mean that lens by which one may take to a system of beliefs when one does not practice it."

"So, you're saying that someone who is too close to something misses what they're looking at. Forest for the trees, and all that?" She smirked.

"Precisely."

"Mm. I'm *sure* that's what you're saying, and it has nothing to do with how much of a *genius* you are. I apologize. Do continue." She waved her hand at him dismissively, like her mother used to do to the young maids in the house when they dallied too long.

A muscle in his jaw twitched hard enough that she could

see it from where she was sitting. And if she weren't mistaken, he might be trying to set her on fire with his mind.

She grinned playfully at him. He turned back to the board and picked up where he left off as though she had never interrupted. She did her best to be quiet for the rest of the lecture, now a little too eager to meet him without an audience.

Annoying the serious ones was always a great deal of fun for her, even if she knew it wasn't healthy for her. But there was something so wonderful about watching Saltonstall's neck go a little red at her sarcastic jabs.

When the class ended, everyone picked up their things and left. She stood and gathered her things before walking up to the table where the professor was also preparing to leave. "Excuse me." *Oh, yes. He really is tall. Huh.* She smiled. "Can we talk for a moment?"

"You do not seem to excuse yourself for much, Miss Emma." Saltonstall eyed her with all the friendliness of a cobra. "And is this for your so-called 'article,' or can we dispense with that little imposturous farce of yours?"

"What, I don't look like a reporter to you?" She huffed. Plucking a pencil from her things, she tucked it behind her ear. "How about now?"

He stared at her silently.

"I thought that was funny. Anyway, no. I'm not a reporter." She put Elliot's books down on the table. "I'm here about my brother, Elliot Mather. He's a student of yours, and—"

"I cannot help you." He turned on his heel and began to walk away from her toward the door into the hallway.

"Wait!" She went after him and grabbed his elbow, pulling him back. "Wait, you know some—"

The wall met her back so suddenly it startled her. He had pushed her into the surface, his arm across her collarbone, pinning her there. He hadn't hurt her—it was just so unexpected that it left her just as dazed as if he had clocked her one.

"I. Cannot. Help you." Those dark, nearly-black eyes bored through her. She wondered if he could see into her soul with how fiercely he glared at her. "Do not come here again." For just a split second, his gaze flicked down to her lips. Then he was gone, storming away from her and leaving the room without even a glance over his shoulder.

She had to stay there, leaning against the wall for a moment, as she tried to process what had just happened to her. Her heart was pounding in her ears, and it was nearly deafening. He was—he was weirdly terrifying. There was something about him that reminded her a great deal of the poisonous snakes that had come to mind earlier.

Letting out a wavering breath, she shut her eyes and rested her head against the wall. He was terrifying, and her body had reacted the same way it did every time she was afraid, whether or not it was appropriate. And in this instance, at the heat that was running through her veins from what he'd done, it was clearly in the "not" category.

But one thing was very clear—Professor Raphael Saltonstall knew something. He knew something he wasn't telling her. And that meant she had to figure out what. *Fine. You don't want me to bother you at work again, Saltonstall?*

I'll do my best.

She grinned as she picked up Elliot's books from the table.

But you never said anything about not following you elsewhere.

CHAPTER FIVE

Emma pictured herself as some kind of sleuth—maybe an International Super Spy—as she followed Professor Saltonstall around for the better part of three days. At first, it was kind of fun, lurking about in the shadows and staying far enough away that he wouldn't see her, but close enough to see what he was doing.

At first.

But as she sat on a bench, twenty yards from the door to Saltonstall's office, attempting to read a book as she glanced in the direction of his door every minute or so, she had a realization.

Wow.

This is boring.

Being an International Super Spy wasn't nearly as much fun as she thought it was going to be. Either that, or Saltonstall was the problem. He followed the same routine—leave his house, go to the University, teach, sometimes go back home for the evening, sometimes work late hours in his office. She would stay there to watch him for as long as she could before it grew too late and she had to head back to the hotel.

Arnsmouth was a safe enough city, and she had both a knife and a gun in her purse, and another small switchblade tucked into her shoe—*you can't ever be too careful*—but she didn't want to take any more chances than she needed to.

The only odd thing about Saltonstall—well, besides the fact that he always walked around the city with such a look of furious annoyance that people parted before him like water in front of the bow of a ship—was the lantern he carried after dark. It was electric, and *extremely* bright. The white light clashed sharply with the amber tones of the gas lamps on the street. It might have been used for trains, or maybe mining. She wasn't sure. But she did know it made him very easy to find at night as he walked home along the brick and cobblestone paths back to his house.

It was a very nice house.

It was a five-story brownstone on Marlborough Street, and it looked like he owned the whole place. Huh. He was a young, genius professor, with a good amount of cash to afford something like that. He would flick the lantern off before stepping inside, and seemed intent on running up his electric bill, as she would watch him go through his house turning what seemed to be every single light on in the entire place.

Handsome, angry, rich, genius, *eccentric* professor. Great. She was just loving the continually growing list of adjectives she was collecting for Saltonstall. After three days of following him around the city, that was all she'd managed to do. *Meanwhile, Elliot might be dying in a ditch somewhere.*

After following Saltonstall home that night, then heading back to her hotel, she decided she just couldn't do it anymore. She blamed her concern for Elliot on her decision to quit her new job as International Super Spy, and not her boredom. Tomorrow, she'd confront Saltonstall at his office and corner him with no one else around.

But she did have one more lead she could follow in the meantime. Sitting on the edge of the bed in her hotel, she picked up the business card that read *Flesh & Bone*, with someone named Gigi's phone number drawn on the back. It was risky to go to a sketchy jazz club—that she guaranteed was also a speakeasy—with nobody there to back her up. Although she had absolutely zero problem with breaking the asinine prohibition laws, she didn't exactly want to get arrested on her first week trying to find Elliot.

Although, where there was alcohol, there was probably also her twin. With a sigh, she changed into a more fashionable, nightclub-worthy outfit. She hadn't packed anything with sequins, not having expected needing anything that slinky on a rescue mission, but the little black dress she slipped on would do just fine.

Some louder makeup than usual, her set of long white pearls, and she looked...well, she wasn't going to be the belle of the ball, but she wouldn't look too out of place.

Making sure she had both her knives and her little Deringer pistol tucked away, and she was off to the races.

Arnsmouth was strangely beautiful, even when the weather was dismal. The fog had rolled in from the harbor, casting the whole city in a haze. The light from the streetlamps created misty circles around the flickering gas flames that shone on the damp stone surfaces and budding tree branches.

The rumble of the occasional automobile engine or the ding of the streetcars were most of the noise out in the city that night. But it was a Friday, and she wasn't the only one out on the town. Her room was right in the center of the city by the Square—Poppa had an account at the hotel—so she didn't have far to go on her own.

The Flesh & Bone was north of where she was staying, in the so-called West End of the city. It was honestly the western part of the northern part. The people of Arnsmouth hadn't been terribly consistent in the way they named their city's neighborhoods. Whatever.

She followed the streets until she had to turn off from the main roads and into seedier, darker alleys. Where she was headed was absolutely not a reputable establishment. Honestly, she loved the sketchier places. She just didn't want to wind up stabbed, mugged, raped, or dead. In any particular order or combination.

But, keeping her fingers on the Deringer in her bag, she kept her head high and looked as confident as she could. It honestly made so much difference in life, simply *looking* like one belonged precisely where one was.

The front of the building on Margin Street was nondescript. A laundromat that was closed for the day. But she could hear the faint hum of the sound of people. Following it, she went around the back of the building, down the narrow alleyway. Ah. There it was. The alley was crowded with people, lit in the glow of the electric sign attached to the awning over a door. She felt bad for the neighbors, but it seemed this was mostly an industrial area.

In a bright, glaring font, the sign that illuminated the alley advertised "Flesh & Bone! Dinner $1.50. Nightly performances by: Gigi Gage."

Oh. The mysterious business card was from the starring act. Huh. *What're you doing getting mixed up with a jazz singer, Elliot?* She shook her head. That was precisely what she was here to find out.

The line into the club was long, and she sighed. She didn't want to deal with it. Quietly slipping around the line, she smiled at the offended people as she passed. "My boyfriend's the bouncer. Just going to go say hi."

The man at the door in question was an enormous fellow, with short-cropped red hair and a scowling expression that was quickly turned on her as she stepped up to him, though to the right of the line proper. "I don't make deals." His voice was just as gruff as the rest of him, and thick with an accent.

"Oh, you're from Kinsale!" She beamed. "I loved it there. Beautiful town, beautiful country. Fantastic beer, even if you lot don't seem to believe in carbonation."

He blinked. "You know Kins—how did you know that's where I'm from?"

"That region's accent is very particular." She kept her smile firm as she stuck out her hand. "Emma. Nice to meet you."

The man stared at her, confused. Clearly, he wasn't used to this kind of interaction. Hesitantly, he put his hand in hers. "Conor."

"Pleasure. Goodness, you have a strong grip. I suppose you would, being a bouncer. I bet you're also probably a boxer, though." She turned his hand over to look at his knuckles, noting the callouses. "I expect you do a lot of face-punching at both jobs. Am I right? I bet I'm right."

"You're—" He shook his head. "Fine. But I'm still not letting you past the line."

"Oh, that's fine. I'm not even sure I want to go in." She let go of his hand and leaned against the wall beside him, as if they were best of friends and she was simply there visiting. "I'm only here because I'm trying to find my brother. He's gone missing. I broke into his apartment—"

"You broke in?" Conor shot her an incredulous look. "You don't look the type."

She paused as he let two people into the club as two people came out. "Yeah, I know. Well, I got into the building via the fire escape, after shuffling along a ledge. I don't recommend it." She shuddered dramatically. "I guess I technically broke into two apartments that night. Anyway! My brother is missing, and I found this in his room." She handed Conor the little red business card. "That's all. Although I'm sure the club is fantastic."

Conor took the card, turned it over to see the writing on the back, and let out a long, heavy, tired sigh. He handed it back to her. "Go home, Emma."

Frowning, she tucked it back into her purse. "You know something."

"I know trouble when I see it. Go home."

"But—"

A man stepped out from inside the club. His dark skin was in sharp contrast to his bright white suit with sharp black pinstripes. "Conor."

The bouncer's back went straight at the sound of the other man's voice. "Yeah, boss?"

"Lady G wants to see Miss Mather. Let her in."

Something like the sensation of cold water ran down her spine. She looked at the newcomer, suddenly distinctly nervous. *I never told Conor my last name. Even if this guy was eavesdropping, he'd never have known...unless he knows my father, but I highly doubt that.* "Do I know you?"

The man in the white suit grinned. It was a hungry, almost feral expression. The words that left him were as suggestive as they were dangerous. "Do you want me to? Come in, kitten."

Suddenly, Conor's warning seemed like a piece of very good advice. "No...I...think not." She took a step away from the entrance to the club. "I think I've changed my mind."

The man in the white suit walked toward her, passing in front of Conor. "But your brother might be inside."

Pointedly, she dug in her heels and stood her ground. She wasn't going to be intimidated by him, even if he was very good at being just that. Making sure he was watching, she put her hand inside her purse and grabbed the handle of her pistol, though she didn't withdraw it yet. "The word 'might' means you don't know. And the fact that you don't know means he isn't."

The motion didn't go unnoticed. The man's eyes flicked to her hand then back to her face. He shrugged. "You caught me. But Lady G has spoken to your brother. She might know where he's gone."

"Then I'll call her. Her number is on the back of the card."

The man clicked his tongue. "Shame. Real shame." His lascivious smile returned. "Name's Mykel. Are you sure?" His gaze raked down her body then back up. "We can have a great night. Elliot wasn't too bad, and you look like twice the lover he was."

There was far more information than she needed to know. "I'm flattered, but no." She turned on her heel, and without turning back, lifted her hand in a wave over her shoulder. "Goodnight, Conor. Nice to meet you."

"Y—yeah," came the confused mutter back.

She smiled to herself, although her levity at the poor bouncer's response didn't last long. Her brother had gotten himself mixed up in some serious business. Mykel made her skin crawl. She didn't know what other kind of nonsense was going on at the Flesh & Bone, but she was fairly certain it didn't stop with drugs, alcohol, and homosexuality.

Organized crime was the most likely answer. And that meant her brother might already be dead. With a long, dreary sigh, she started her walk back to the hotel. She decided to cut her trek back in half by ducking through more alleyways and shortcuts.

She walked with nothing but sour thoughts to keep her company.

Right up until the moment something *else* wanted to keep her company.

I should have stayed on the main streets.

It was halfway down an alleyway that she heard something behind her. It was a heavy, wet sound. *Shlorp.* Like a pile of wet clothing smacking into the pavement. Or wet clothes with bricks inside.

She turned, her hand now firmly holding her pistol in her purse. Nothing. She narrowed her eyes, searching the darkness and the shadows for whatever had made the noise.

Shlorp.

The sound came again, closer than before, and she jolted in surprise. The puddle in front of her, some twenty feet away, distorted as though something very large had stepped into it. The rainwater and condensation from the fog shifted away in all directions.

The shape that it made was…a foot. Of sorts. Its toes were long and pointed, and the size of it was far larger than it should have been.

Shlorp.

Another step closer. The thing—whatever it was—however it was invisible, was getting closer. She shut her eyes as tight as she could and took a breath. She tried to center herself. This was just her shadows acting up. A new and fascinating monster had decided to appear in her mind. "Not now, please. Later tonight, when I'm safe in my hotel, please. Then you can come back," she murmured.

Shlorp.

The hallucination was right in front of her now. Judging by the sound of the heavy, wet steps, she could picture it in her mind's eye as having skin sloughing off in bloated sheets, like a corpse her boat crew had pulled out of a jungle river once.

She could smell the rancid flesh. That was where this was coming from. It was just another memory of the buzz of mosquitos and a poor man who had been *mostly* eaten by a school of piranha, only to have the rest float off and be found by their expedition.

Just another memory. Another shadow, brought on by stress and worry. She opened her eyes. "All right, if you want to be a pain in the ass and follow me, I guess I can't stop you." She turned and walked away from it. "You'd be surprised how little I care, though."

Her shadow didn't follow her. There were no more heavy, wet steps approaching. She smiled a little in victory. She always tried being polite first, but dismissive was always a good plan B.

But she did stick to the well-lit, main streets after that. Even if it did take her another ten minutes to get back to her hotel.

Just in case.

CHAPTER SIX

Today, Emma was going to make progress. She could feel it. She gathered up her things in her hotel room, opting to leave Elliot's books behind. She wasn't going to pester Saltonstall during his lectures—she was going to catch him during his office hours instead. He had told her not to come back "here" when he'd been standing in his lecture hall.

He hadn't been specific, after all.

She put on her reddest lipstick, deciding that if she was going to kick his door in and make him listen to her, she wanted to look her best when she did it. She kept her attire a little less sexy than what she had worn the night before, but not by much. Saltonstall was a handsome man. A very, very handsome man. And the rush she had felt after he had slammed her up against the wall lingered with her longer than it should have.

But it had.

And so, she donned her best stockings…with a switchblade tucked into her boot. *Just in case.*

He was a handsome man with the distinct air of danger

around him. That made him both precisely her type, and exactly why she wanted to make sure she had some kind of defense against him.

It was late in the afternoon as she struck across town to reach Arnsmouth University. By her watch, Saltonstall would be finished with his classes just as she arrived, and she could follow him to his office. He'd be there for most of the rest of the night, if his pattern held true.

She hummed to herself as she walked along the brick streets, the lamp lighters just going about their duties of setting the gas flames ablaze. She smiled and wished the ones she saw good evenings as she passed. She received a few tips of scally caps and a polite "miss" or two in reply.

It was terrible, the way people ignored each other on the street. She hated that about city life. Out in other parts of the world, people were much more likely to smile and say hello, or wish each other a nice day or evening. But in Arnsmouth, everyone kept to themselves. In fact, some of the people she would say hello to looked positively startled by the action.

The whole city always seemed to have this...cloud over it. Like there was some kind of pervasive gloom that came with the harbor fog. But it was probably in her head, like most of the rest of her life.

Like clockwork, she smirked as she caught sight of Saltonstall walking from his class, a stack of papers and books under his arm. He wore a long, dark gray peacoat, with the collar popped to keep the pervasive misty April weather off the back of his neck. He struck an imposing figure as he walked through the trees of Arnsmouth University's central greenway. She followed him, some fifty feet behind, as he walked into the smaller, squatter building that was used for administrative purposes and offices.

She snuck in after him, daring to get a little closer as she could duck behind corners within the building. When she watched him pause to pull out the ring of keys for his door, she walked up to him. "Professor, we need to talk."

He flinched as if she had slapped him. The look he gave her as he turned to her could have withered flowers. "Go away, Miss Mather. You have no idea what you're doing."

"I'm not leaving." She lifted her chin in defiance. "We're talking. If you want to call security, I'll just tell them I'm carrying your baby out of wedlock." She smirked. "That would get the attention of a *real* reporter, don't you think? I wonder what the University would say, belonging to the Church and all."

The muscle in his jaw twitched. The look in his dark eyes should have been terrifying. And she supposed, to a certain extent, it was. But it also sent a shiver down her spine that lingered low in her body and turned into something distinctly like excitement. Excitement, and something sinful. She loved it.

He opened the door. Without a word, he stepped inside his office, leaving it ajar.

She followed him and shut it behind her with a click. "Look, I just want some answers. That's all. Then I'll leave you alone, I promise."

"Knowledge is dangerous." He dropped his stack of papers on his desk and turned the lights up as high as they would go. She wondered if he had a hard time seeing in the dark. The sun was just setting, but it wasn't that bad yet. "But I suppose now you will stop following me about like a stray animal." He shrugged out of his peacoat and put it over the back of his chair.

"You knew I was there?" She frowned.

He pulled the thin-framed glasses from his nose and wiped a palm over his face before replacing them. "You have all the stealth of a steam train."

Now she was pouting. "I thought I was doing quite well, actually."

"No."

She sighed. "Well. Whatever." She reached into her purse and pulled out the letter she had found in Elliot's apartment. "My brother sent you this, and you never opened it. He was begging you for help. He's gone missing, and I need to know what's happened to him."

"It would be best for you and all involved if you considered him dead and gone, Miss Mather." He sat down at his desk and picked up his fountain pen, sorting through his papers and setting to writing something as though she weren't still standing there. "I couldn't help him, so he sought out those who could, despite my warnings to the contrary. He is dead to you now. That is all I know. Go away."

Now it was her turn to get angry. "Couldn't help him, or *wouldn't* help him?"

The scratching of his pen paused for a moment. "Wouldn't." The writing resumed. It seemed he could carry on a conversation and keep writing at the same time. But she wasn't going to be so easily dismissed.

Storming up to the desk, she plucked the pen out of his hand. "I saw a symbol on a piece of paper in his apartment." Snatching the piece of paper he was using, despite his grunt of annoyance, she began to draw the symbol right in the middle of his paragraph. "And you need to tell me what it—"

She hadn't made it even two lines into the symbol before he shot up from his chair with such speed it nearly knocked her to the ground.

"Hey!"

He grabbed the piece of paper back from her and, crumpling it into a ball, reached into his pocket and pulled out a lighter. He wasted no time in setting the piece of paper on fire and tossing it into his empty metal trash can.

"What're you—" She didn't get the rest of the words out before he had her by the front of her coat and had her backed up into his desk, nearly sitting her on the surface.

"*Enough.*" He stepped into her, using his considerable height to his advantage. His words were a quiet, seething hiss of anger as he glowered down at her. "You do not know what you are meddling with. These things—these *people* your brother sought to involve himself with are dangerous beyond your comprehension. It is bad enough you risk your own life by hunting him down. But now you risk mine, as well. And anyone else you're foolish enough to involve in this doomed quest of yours."

"I—but—" She knew her eyes must have been saucers. She stammered uselessly, finding that same terror rushing through her at his intensity. But it, like before, simmered low in her stomach, and turned to something else entirely. She was afraid. But that wasn't all. "He's—he's my twin. I—"

"No." His grip on the collar of her coat tightened as he twisted the fabric, pulling her closer to him. He smelled like crisp cologne and aftershave, sharp and woodsy, mixed with something else that she couldn't identify. But his next words jarred her out of her fascination with him. They were dark, and low, and almost a whisper. She could feel his deep voice reverberating through her. "He is not your brother anymore."

"W—what?"

He opened his mouth to reply, when they both jolted in surprise.

Wham, wham, wham! A loud and insistent knock on the door. "Saltonstall."

The professor turned his attention to the door, swore vehemently under his breath, before snapping his head back to her. "Do as I say. Play along, or we're both meant for the noose."

"I—" She didn't get the words out.

He kissed her.

She was glad she was basically sitting on the edge of his desk, because her legs would have gone out from under her. He still had her by the front of her coat, one of his legs between her knees as he tilted his head to deepen the embrace.

She'd been kissed before. Many times. By people from all over the world. But not one of them knocked the wind out of her like this embrace did. She felt lost, one hand pressed to the surface of the desk behind her, and the other against his chest. The kiss was vehement, passionate, and like the rest of him, *intense.*

The door swung open, and he broke the embrace almost instantly, straightening his back and turning to look toward the intruder. "Dean—"

"What're you—" A man stepped inside. He was maybe in his late forties with a physique that had once probably been perfectly average was just starting to slide into a softer one. His beige suit looked like it had a hard time containing his new girth. His beard and his hair were both more gray than not, and he looked at Saltonstall with a tired, annoyed expression. "What're you doing?"

Play along, he said. So play along, she did. She laughed. "What's it look like?"

The Dean—she assumed he was Dean of Saltonstall's college within the university—glanced at her and cringed. "A student, Saltonstall? I can finally have you fired, though I didn't think *this* would be why."

"Joke's on you." She chuckled. "I'm not a student."

The Dean blinked.

With a lift of her chin and a proud smile, she introduced herself. "Emma. Emma Mather. Yes, *that* Mather. I'm here visiting my paramour. Nothing illicit going on here…not legally, anyway."

That seemed to drain some of the blood from the Dean's face. He cleared his throat, and then looked to Saltonstall. "You sounded angry." He wrinkled his nose. "And what's burning?"

She cut the professor off before he could answer. "An explicit love letter I sent him. He was in the middle of lecturing me about why I can't send such things to a religious institution. I was about to reenact the contents of the letter before you barged in." She smiled at the Dean as she slyly, without either man noticing, slid her hand to Saltonstall's belt buckle. She rested her other hand on the professor's shoulder, running her thumb along the fabric in a slow circle, as if the Dean's presence wasn't going to do a damn thing to slow her down. "And who're you, exactly?"

"This is Dean James Toppan," Saltonstall muttered. He looked a little uneasy, but not furious. He straightened his back and loosened his grip on her coat. "He believes I am involved in illicit affairs and has been trying to catch me in the act for three years or more. He clearly hasn't succeeded."

"Yet." Toppan wrinkled his nose and glanced between the two of them. "Haven't succeeded *yet.*"

"Well, no illicit affairs here." Emma laughed. "He's not married, and I'm not a student. Although…I guess we aren't married, so there's that."

"This—" Saltonstall stepped away from her and turned to face the Dean. Both men looked down, and Saltonstall swore, quickly redoing the button to his fly and refastening his undone belt buckle.

Emma grinned in triumph and tried very hard not to laugh.

"I—uh—auh—" Toppan coughed and turned away, his face turning red. "I'm—" He shook his head. "Have a good night, Miss Mather. Take my advice, stay away from this man. For your own good." He walked out of the room with that, heading down the hallway, muttering to himself.

It wasn't until then that Emma noticed the three white-robed Investigators that had been standing in the hall, who now followed the Dean silently. She frowned. Why had *they* been there?

Saltonstall shut the door and rested his palm on the wood surface. He lowered his head. "How did you unfasten my belt buckle?"

"I have a whole lot of skills." She slid from the desk and straightened out her clothes. "I even lifted your wallet while I was at it." When he went to check, she snickered. "Not really. But I could've. I learned to pickpocket from some of the best street urchins in the world."

"Charming." He frowned. "Now…go away."

"After all that, you're just going to send me out the door?" She folded her arms across her chest.

"Yes. You're already in deeper than you know." He shook his head. "Emma." For the first time, something like compassion, or maybe concern, creased his otherwise sharp, exacting expression. "For what it is worth, I tried to save your brother from his fate. And I find myself trying to do the same for you. Now *please,* for both our sakes…go away."

She watched him for a long moment and found herself believing him. "I won't stop trying to find him, whether or not you help me, Saltonstall." She wrinkled her nose. "Can I call you something else, now that we've kissed? Please?"

Something odd crossed his expression. It was dark, but it was otherwise unreadable. She stepped up to him and ran her hand over the lapel of his vest. "I'd like something to moan out tonight that isn't *oh, Professor Raphael Saltonstall.*" She was playing with fire. She knew she was. But that was what she did best.

The color of his neck went just a little bit red. He said

only one word. "Rafe." And without further ado, he opened the door and pointed out into the hallway.

She sighed. "This isn't over."

"I fear you are right."

Pushing up onto her toes, she placed an innocent peck on his cheek and murmured, "The kiss was wonderful, by the way."

The only movement he made was the twitch of the muscle in his jaw. She dropped down from her toes and headed out into the hallway. "See you soon, *Rafe.*"

It wasn't until she got outside into the mist and drizzle that she pulled his wallet out of her coat pocket with a grin and idly began to leaf through it.

She'd see him real soon.

Whether he liked it or not.

CHAPTER SEVEN

Emma decided she should very much learn to not keep cutting through alleyways late at night. It was halfway back to the hotel when it began again.

Shlorp.

She froze. That wet slap of something heavy and thick on the stones behind her. She shut her eyes and took a deep breath. "No. Not now. I'm in the middle of something, thank you."

Shlorp.

She turned toward the sound and squared her shoulders. There was nothing there behind her. Nothing, save the sound of the viscous footsteps. "I will have to give you this much credit, you're far more unique than my shadows usually are." She smiled. "Would you like a name? I've named a whole bunch of my monsters over the years. Momma used to say it helped give me power over them."

Shlorp.

"I've had a Herbert, Charles, Henry, Jacob, Obed, Randolph…" She shrugged. "How about Jim? You sound like a Jim." When the heavy steps stopped, just a few feet away from her, she smiled. "Jim it is, then. Nice to meet you. I'm Emma, though I'm sure you already knew that."

Silence.

She shrugged. "I just have a few ground rules. You can follow me about all you like, but please don't interrupt me when I'm sleeping. I don't sleep well generally, as you can imagine. Otherwise, you're free to do what you like. I understand that you want to be seen and heard, and that you're trying to tell me something. And that's okay. I validate your existence, even if you aren't real to anyone else." She recited a speech she had given her shadows a thousand times. "You're real to me."

Something moved in front of her. She could feel its breath wash over her, huge and hot like an elephant. A thick, heavy *creeeaaaak* filled the air around her, like wood. No… like bone.

Then, the sound of twisting metal. Of iron being bent and warped. She knew the sound from the time their steamship had run aground on some rocks. But it was the fire escapes attached to the buildings on either side. The bars twisted, as if being gripped by enormous, invisible hands.

Her breath caught in her chest. Her heart might have stopped beating. She took a staggering step back from the thing in front of her. *It isn't real. It isn't real. It's just an illusion. A trick of the mind. Those bars haven't changed. I'm just seeing things. It's okay.* She shut her eyes. *It isn't trying to hurt me.*

The sound of heavy breathing was close to her now. The stinking, rancid breath of something that smelled like a rotting corpse hovered near her. She could have sworn her hair moved with its exhales.

"You aren't real. You aren't. And that's all right. I'm all right." But her voice wavered more than she'd like. She was holding on to her purse just a little too tightly. And before she even realized it, she was holding her gun, though it was still tucked away. "I'm all right."

Something touched her cheek. Something thin, and pointed, and sharp. It felt like a knife. But in her mind's eye, she imagined it as the tip of a jagged, inhuman fingerbone. Like a scratch from a cat, it burned.

Now she was shaking. Positively trembling. She opened her eyes. "That's enough, Jim."

Nothing was there. Nothing that she could see. *Nothing that was real.*

There was no more rank breath washing over her. The fire escape railings were still bent, but she honestly couldn't have promised anyone that they hadn't been that way before she got there.

Her cheek burned. But maybe she had just caught herself with her fingernail without realizing it. Or had scraped against something on her walk.

The problem with having a broken reality was...well, she had a broken reality. She couldn't put her hand over her heart and promise anything that she had ever seen her life had actually been the way she had seen it.

Had Rafe actually kissed her?

Was she actually standing here in an alleyway?

Did she even exist? Or was she just some poor urchin, locked away in an insane asylum, suffering whatever "treatment" was in vogue that day? Was she submerged halfway into a tub of water? Were leeches covering her entire body?

She never could be certain.

"Nobody can ever be certain." The words of her momma sounded like they came from right beside her, and Emma wrapped her arms around herself, mimicking the hug she wished she was receiving instead. It was easy to imagine her mother was right there with her. *"The things you see are just as*

real to you as anything is to me. It's just different. It isn't wrong. You are you. Everything else is subjective."

Emma let out a wavering breath. Everything else was subjective. And everything was a double-edged sword. She could hear the voices of the people she loved in her darkest moments, even if it was because she was being terrorized by a creature from her imagination.

Pros and cons. To everything. Always.

"Okay, Jim. That was fun. We'll talk again later, all right?" She smiled at nothing. As she turned to leave the alleyway, she heard a creak from behind her. Like the sound of old bones, shifting.

She decided not to look back.

THE NEXT MORNING, she felt as though she'd been hit by a streetcar, and she wasn't even sure why. She hadn't drunk anything; she hadn't been out late. But she felt almost worse than when she had gone to bed. Emma opted to stay horizontal for another hour or two, just lazing about beneath the comforter.

She knew she was spoiled.

She knew.

Sometimes, she did feel guilty about it. Being able to lie about for as long as she liked, never having to work a damn day in her life. She wasn't blind to the lives of others. And she helped people whenever she was given an opportunity to do so. But what else was she supposed to do? Live the life of a monk?

Do as the Church of the Benevolent God asked Poppa to do every year, and give literally *all* his wealth and property to them? No, it made no sense. Her father was prone to donating money to worthy groups and causes. Hopefully, that was enough in the end.

She jolted as the phone in the other room of the hotel suite rang. She furrowed her brow. *Who would be calling her? Maybe it's Elliot.*

That spurred her out of bed and had her half-racing to the phone, entirely naked, which was how she preferred to sleep if she wasn't in the presence of an expedition team. It wasn't like anyone could see into her window on the tenth floor. Scooping up the phone, she answered it. "Hello?" She expected the front desk.

What she received was a woman, the voice sultry and smooth. "Good morning, strawberry. Afternoon, I suppose. You and I both like to sleep in, I see." She hummed. "And see, I do. Goodness, you are a pretty thing."

Emma whirled about, half expecting to see someone lurking in the corner of the room, somehow also on a phone. Her hotel room was near the top floor. There wasn't any possible way anybody could—scrambling for the blanket on the sofa, she wrapped herself up in it. "Who are you? How...?"

"Gigi Gage, at your service." The woman chuckled. "As for the rest, don't worry about it."

"I—but—" Emma sat down on the sofa, feeling suddenly very nervous. Even if the woman was on a nearby roof with a spyglass, she wasn't anywhere near any of the windows. It wasn't possible. She broke out in a cold sweat and pulled her legs up under the blanket. "What is happening?"

"A great deal I'm afraid you don't understand. It's all right. I'm not your enemy—in fact, I'm calling to help you. You're looking for your twin, correct? Elliot?" The woman sounded friendly enough. There wasn't any sort of dangerous overtone in her voice. But that didn't mean anything.

"Y—yeah."

"Sweet boy. Sweet, poor, misguided, broken boy." Gigi sighed. "Tell me, do you suffer from the same—what did he call them—shadows? Are you afflicted as well?"

Emma went quiet for a moment. "That really is none of your business."

"That's a yes. Well, from what I can tell, you've wound up far more at peace with your *issues* than your brother. I would love to know more, if you ever want to sit and have a drink or two." Gigi chuckled.

Emma began winding the cord of the phone around in her fingers. "Who are you, and what's happened to my brother?"

"I told you my name, and I own the Flesh & Bone. But that's not what you're asking. And what you're asking, I'm afraid I can't tell you. And it's for your own good, strawberry. Trust me. That's precisely why I'm calling. I have a piece of advice for you."

Emma shut her eyes. "You're going to tell me to give up. That he's as good as dead, and I'm putting myself in danger."

"Why, yes." Gigi laughed. "Let me guess…Raphael?"

"You know him?"

"I know *of* him, and more importantly, I know you've been following him around like a kitten. Not that I blame you. Fetching man, isn't he? Too bad he is so very stern and exacting. Unless you like that kind of thing. I do think you're a bit of a daddy's girl, aren't you?" Her voice dropped to a purr. "I love that."

She shook her head. She didn't know what was happening and couldn't even begin to process half of what Gigi was saying. "I can't give up on Elliot. I can't. I won't just leave him to whatever mess he's gotten himself into."

"It's too late, strawberry. I'm so sorry." To Gigi's credit, she did sound remorseful. "I warned him, but he was like you—too stubborn to listen to advice." She sighed.

"No. He can't be dead. He can't be. I refuse to accept that until—until I see the body myself." She cringed, tears stinging her eyes.

"Oh, he isn't dead. Not properly, not the way you're thinking. If you keep at this, you'll see his body. But if that happens, it'll be too late for you, darling. Far too late. Go home. Go back north to the country and hug your father. Cherish the family you have left and mourn the ones you've lost." Gigi's tone was insistent. "Please, Emma. For your own sake, go home."

Emma shut her eyes and felt the tears stream down her cheeks. "I...can't. I just can't."

Gigi let out another long, heavy sigh. "Come see me tonight. You and I need to talk in person. I have something to show you. Don't worry about Mykel or the others—I'll tell them to leave you alone."

"I can't trust you."

"No, you most certainly cannot." Gigi laughed. "You can't trust anyone, Emma, darling! Most assuredly not me, and even more so, not the handsome professor. Keep away from him." The woman yawned. "Now, if you'll excuse me, I suppose I should crawl out of bed." She paused. "Oh. One more thing. Stay out of dark alleys."

Emma furrowed her brow. "Are you afraid I'm going to get mugged?"

"No. But the thing that's following you won't come out into direct light." Before Emma could say anything else, or follow up with any questions about how Gigi could have possibly known about what she had thought she had seen, she kept talking. "Ciao, darling! See you tonight."

Click.

Emma sat there, stunned.

Stunned and terrified.

She decided she wasn't going to sleep naked in her hotel

room anymore. Shutting her eyes, she debated her options. She knew she should pack up her things and do exactly as Rafe and Gigi demanded—get on the next train north to the country and go back to Poppa's estate on the coast. She knew what she was doing was dangerous. Elliot had found himself embroiled in some sort of drama with organized crime; she was sure of it now. But the strangeness with Gigi sent shivers up her spine. The things the woman had said that she couldn't have known—the bizarre statements about her brother not being dead, but being gone.

I need answers.
And I need them now.
She knew who had them. And she had his damn wallet.

EMMA SAT at the little metal table outside the coffee shop and waited. She knew his patterns, after unsuccessfully sneaking around after the professor for almost four days. *I thought I made a great spy.* She frowned into her drink and pouted. *Stupid Saltonstall. Stupid Elliot. Stupid everybody.*

She looked up as she saw him walking up the street on his way to his lecture. He always left hours early, preferring to spend some time in his office before teaching. When he got close enough to the cafe, she called out to him. "Afternoon, Rafe."

His steps hitched, and his look of surprise was almost instantly overcome with one of annoyance. He sighed, shut his eyes, and clearly took a moment.

Emma snickered. "Would you like something to drink? A scone, maybe?" She picked up his wallet from the table where she had put it. "You might as well, you're paying for it." The way he glared at her only made her smile. Well, it did something *else* to her as well, but she pushed those thoughts away for the time being.

The memory of their kiss made that a very difficult thing to do.

Clearly giving up, Rafe approached the little metal patio table and, pulling out the other chair with a scrape along the bricks, sat down.

"I'm kidding, by the way. About paying for the coffee." She softened her smile. "I like to joke around."

"I can tell." He reached for his wallet, and she let him take it back. For a moment, she wondered if he was going to stand up and leave again. It looked as though he was considering it. He watched her, dark eyes boring into her as if he were trying to unravel her just by staring at her. But with a sigh, he sat back against the chair. Whatever he just decided, she didn't know what it was. But it meant she had a chance to get more information out of him. "Miss Mather, this has to stop."

"Emma. Please. We've kissed, after all." She smirked. "And it was a very nice one, so you may call me Emma."

The muscle in his jaw twitched, and if she weren't mistaken, his neck went just a little red for a moment. "Your brother is gone."

"So I've been told. By you, and now Gigi Gage." Emma grimaced at the memory of the call.

Rafe's eyes went a little wide. "You spoke to her?"

"She called me."

"*Damn* it." He cringed and turned his gaze down the street. "What did she say?"

"Exactly the same malarky you've told me. Elliot is gone. Go home. Although she did say that he wasn't…dead. Not exactly. But I don't know what that *means*." Tears stung her eyes again, and she held them back, even if she had to bounce her leg a little and fidget to do so. "I—" She paused as the waiter came up, took Rafe's order of coffee, and then walked away. It meant he was going to stick around for a few minutes, at any rate. "Elliot is my twin. We've always been there for each other. Always. In the darkest hours, when we—when we were so scared of the things we saw—" She broke off.

"You share the disease." It was a statement, not a question.

She nodded. "The shadows that follow us. The voices. Mine are just…different. They aren't as bad." *Correction, they weren't as bad. After what I saw last night, they might be getting worse.* "I…had more opportunities to learn about what I see, and how to better cope with them. It's a long story." She shook her head. "But when we were little, we had each other. And I won't let him get lost into whatever organized crime ring nonsense he's gotten himself into."

Rafe frowned. "It isn't organized crime." He said it as though it were meant to be a comfort. It wasn't. "It's worse than that."

"Then what is it?" She hated how desperate she sounded. How small and little she felt all of a sudden. "Please, Rafe. *Please.* Whatever you're trying to scare me away from, it won't work. I need your help."

Regret, or perhaps remorse, passed over his sharp features. "Your brother asked me to help him, and I said no."

"And now he's gone."

That made him wince. "I am trying to help you. To help him. What this is—what he became involved in—is dangerous. And if you don't leave now, you might suffer the same fate."

"Which is *what?* That's what I want to know. You tell me to run away from some terrible thing, but you won't tell me what it is!" She shifted closer in her chair. "Whatever that symbol was on that piece of paper scared you, and—"

"It didn't scare me." He seemed very annoyed at the notion. "But you cannot come around my office waving those things around, Emma. I have no desire to be hanged. And neither should you."

"What do you mean, hanged? Over a symbol? What is going on?" She wanted to punch him in the face. She hated these half-answers and non-statements. "If you won't tell me, Gigi will. Or perhaps the Investigators I saw last night."

Rafe sighed, heavy and drawn out, and he bowed his head. "You will not stop, will you?"

"No."

"Very well." He paused and lowered his voice. "Your brother became involved with a group with a particular set of beliefs that he felt could save him from the voices that plagued him his entire life. A very dangerous set of beliefs."

A group with a particular set of dangerous beliefs.

She groaned. "Oh, Elliot." She slapped her hand over her eyes. It was worse than organized crime; Rafe was right. It was organized religion.

Emma leaned over the table toward the professor. "He joined a *cult?*"

CHAPTER EIGHT

With every ounce of her being, Emma wanted to reach across the table and slap the man across the face and tell him that the Dark Societies of Arnsmouth hadn't existed for over three hundred years, if they ever existed at all.

Was *he* insane? No. There was no possible way that her brother had fallen into—who was she kidding. Yes, there was. There absolutely was.

Even though it was all just a legend and a story to tell people to scare them into joining the Church. That *darkness* lurked in Arnsmouth that must always be defended against. It was a load of absolute bullshit.

Elliot would start worshiping a stuffed turkey with a lightbulb shoved in its mouth if it meant he was saved from the voices and the shadows that haunted him. If there was a pack of people in the city who had started pretending they were one of the Dark Societies...there was a real good chance Elliot would join them.

But there was something else that made her believe the man across from her about where her brother had ended up

—something that didn't have anything at all to do with her brother's mishaps and idiotic choices. Because she would have thought that with that single word, "cult," she'd fired a bullet straight at the professor's head.

His reaction was instantaneous and violent. Emma stifled a squeak as Rafe snatched her wrist with such force that it rattled her cup of coffee on the metal outdoor table and nearly knocked the whole thing over.

"Are you out of your damnable *mind?*" His words were an angry, hissing whisper. There was an edge of panic to his voice, as if she had just popped open the door on an aeroplane in mid-flight.

She most certainly was out of her mind, actually, but that was beside the point. She blinked at him, stunned at his reaction. "Wh—"

"Do you want to get us both hanged?" He yanked her wrist, forcing her to bend closer to him over the table, jostling it again. There was such fury in his features that it took her a second to process everything that was happening.

Her first thought, which was probably not the most important one to have, was that there were people staring at them. Rafe was making a scene. She pressed her wrist to the table like they were arm wrestling, then put her hand over his. She tried to make it look as if they were just two lovers on an early spring date. She smiled sweetly at him, keeping her words low and overly pleasant. "If you don't go easy on your grip, Rafe...I'm going to shove my mug of coffee down your throat. The entire mug. Then the saucer."

His anger faltered for a moment, and he studied her, dark eyes flickering between hers. Her threat didn't exactly have the effect she was looking for. She wanted him to be afraid of her—or to let her go. But instead, he seemed...puzzled. After a moment, he relaxed his grip, but left his hand where it was.

That was fine. She was enjoying his touch just a little

more than she should. Even if it was violent. *Especially because it's violent.* She mentally kicked herself. *Get your mind out of the gutter. We have work to do.*

"Don't say the *magic* word. Got it." She smirked at him. His hand twitched beneath hers, and so did the corner of his eye. She tried not to laugh. He was so easy to annoy, and it was becoming way more fun than it had any right being. But she knew he was right. She should be taking this more seriously. With a sigh, she sat back in her chair, though she let her hand linger atop his. "So, he's mixed up in real trouble, is what you're saying."

"I'm saying your brother is gone, Miss Mather. That you should leave here and go home." Rafe sighed. "And I want you to stay away from the Flesh & Bone. Stay very away from Gigi Gage and all the rest."

She shook her head. "I can't leave until I know where he is. Or—or whatever you all think is left of him." She kept her voice quiet, not wanting to be overheard. "Please, whatever you know, just tell me."

He shook his head. "I honestly have no inkling of where he is."

"But you know what's happened to him."

"Yes."

She shifted closer in her chair. "Tell me."

"No."

She glared at him. It was her turn to tighten her hand atop his. "Rafe."

After a moment, he looked down at where his hand was on her wrist. It seemed he didn't feel any need to separate them. He paused for a long time as he thought, clearly debating something. The muscle in his jaw ticked again before he spoke. "I can't stop you, can I?"

She wasn't sure if she could trust Rafe, any more than she

could trust Gigi. Hell, she *knew* she couldn't. But damn her to smithereens, she couldn't help but be distracted by the sensation of his warm hand beneath hers. How nice he smelled—crisp, and spicy, and minty. How it sent a shiver down her spine when he turned those midnight eyes in her direction and stared *through* her, like she was just another puzzle to be solved.

Or a mystery to be undone.

She really, really wanted to be undone by him. The memory of his kiss threatened to come back to her, before she slammed the door in its proverbial face. Focusing on the moment, and her damn brother, she answered his question. "No. You can't stop me."

Rafe shut his eyes and, dropping his head, let out a breath. When those dark eyes finally lifted back to hers over the rim of his thin-framed brass glasses, his expression had changed. He was still as imperious as before, but perhaps a little less harsh. Or maybe not—maybe there was just something else coloring the edges. Something smoldering that made her shift in her chair. His words were quiet again, deep and rumbling, and that didn't help at all. "How much did Gigi tell you?"

He could be reading her the phone book and she was pretty sure she'd want to crawl under the table and—*Focus, Emma. Focus!* "Nothing. She said to come see her tonight after her show—that she wanted to tell me what was going on." Emma cringed at the memory of her first attempted visit to the Flesh & Bone. "That place gave me the willies. Something wasn't right about it. I went there once already, and I didn't feel safe. I left, despite them inviting me inside. I was pretty sure I wouldn't come back out."

"So, you *do* have a brain in your head. How charming." He smirked.

"Hey." She shot him a look. "That wasn't very nice." But she suspected he was half teasing her and only half actually mocking her, so she let it go. She couldn't hold her glower, and it cracked into a faint smile of her own.

His expression faded back to his more common dour and drastic one. "Do not go see Gigi. Do not seek her out. Do not even talk to her. She's dangerous, as is everyone who works for her."

"Then talk to me and I won't have to." She shook her head. "The only reason I'm tempted is because she, unlike *somebody here*, is willing to tell me what's going on."

Finally, as the waiter appeared with his coffee, Rafe let go of her wrist and sat back. He muttered a thanks to the young man before turning his attention back to her. "Telling you what I know will result in your death."

"Not telling me will get me killed too, apparently." She rolled her eyes. "I'm already dead." She threw up her hands in frustration. "And as you've already figured out, I'm not leaving until I know what's happened to my twin. So you might as well 'fess up, if I'm dead either way."

Rafe's sigh was as though he were an ancient god with the whole world placed atop his shoulders. He took the glasses from his nose and, plucking a handkerchief from his pocket, began to slowly clean them as he clearly measured out his thoughts. "You know where I live."

"Mmhm."

"Meet me at my home tomorrow night." He moved to stand. "We'll discuss your brother over dinner."

"Wait, you're just going to leave without drinking your coffee?" She gestured to the brand-new cup of the hot substance. "Come on. I thought we were on a date."

His quizzical expression was almost comical, and he sat back in his chair. "Excuse me?"

"Well, you kissed me yesterday. Tomorrow, we're going to have dinner at your home. I figured, since we're doing this all out of order, we might as well have our coffee date now." She smiled, leaning her elbow on the table and propping her chin in her hand. "I'd like to spend more time with you, Professor Saltonstall, before you invite me into your abode."

Rafe stared at her, and she would have thought him stunned if it weren't for the dubious but deeply curious expression on his face. As if he saw her open a door and found himself wondering what was behind it. "What is your game, Miss Mather?"

"Game?" She puffed out a breath. "You're accusing *me* of playing games? You, who won't tell me a damn thing without resorting to spying on you—"

"Very poorly."

She narrowed her eyes at the interruption. "—following you about, and then stealing your wallet in order to get you to take me seriously."

"I don't think you want me to take you seriously. I don't think that's ever your goal, if I might presume." He picked up his coffee cup and, blowing on the top of the liquid, took a sip. "I think you want attention."

"I want answers." *And I want you to kiss me again.* He was clearly the dangerous type, with something dark lurking in those fiery midnight eyes. She knew she was attracted to the wrong kind of men, and here she was adding to the list of her mistakes.

Rafe arched a thin, incredulous eyebrow.

She smiled. "I mean, I wouldn't say *no* to attention. You are quite the kisser."

The flinch on his face was almost imperceivable. "It was under duress."

"Oh, so you're saying you're even better when you're not?

Or does the idea of getting caught flip your switches?" She grinned. "I won't judge. It was kind of exhilarating."

His neck turned just a little red. She couldn't tell if that was him blushing or getting angrier, or both, and she honestly didn't care what combination it was. It was a victory for her all the same. He sighed. "Miss Mather."

"What? Does a woman stating that she enjoyed your amorous embrace make you uncomfortable? It's a new modern era, you know. We can vote now. We can even *drive.*" She picked up her own coffee and sipped it, though it was probably far colder than his. It was still perfectly tasty.

"I am aware. And while I have no problem supporting women's rights at all turns—"

"Good."

It was his turn to look annoyed at the interruption. "—your attempt to procure my 'attention' is not in your best interest. Your insistence in trying to pry answers from me is deadly enough. I highly recommend taking it no farther than that."

"Noted." *And promptly ignored.* "Tell me one thing, Professor, before you go, since now that I think about it, I believe you're about to be late for your first class today if I'm not mistaken." She grinned as his expression darkened somehow even more. Yeah, she might have spied on him poorly. But she knew his routine now, and that seemed to bother him. She rested her arms on the table and leaned forward as far as she could go. She beckoned him in with a crook of her finger.

He leaned into her after a moment's hesitation. She tilted her head toward his ear, as if she were going to whisper to him, before, with a mischievous smile, she pressed her lips to his, kissing him.

She expected him to recoil in surprise. She expected him to scold her for being outrageous.

That was not even close to what Professor Saltonstall did.

Not at all.

RAFE WAS NOT certain of what to make of Miss Mather. Her impish smile, her dark curly hair that reached her chin, and the way her lithe body had felt against his when he had pressed her up against his desk...

She was beautiful. Feisty, fiery, and *alive.* Very different from the moldering stacks of ancient books and bits of paper that he spent his days with. Very different from the mumbling, frightened children he taught or his pompous, highfalutin, ignorant colleagues.

There was intelligence that flashed in those amber eyes. A wicked kind of cunning that he was deeply relieved she seemed to employ entirely toward her childish pranks and roguery. She was perceptive. But she was also a fool, scratching at the surface of things that she should know better than to tamper with. She should listen to the warnings of others. And yet, there she was, sitting before him. The little devil was taunting him.

Tempting him.

His body reacted to her nearness each time she came close. It had been a long time since he had been with a woman, though that was not by choice. It was simply because he did not wish to watch what would happen to them before or after the fact.

But if she wished to die...so be it. He had done his due diligence. He had warned her to the extent to which he was capable. Now, he would not stop her from reaping the *rewards* of her idiotic behavior.

Especially if it rewarded him, as well.

As she had just said, she would be dead either way. Why not let them both enjoy the moment?

He slipped a hand into her hair, tightening it into a fist, as he pulled her deeper into the kiss she had intended to mischievously steal. The people around them at the cafe, and those passing them on the street, would stare at the incredibly inappropriate display they were making.

He paid them no mind. If there were rumors of his salacious behavior, it would only do him a small favor. He wouldn't turn down any opportunity to hide his...other interests. And if he could convince the Investigators and the University that he was, in fact, simply illicitly involved with the imp in front of him, it might deflect some of their curiosity. For a time. It would explain her appearance in his life and deter some of the Dean's wonderings as to why she was in his office and following him about like a lost dog.

Besides...

She tasted divine, like honey and exotic spices, with just a tinge of the coffee she had been drinking. There was a pragmatic reason behind his paying *attention* to the young woman. There was also now a personal one, as brief as it might be. This little diversion would not last for long. One night would be all they had, before the Things came from the dark to take her. Like they did all the rest.

But it would be a glorious night; he could tell that already. The image danced in his mind of her writhing beneath him, crying out his name in pleasure, before it turned to screams of terror. What did it say about him that both moments sent the same thrill through him?

Nothing I do not already know.

He broke away from the kiss and stood from the table. Gathering his things—and his wallet—he looked down at the young woman. Emma was watching him, eyes the size of saucers, in complete shock.

Good. Finally, he had shut her up. *Two can play this game, Miss Mather.* "I will see you tomorrow night. Seven." Turning, he left without another word.

By midnight tomorrow, Emma Mather would no longer be a concern.

By midnight tomorrow, she would no longer exist at all.

CHAPTER NINE

What am I doing with my life?

That was the question Emma couldn't help but ask herself as she walked back to her hotel, in rather a bit of a daze. She couldn't help but dwell on what had just happened. If the first kiss with Rafe had been intense, she had no words to describe the second one. She touched her fingertips to her lips as she walked.

There was something about the way he stared at her. The way his gaze cut through her. But she couldn't deny that when he snatched her hair in his fist that it hadn't done primal things to her. She was looking forward to their dinner tomorrow night. Greatly looking forward to it. She smiled to herself as she headed along the brick sidewalk, careful not to trip over the portions that had been lifted by tree roots along the way. Just a side effect of living in an old city.

The encounter with Rafe left her excited with anticipation as she finally reached her hotel. But she did have one thing she needed to resolve—Gigi and the Flesh & Bone. She had been invited to the club tonight. Rafe had told her specifically to stay away, and a large part of Emma wanted to listen, knowing it was the right decision.

But Gigi had information. And while she couldn't trust either party to tell her anything remotely close to the truth, she wasn't sure if she was in the business of picking sides. She had to follow every lead she could get. But she believed Rafe that the Flesh & Bone was dangerous. She had felt it herself.

I'll give Gigi a ring, tell her I can't make it tonight, and see if she'll meet me later in the week. I can always cancel on her then, if Rafe tells me what I need to know. It sounded like a logical plan. A great plan.

Right up until she reached her hotel room. It wasn't until her hand was hovering over the knob that she realized the door was just ever so slightly open. She froze. She had shut and locked the door—she *knew* she had.

Someone had broken in.

Slipping her hand into her purse, she grabbed her gun and pulled it from the small pocketbook. Holding it down at her side—for now—she carefully nudged the door open with her foot. "Hello?"

Silence.

Stepping inside, she kept her back to the door. Her heart pounded in her ears, and she had to force herself to breathe regularly. She'd been in sticky situations before, and she always tried to focus on her breathing every time. It helped slow down moments that seemed to whip by too quickly.

Like this one. Like having her hotel room broken into after learning her brother was probably up to his eyeballs in the Dark Societies of Arnsmouth—or a group pretending they were. And after making out with a *very* sexy professor with serious secrets. Her day was only going from *weird* to *wild*.

It'd be fine. She had a gun. That would keep her safe. She held it aloft as waited by the door. "Hello?"

"Come on in, dear. Stop *lurking* in the hallway. It's rude," a female voice called from her rented living room. The woman laughed. "It is your suite, after all."

She knew the voice. She'd heard it on the phone. She lowered the gun, though she wasn't sure she should. She shut the door behind her with a kick, latching it that time, and took a few more steps into the room.

The most beautiful woman she had ever seen was lying on her sofa, draped out as though it were her own personal smoking lounge. She wore a gossamer dress that flowed around her, all in shades of crimson and golds. Her hair was a perfect shade of blonde, resting around her face in curls, and her makeup was the absolute height of fashion. The smell of smoke tinged the air, and it came from a cigarette holder that dangled from the woman's fingers as she lazily puffed on the ivory.

It seemed she was alone. There weren't any hulking bodyguards that Emma could see. Emma glanced this way and that, just to make sure.

"I'm here by myself, strawberry." The woman chuckled. "I figured I wouldn't need any help."

"Gigi Gage, I take it?" Emma frowned and kept a firm grip on her gun, though it was still lowered.

The woman almost purred as she shifted on the sofa. "The one and only." Crimson lips parted to puff on the ivory cigarette holder again, before lazily letting the cloud of smoke out into the air above her in thin gray wisps.

"Why're you here? In my hotel room?" Emma kept her back to the door, just in case she had to make a quick exit. There wasn't a fire escape this far up the building. If she had to make a secondary exit...it'd be a permanent one. The pros and cons of renting an expensive suite.

She wrinkled her nose. "I'm not a fan of cigarette smoke."

"Oh, my apologies!" Gigi sat up and immediately snuffed the lit object out into the ashtray on the coffee table. Emma idly noted the fact that the ashtray had been in the kitchen, empty and unused. Now, it had a decent amount of ash, collected in the little glass depression.

Gigi had been here for some time. And she was kind enough to find an ashtray to use. And she was generous enough to extinguish her cigarette when asked.

All right...dangerous but *polite.*

Emma kept her position with her back to the door, regardless of how gregarious the beautiful woman seemed to be. "I'll ask my question again. Hello, how can I help you? Why've you broken into my hotel?"

Gigi laughed. It sounded somehow both sultry and innocent at the same time. Emma had no doubt that the woman commanded any room she entered. She was a perfect example of beauty, and a sharp intelligence flickered in her bright green eyes. "I'm not here to hurt you, strawberry. I promise. I'm here to help you." She gestured at the chair across from her on the other side of the coffee table. "Sit."

"I thought we had an appointment to meet tonight." Emma didn't budge.

"An appointment you"—Gigi pointed at her with her now unlit cigarette—"were just about to cancel."

Emma furrowed her brow. "How did you..."

"I had someone sitting next to you at the cafe where you met your new *extremely* uncharismatic friend." Gigi let out a quiet hum. "And saw you kissing him. And more importantly, him kissing *you.*" There wasn't any judgment in the other woman's tone. In fact, if Emma weren't mistaken, there was a level of respect. Gigi seemed impressed.

"Does Professor Saltonstall not usually dally with the

fairer sex?" Emma smirked. "Can't imagine why he's not extremely popular."

Gigi laughed and sat back on the sofa, draping herself out again as if she owned the place. She gestured at the seat. "Sit, strawberry. You and I are going to be friends."

"Right..." Emma sighed. Well, she had just been debating whether or not it would be worth following both of her leads —Rafe and Gigi—and here one was, willing to talk to her. She could hardly look a gift horse in the mouth.

Until you find out the gift horse has a plague that'll wipe out the rest of your team. With a shake of her head, Emma walked over to the chair and sat down, if very slowly. She didn't let go of her gun. "What do you want?"

"To talk, dear. That's all. Just to talk." Gigi plucked the snuffed cigarette from her holder and dropped it into the tray before tucking her holder into her small, delicate, and extremely expensive-looking purse. "You were going to cancel our appointment, though."

"Yeah. Your club gives me the willies." Emma wrinkled her nose. "Mykel gives me the creeps."

Gigi laughed again and draped an arm over her head as though she were about to take a nap. Her casual nature was both disarming and alarming. "Mykel can come off a bit strong, but oh, he knows how to run a tight ship. And a whole lot of other things."

Emma had no idea what that was supposed to mean, but she assumed it was sexual. "Good for him."

Gigi chuckled again and shut her eyes, seemingly entirely unalarmed by the fact that Emma had a gun. "I'm sorry that he bothered you. I'll tell him to calm down next time he sees you. He just can't help it when a pretty woman is involved. And oh, strawberry, you are something *delicious.* I honestly can't say I blame him."

The overt nature of Gigi's tone left nothing to the imagination. She was that kind of woman. Emma shrugged. To each their own. "I don't sleep with women."

"That's a shame, but good to know." Gigi tilted her head to watch Emma through heavy, lidded eyes. "Have you ever really considered it, though? Have you ever been tempted?"

Emma faintly smiled. "There was that time in Marrakech. It was close. But...eh. We kissed, but it just doesn't do it for me, I'm afraid."

Gigi smiled, far more broadly than Emma did. "Good for you for having tried. That's all I ask. Sample the dish before you judge it. Although I'm not surprised you'd be open-minded, given the nature of your brother."

Emma shrugged. "Never saw what was wrong with it."

"Good girl." Gigi shut her eyes and relaxed farther into the pillows on the sofa, looking perfectly resplendent, like any of the movie stars Emma loved to go see. "You *were* going to cancel our date, though."

"I was."

"Why?"

"I don't trust you, and I get the distinct impression you're dangerous."

"I get the feeling you love danger." Gigi cracked open an eye to smirk at her. "Don't you, my adorable, delicious little adventurer?"

Emma wasn't quite sure which one of those adjectives she was supposed to be more offended by. She opted not to be offended by any of them. She shrugged again. "I suppose."

"More importantly, *I* get the 'distinct impression' that fear turns you on..." Gigi's voice turned low and sultry again, and Emma watched as the woman arched her back on the sofa, miming pleasure, and ran a thin, delicate-fingered hand down her gold and crimson dress. "Doesn't it?"

Emma knew she was blushing. The burn in her cheeks gave it away. She wasn't quite sure what to say to that. She could deny it, but it'd be a lie. And judging by the smug, all-knowing smile on Gigi's cardinal-painted lips, it wasn't worth trying to fib. The other woman already knew.

Somehow.

Emma's reaction to dangerous situations wasn't anything she was terribly proud of, but it also just seemed to be part of her personality. Like her shadows and the voices of her past that followed her around, she could either fight it and lose, or accept it. She chose the latter.

"Aren't you going to pretend I'm wrong?" Gigi chuckled.

"No." Emma made a face. "I'm just more concerned as to how you know that. And even more importantly, why do you care?"

Gigi laughed, a true and genuine sound. Emma's response had clearly truly amused the other woman. She sat up and shifted so she was draped sideways in a half-lounge, resting on the arm of the sofa, her blonde curls looking wonderfully tousled from having been horizontal a moment earlier. "I can see why the professor likes you. I think you challenge his expectations. That's unusual for him."

"Can't challenge the expectations of somebody you don't know."

"You don't know him?" Gigi arched an eyebrow. "Seems like you know him plenty well to me."

"No." Emma snickered. "We've just kissed. There's a difference, and I'm pretty damn sure that's a difference you know quite well."

"Right you are." Gigi laughed again, bright and cheerful. There was a surprising amount of affection in her expression. "Oh, Emma. Emma, Emma, Emma. What am I going to do with you?"

"What do you mean?"

"I have a bit of a predicament." Gigi began to idly toy with one of the beaded tassels of her dress, curling the shining objects around her painted nails. "Your brother came to me for help. When I said no, he went and found himself tangled up with a group of people I deeply and adamantly dislike."

"Looks like you and Saltonstall have something in common." Emma rolled her eyes. "Turning down my brother's requests for help."

"That's not all we have in common." Gigi chuckled, her voice a purr again, though marred with a layer of playfulness. "I believe we'd both love to get you in bed, also."

Emma laughed. "I'm flattered, but no."

"So you've said. Ah, well." Gigi sighed dramatically before continuing. "But the professor and I have more in common than you'd think, going far beyond our mutual interactions with the Mather family." She waved her hand. "But that's neither here nor there. Where was I?" She furrowed her brow.

"We were talking about your predicament." Emma couldn't help but smile. She rather liked the woman across from her, all things considered.

"Right!" Gigi smiled beatifically, resting her elbow on the arm of the sofa and her curled fingers against her temple. "My predicament is this—I think I rather like you, Emma Mather."

"Why is that a problem?" Emma was suddenly very glad she had kept hold of her pistol.

The tone of the jazz singer's voice for what she said next was that of Emma's absolute best friend in the world. "Well, you see…I came here to kill you."

CHAPTER TEN

Emma was on her feet and had the chair between her and Gigi, with her gun now pointed squarely at the woman's face, before the words even finished leaving the jazz singer's mouth.

Gigi chuckled and sat back cozily into the cushions. "Oh, strawberry." She waved a hand. "Calm down. I've changed my mind."

"I'm going to say this gently—I don't *fucking* trust you." Emma didn't budge from where she was standing.

"And you shouldn't. And I don't blame you." Gigi looked around the room and sighed. "Do you have anything to eat? I'm starving. Let's go get lunch. I don't think either of us have eaten anything today."

"I'm becoming more and more alarmed by how much you know about me, Miss Gage." Emma refused to let the tension leave her, or to let her guard down, no matter how casual the other woman was. "How?"

Gigi let out a long breath. "First, call me Gigi. Please. Second…well, half of it is just good ol' fashioned snooping. I've had people following you since you arrived in the city.

And it was absolutely *adorable* watching you follow the professor around, can I say that?"

"I know, I know, I did a bad job of it." Emma fought the urge to roll her eyes. She didn't want to take her attention off the woman who had just confessed to plotting her murder. "I'm a shit spy."

"But a fantastic lockpick." Gigi smirked.

"That brings me to the second half of how you know so much about me." Emma shifted her grip on the pistol, keeping it ready to fire.

Gigi chuckled. "You haven't guessed?" She draped an arm over the back of the sofa. "The darkness whispers to me about who you are and what you're doing. It tells me everything I need to know."

"The darkness." Emma repeated the words dumbly, not knowing what to make of them.

"Well, to be more specific, the things that live in the darkness. They're curious about you. Very curious. And when they whisper of such a tasty morsel wandering around the city, poking at things she shouldn't be, I get curious, too."

"You're insane."

"I wouldn't throw stones, there, dear." Gigi began to toy with her long set of pearls, winding them around her fingers as if she had every business being there. It was clear she had no concerns about the gun pointed at her.

"If I shot you, what would happen?"

"I'd die, of course." The woman let out a huff. "I'm not invincible. Or immortal. Or inhuman. I just have a modicum of control over things in the world that other people don't, that's all." She shifted to sitting and began gathering up her things. "No, that's not why I know you won't shoot me. I know you won't shoot me because you need me. You need the answers I can give you, and you need my protection."

Emma squinted an eye in incredulous confusion. "Excuse me? Why do I need your protection?"

"Because there are others who have taken notice of you, dear girl. More than just our grumpy, pent-up professor." Gigi shut her purse with a snap. "There are people and forces in Arnsmouth that want to consume you, in every sense of the word."

"Are you on the list?"

"Most certainly." Gigi laughed cheerfully. "But I promise, strawberry, I've changed my plans. I'm not someone who likes to scheme and deal in back rooms. I leave that for people who're better at it. No, I deal in very sharp lines. What I tell you will always be the truth. It's just a matter of whether or not I tell you anything at all. Now, put your gun back in your bag, and let's head to the hotel's restaurant. I am positively *famished.*"

Emma shut her eyes and finally surrendered to the notion that Gigi was right. Shooting her would be pointless. And besides, then she'd have a body to deal with. With a long, weary sigh, she put her gun back in her purse and rubbed her temples. "This is all going to give me a headache."

"Do you know what solves that? Whisky." Gigi stood and brushed out the lines of her dress.

"It's one in the afternoon. And it's illegal." Emma felt tugged along by a streetcar. What was happening? She shook her head. She shouldn't be going to lunch with a woman who had threatened to kill her, and now claimed she could use *dark magic* to spy on her.

But Gigi had information. Information Emma desperately needed.

"All right, fine. Coffee and vodka. And never mind that stupid law." Gigi walked around the coffee table and the chair and approached her. Emma went stiff, not knowing what to expect. Part of her expected a knife to the ribs. Or for her to turn into some terrible monster and rip her face off.

Instead, Gigi pulled her into a hug. One that Emma didn't return. But that didn't seem to bother the beautiful jazz singer in the slightest. Gigi took Emma's face in her hands, seemingly studying her eyes.

Gigi had perfect, ice-blue eyes that were just as flawless as the rest of her. They studied Emma thoughtfully. She smiled. "You're just the sweetest thing, you know that?" She leaned in and placed a kiss to Emma's cheek, just a little too close to Emma's lips for it to be perfectly benign. When she parted, she whispered, "I do hope you live through this."

That sent a shiver down Emma's spine. It bothered her far more than the woman's threat of murder. It made her skin crawl, and she didn't know why. But there was something in the way she said it that made Emma feel as though she had just taken a step toward the edge of a cliff and stared into a deep abyss.

Her face went cold, and she must have gone pale. Gigi tutted and patted her cheek. "Vodka, coffee, and a nice big steak. That's what you need. Come, dear. My treat."

She wasn't quite sure what to do with herself as Gigi took her hand and pulled her out of her hotel room. Tugged behind a streetcar, indeed. She just hoped this one didn't suck her under the wheels and kick her out the other side as a mangled corpse.

When they were in the elevator, Emma had to ask the question that popped into her head. She had to know. Even if she wasn't sure she really *wanted* to know. "How many people have you killed, Gigi?"

"Recently? Or total?" The woman laughed at Emma's horrified expression. "Oh, strawberry." She leaned back against the elevator wall. "I've lost count."

What am I doing with my life?

Emma found herself sitting in a corner booth of the restaurant, private and set away from everyone else, listening to Gigi flirt with the blushing waiter. The hotel's establishment was more than eager to sit the local celebrity wherever she liked, and the dark fabric curtains that draped alongside the booth would ensure they weren't seen or heard.

It didn't make Emma feel safe in the slightest.

"And my dear friend, she'll have coffee, a tonic light on the ice, and the filet mignon, rare." Gigi reached out and let her hand run slowly down the waiter's arm, from elbow to wrist. "She's just had an *awful* few weeks, you know. She needs to get some blood in her system."

"Y—uh—of course," the waiter stammered, his face almost the shade of the deep burgundy upholstery. "Right away." The man took a step back and hastily began to beat a retreat.

"Oh!" Gigi called after him. "And some of those dinner rolls—they really are amazing." Once the waiter was gone, she turned her attention back to Emma. "Hope it wasn't terribly gauche of me to order for you."

"No, it's…fine." Emma felt suddenly small and out of her league. She wasn't sure why. Maybe it was the overbearing curtains that were surrounding them. Maybe it was the fact that she really, really didn't know what she had gotten herself into. "Probably what I would have ordered, anyway."

"Grand." Gigi scooted around the booth until she was sitting shoulder-to-shoulder with Emma and smiled. "That's better. Much cozier this way, don't you think? Especially if we're going to be whispering secrets to each other."

"People might start rumors, seeing us sitting like this." Emma reached out and picked up her glass of ice water. She needed something in her system, even if it was just that.

"Do you mind?" Gigi smiled.

"Not particularly." She sipped the water. "I've had worse rumors started about me."

"How many were true?"

She paused. "Most of them."

Gigi smiled wryly. "Like what?"

"That I spent my youth stomping around the house in men's clothing, because I have a severe hatred for skirts. It won't be the first time people assumed I preferred the company of other women." She sipped her water, glad for its presence. "To be clear, I don't hate skirts. I just think they're entirely impractical. And when you want to climb a tree or go boating in the lake, they're absolute death traps."

Gigi laughed and leaned back on the velvet upholstery. This was where the woman belonged—surrounded by expensive things, lounging in the most comfortable places, being fawned and poured over by everyone around her. Emma was meant for adventures, the smell of engines, the discovery, and the wind.

She had never been a very feminine girl, even at a young age. She was always playing at fencing with her brother's friends, and always ready to climb the tree right behind them. She was always coming home with scrapes and bruises. Her brother loved all the things Emma didn't, and vice versa—fancy clothing, hosting tea, social events, flowers, and delicate things.

Neither was right. Neither was wrong. It was just how they were. But sometimes, just sometimes, Emma saw women like Gigi and found herself being extremely jealous of them. She knew she was attractive; she knew she was beautiful. But Gigi was something else entirely.

"You're staring." Gigi tapped the end of Emma's nose with a fingertip, jarring Emma out of her thoughts. "I'm flattered."

Emma chuckled and looked down into her water. "I just miss my brother."

Gigi frowned. "What do you mean?"

"My mother once told me, a few years before she died, that she had always wondered if Elliot and I had our souls swapped in the womb. That I was meant to be a boy, and he was meant to be a girl." She let out a sigh. "Sometimes when I see really beautiful women, like you, I wonder if that's not what I'm supposed to be like. I guess everybody's always envious of the things they aren't. Don't get me wrong, I love lipstick as much as the next gal, but you look like it was *made* for you."

Gigi studied her face for a long time, an unreadable expression on her face. It almost looked as though whatever Emma had said had touched her. It...almost looked like the singer was going to cry. She smiled after a moment, a mournful thing that Emma hadn't seen on her before. She pulled Emma into another hug and kissed her cheek. "Sweet girl...sweet, wonderful girl. I can see why they all want you so badly."

"I really need to know what you mean by that." Emma shifted in her seat to half-face Gigi. "You can't possibly be referencing what I think you are. That the Dark—" She stopped as the waiter arrived. A coffee and tonic for her, and another tonic water for Gigi. And a basket of rolls that smelled fantastic.

Her stomach grumbled. Apparently, she *was* hungry.

Once the man left, Gigi lifted her finger to her lips in a sign for her to be quiet. Rustling through her purse, she pulled out a flask. Pouring a clear white liquid into both of their tonic waters—Emma assumed it was vodka of some kind—she flipped the cap back on. Picking up her drink, she sipped it. "Oh, that's much better. I positively *hate* that damn law."

"Same." Emma hesitatingly sipped her own drink. Definitely vodka. But it was good, and honestly, she'd be glad for something to help her settle her nerves.

Gigi sighed. "I will tell you this in full honesty, Emma. I'm telling you this because I am suddenly very, very fond of you. And the idea that you might fall to the same fate as your poor, misguided brother breaks my heart."

Emma picked up one of the rolls and began to pull it apart into smaller pieces. It gave her something to do, before she began fidgeting nervously with her purse or her sleeves. She waited for Gigi to continue.

The singer half shut her eyes and leaned back against the seat, watching Emma carefully. "The Societies are real. They are very, very real. Think what you want about them being myths and legends, but they've never left the city. The darkness in Arnsmouth lives. It breathes. It's a tangled ball of worms, writhing and squirming through every pore of this damnable city. And there are those of us who are foolish enough to tap into it, to wield it, and even worse, sometimes seek to control it."

Emma stared at her. Swallowing the lump in her throat, she fought the urge to down the glass of vodka tonic in one go. "Can I politely say that I don't believe you?"

Gigi chuckled. "But you do. I can see it. And it doesn't matter if you believe me or not—your brother did. He went and got himself into trouble with the Idol, and they—" Gigi cut herself off. She waved a hand dismissively. "Details."

"Wait. The Idol?"

Gigi sighed. "It's complicated, strawberry. More than you need to know. Simply stated, I'm not part of the Idol. And if anyone comes to you, whispering about them, *run*. Run as far and as fast as you can." Reaching out, she took Emma's hand and squeezed it. "They are already hunting you. And if they take you, there's nothing anybody can do."

"Why are they after me?"

"Because your twin was something special to them. And I suspect they believe you have the same connection to the Ether that he did." Gigi shook her head. "I know none of that will make any sense to you. And I won't go into more detail, no matter how nicely you ask."

Emma ate a piece of the bread to help quiet the churning in her stomach. It didn't work. She ate another as she tried to think. "How many different Societies are there?"

"Five."

"And which one are you a member of?"

"The Blade." Gigi reached out in front of her and picked up a steak knife from the table. She turned it over in her hand thoughtfully, and in Emma's mind's eye, she saw the singer turn and drive the knife deep into her throat. She had to struggle to keep the vision from overwhelming her. But the image of her blood pooling on the white linen tablecloth lingered with her.

Her blood would be the same shade as Gigi's lipstick. She had to shut her eyes and focus on her breathing. She felt dizzy, lightheaded.

Lips pressed to her cheek. "Easy, now, strawberry. It'll be all right."

"And—and Rafe?"

"I'll let him tell you that over your dinner tomorrow."

Emma frowned. She felt very strange all of a sudden. When she opened her eyes, the room swam in front of her a little. "Did you…"

"Drug you? Hm. No. Not exactly." Gigi pulled Emma against her side. "We're going to have a lovely lunch, you and I. But I'm afraid you're not going to remember a damn thing about any of it."

"I…"

"I said I'd tell you the truth." Gigi smiled. "I never said you could keep what I told you."

Everything that happened after that…was all a bit of a blur. She remembered the steak was fantastic. She remembered having a wonderful conversation. She remembered the softness of her bed as she went to sleep in her hotel room after.

And she remembered the press of lips to hers that tasted like blood.

CHAPTER ELEVEN

It was dark when Emma woke up in her bed, feeling both cozy and warm, and as though something was very, very wrong. She groaned and rolled onto her side, rubbing a hand over her face.

She remembered Gigi in the apartment. She remembered going to lunch. She remembered sipping a drink, and then… bits and pieces. Laughter, and stories, and serious moments where she knew that Gigi had told her important things. But none of it seemed to have stuck.

Gigi Gage, I'm going to slap you next time I see you.

Shutting her eyes, she tried to focus. Tried to recall anything that she could from what Gigi had told her. Something about Dark Societies. Something about an Idol, maybe? Growling in frustration, she pulled a pillow over her head and wished the world would just go away and leave her alone.

"Emma!"

She jolted at the sound of the voice. It was so real. "Elliot?" She sat up, searching the room for her brother. She winced. It was just one of her shadows. He wasn't really there. She let out a long sigh and lay back down on the bed, shutting her eyes once more. "Go away. Please."

For a moment, it seemed her polite request had worked. She began to fall asleep again, this time of her own accord. But it was just as she was entering that place between awake and not that she heard his voice again.

"Emma, help me!"

She sat up again, letting out a wavering breath. "You're not really there. You're not real. You're just my mind."

"Please...It's dark, and I don't know where I am." He sounded so afraid. So desperate. These weren't the sounds of her memories playing pranks on her. She had never heard him say those words before.

Climbing out of bed, she was distracted for a moment as she was wearing only her shift and underwear, which was very disconcerting. Gigi had undressed her. Or she didn't remember doing it herself. No, she wasn't just going to slap Gigi. She was going to slap Gigi with a brick.

"Find me, please!"

Cringing at the sound of Elliot, that felt so very close and yet just out of reach, like he was around a corner, she got dressed and slipped on her coat. Tucking her gun into her coat pocket, she stepped out into the living room area of her hotel suite.

There was a good chance the voice in her mind was just a hallucination—part of her psychosis. But there was also a chance it wasn't. And *if* it wasn't? She couldn't let her brother suffer. "Where do I start?"

"Follow my voice." The sound of him was coming from her hallway, leading her out of the room. Gritting her teeth and steeling herself for what might be a task that was both stupid and likely—literally—insane, she left the room and made sure to lock it behind her.

Not like it'd do much good.

Elliot's voice was quiet until she left the hotel lobby and stepped out into Arnsmouth at night. It was a beautiful, crisp, early spring evening, with the moon full and high in the sky, and only a few wistful clouds to interrupt the view. The drizzle had ended, but she felt no less cold for it.

"This way!" Elliot's voice called to her from her right.

This was stupid. This was extremely stupid. But she had to try. If he was calling to her, either through their intrinsic link or through some kind of dark magic, she had to try to save him. With a whine, knowing full well that the thing she was going to do would probably wind up with her dead in an alley somewhere, she followed the sound.

Turn after turn, street after street, she followed him as he called to her. And with each step, she knew she was walking farther and farther into a trap that she had no ability to avoid. It was her brother. Her *twin*. Elliot had always understood and accepted her, even more than her father and mother ever had. They knew each other in ways that nobody else ever would.

They were always there for each other. When each of them had been teased for being different, for being *weird*, they had each other to confide in and take solace in. There was never judgment between them.

And it meant she would die for him, if that was what it took.

His voice took her west, away from the center of the city, and down toward the back bay area that had been filled in and developed decades earlier, but that had originally been entirely water. The buildings weren't as old, but they were designed to impress. To make the people walking by them feel small. And it worked.

It was as she was passing through a pitch-black alleyway between two buildings, with only the streetlamps on either side to provide any illumination, that she froze.

Shlorp.

She could feel herself shaking. "Not now, Jim. Please, not now. Please, go away." She shut her eyes. This was all in her head. This was all in her head.

Shlorp.

"Please, please, please..." But her pleading wasn't obeyed this time. There came the stink of rotting flesh, so heavy and thick in the air that she had to cover her face with her hand. It began to sting her eyes.

Shlorp.

She could feel its breath on her, hot, and rancid, and terrible. Something knocked over a trash can. The sound of more metal warping as "Jim" decided to break another fire escape. *Don't open your eyes. Don't open your eyes. Don't open your eyes. It isn't real. It isn't there.*

Something touched her. A hand on her shoulder—or a claw. The feeling of it made her knees want to buckle, like it was somehow pushing her down, or dragging her forward. It felt as though it weren't touching her body at all, but instead touching her soul.

She opened her eyes.

And she screamed.

The thing in front of her was unlike anything she had ever seen before in her life.

It was enormous. It filled the alleyway with its skeletal, *dripping* form that loomed some ten feet above her in its totality. Bones stretched in all directions, seemingly made of hot wax. It appeared and disappeared in waves, oozing and splattering to the bricks before building out again. And before her, hovering only a foot away from her face, was a distorted skull that melted and appeared like the rest of it. If she could imagine a warm wax skull, and pictured sticking her fingers into the socket and dragging downward, stretching the shapes into distorted, slimy, inverted tears, it still wouldn't be quite accurate.

It had no legs, only a torso, sticking up out of a puddle that was the color of a bloated corpse. It had six arms, if she could call them that. It was using the fire escapes to pull itself along down the alleyway like a wounded soldier.

The "hand" that touched her was both rigid bone and gloopy, gelatinous, fleshy mud. The hand itself was also twice the size of her body, and she watched as it began to curl its talon around her. It was going to grab her. She screamed again and, lifting her gun from her pocket, took aim and fired.

The bullet hit Jim square in the head, but it was as though she had shot a jelly mold. It parted for the projectile, and then squeezed back together in its amorphous form as though it had never existed at all.

It didn't stop her from firing again. And a third time. And then she decided it was time to run. She turned on her heel and went for the exit of the alley as fast as she could. She didn't know if it was real, but she didn't want to find out.

Shlorp.

Shlorp.

Shlorp.

She glanced over her shoulder. The sound was the creature pulling itself along, its wet, claw-like hands slapping into the surface as it dragged itself toward her, deformed skull opened wide in a silent scream. *"Emma! Emma, it's all right. It's safe! It won't hurt you. Come save me! Save me!"* The voice seemed to come from the monster itself. It had been a trap all right.

It was just as she exited the alley that she ran into someone. She hadn't been looking where she was going. She couldn't take her eyes off what she saw. Her pistol clattered to the ground as she impacted the poor person.

"I—Oh—Oh, God, I—"

A hand grabbed her shoulder, steadying her. "Emma?"

She blinked up into the face of Professor Raphael Saltonstall. He was looking at her with a furrowed brow, and an expression that was both studious and concerned. It was as if he were trying to pull some kind of secret out of her. He lifted that battery-powered lantern of his and peered down the alleyway from which she had come.

"R—Rafe?" Relief flooded her, though perhaps it shouldn't. There was no telling if he was just as bad, or worse, than the monster that had just been chasing her. She ducked behind him, pressing her back to his, using him like a shield. She shut her eyes tight. Her heart was going a mile a minute, and her breathing was short, fast, and shallow. "Fuck —just—*fuck*."

"I would ask if you are all right, but I believe I know the answer."

She reached behind her and found his free hand. She took it and squeezed it tight. She needed something to hold on to. The presence of him at her back was strong, and she leaned on him. To her shock, he squeezed back. "I...I need you to tell me something. I need you not to lie. If you never answer another one of my questions ever again, I need you to answer this one. Please, Rafe. Promise me."

Maybe it was the desperation in her voice that did it. Maybe it was because she was crying, and she hadn't even noticed it. But after a pause, he answered. "I promise."

"Is—is that thing—" She could barely catch her breath enough to speak. "Is that thing that chased me—is it real?"

Another long, pregnant pause filled the air between them before he spoke. "It is."

Leaning her head back against him, relying on his presence, she let out a long, wavering breath that felt and sounded more like a sob. "Oh, thank fuck."

"What?" Finally, he turned toward her, forcing her to face him. Now he was looking at her in abject confusion, and a little bit of horror. "You're *relieved?*"

"I—" Tears welled in her eyes, and she sniffled through another sob. "I've always—I've seen things—but not like that, and I was afraid…I was afraid I was going to be like Elliot, seeing things, and…" She didn't know what to do. He was right. She should have been happier to know the huge, evil, terrible monster had been in her head. That meant she would be safe. That meant there weren't creatures of the dark trying to eat her.

But things that were real could be defended against. Could be avoided, could be run away from. She could go to Egypt or Marrakech, travel to Ireland or England, and escape the thing that chased her.

Things that weren't real would follow her everywhere. Because the darkness in her head would always be with her. She didn't know how to explain it to Rafe. She didn't. She could barely even explain it herself. With another broken sob, she threw herself into his arms, hugging him as tight as she could.

He went rigid. She buried her head into his chest, taking solace in the smell of him. Of the crisp spices, and clean, minty aftershave. She cried, not caring if her tears stained his shirt. She needed something. Anything.

After what felt like forever—and probably realizing she wasn't going to let go—Rafe wrapped a single arm around her. He held her close and rested his chin atop her head. He said nothing, and that was fine.

She didn't know how long she stayed like that before she finally pushed away from him a few inches and wiped her face with her coat sleeve. "I'm—I'm sorry. That wasn't appropriate of me."

"I would never use that word to describe anything you do.

It is hardly a surprise." Rafe looked off down the alley and lifted his lantern, pointing the light toward the shadowy space. "It's gone. Come."

He began to walk away, leaving her standing there for a moment in stunned silence before running to catch up with him. She fell in step beside him. "Were you following me?"

"Yes."

"Huh." She couldn't exactly be mad about it. Turnabout and fair play, and all that. "Why?"

"Because you are in trouble, and you are an idiot." He pushed his glasses up his nose with a press of his ring finger to the bridge. "First, you're foolish enough to associate yourself with Gage. Now, you go running off into dark places."

"It...sounded like my brother. I couldn't help it." She wrapped her arms around herself. "I had to try. I know it was stupid. But if—if it was really him, and he was real, I couldn't just ignore him." She frowned. "Besides, I thought he was only in my head."

"Then you would have wound up mugged or worse."

"I can handle myself, thank you very much." She stuck her tongue out at him.

To her surprise, he chuckled at the childish gesture. He shook his head. "What am I to do with you, Miss Mather?"

"Everybody asks me that." She smiled up at him. "Let me know if you figure it out. I'll telegram my father."

He huffed a laugh again and sighed. They fell into silence as they walked, the sharp white light of his lantern cutting drastic shadows on the world around them. Each railing and tree, brick and lamppost, felt somehow all the more surreal because of it.

"I had no say in Gigi coming to see me. She broke into my hotel room. We had lunch, and she drugged me."

"I doubt it was drugs. It was likely—" He let out a small noise. "Never mind. The difference doesn't matter."

It wasn't until they had gone a few blocks that she spoke up again. "Where are we going?"

"You can hardly return to your hotel. And your brother's apartment will be even worse." His expression looked pained, as if he just realized he had forgotten to take out the trash and there was something foul growing inside of it. "We are going to my home."

"Huh?" She blinked in surprise. "But—"

"Yes. I know." That time he grimaced. "But it is the only place you will be safe."

Safe. She laughed. When he looked at her with a raised eyebrow, she waved a hand as if to say she didn't mean to offend him. "I don't think I'll ever be safe again. Not as long as I'm in Arnsmouth."

His smile was thin but approving. "Indeed."

Before he asked the question, she grinned. "And no, I'm not leaving. I haven't changed my mind."

"Even after what you just saw?"

She hesitated. She rubbed her shoulder where the thing had touched her. It felt off. Somehow wrong. She hoped it would fade. "If that's what my brother is fighting against...I can't leave him to do it alone. I have to find him."

"It is too late for him, Emma." Rafe placed his hand on her other shoulder. "But it is not too late for you."

Part of her believed him. A part of her that was slowly growing larger by the minute. But she shook her head.

Nodding, Rafe seemed to accept her silent answer.

And together they walked in silence to his home.

CHAPTER TWELVE

The walk to Rafe's house was spent in silence. Even Emma, for once, didn't feel like talking. After what she had seen...after how it had somehow seemed to have touched her soul? She couldn't find the conversation.

It wasn't like Rafe seemed to mind. He walked beside her, bright lantern shining, as they headed through the city of Arnsmouth. It almost would have been romantic to stroll beneath the moonlight and the amber light from the gas lamps, if it weren't for how they struggled to compete with the overbearing white light.

She finally had to ask. "Why are you using a lantern?"

Rafe didn't answer and simply kept his gaze on the road ahead of her. She frowned at him and nudged his elbow. He glanced at her and then sighed. "I have difficulty seeing in the dark."

It could be a lie. But she remembered watching him turn on the lights in his home one at a time until every room was painfully bright. Maybe it was true. Or maybe there was something else going on. She opted it was probably better for her not to know. Not tonight. Not after seeing "Jim."

Instead, she shut her eyes for a moment and tucked that mystery away for another night. When they reached the steps of his home, she almost felt a modicum of relief. She was going to be inside soon, and inside hopefully meant away from the monsters that wanted to hurt her.

Unless he's a monster that wants to hurt me.
My money would still be on "yes."

But Rafe looked human. She wasn't sure—she wasn't sure of anything anymore—but he appeared mostly normal. Eccentric, yes. But certainly nothing like the creature she had witnessed.

As he climbed the stone steps of his home, he reached into his pocket for his keys. When he went to open the door, he hesitated and turned to her. The white light flashed across the lenses of his glasses. "Miss Mather."

It felt like she had been called on in class by her teacher. There was a certain level of authority to the tone of his voice that had her back going straight. "Y...yeah?"

"I feel I must take a moment to explain something to you."

She narrowed an eye at him. "If you prefer the company of men, first, I don't believe you. And second, you needn't warn me, as Elliot—" She shut up as he growled in frustration. This was a serious moment. She tucked her chin a little but didn't apologize.

He watched her in silence for a moment, and it hung between them like the pause between breathing. His deep voice sent a shiver up her spine. "There is one rule you must follow in my presence if you wish to survive. *Do not scream.*"

He turned without waiting for her to reply and opened the door to his home. He stepped into the darkness beyond, flipping switches as he walked, the austere setting of his abode otherwise only illuminated in the eerie, stark shadows of his lantern.

The door remained open. Waiting for her either to go inside, or to leave.

Oh. Yes. He was most certainly a monster. But the question simply was whether he wanted to hurt her.

Or if she even had a choice whether she should step inside his home. She pulled her coat closer around her, suddenly feeling a chill. Rafe had finished with the first floor, and without even glancing at her hesitating at his doorstep, he walked up the stairs to do the same routine with the lights on the second.

If she walked away, Jim was certain to come back to hurt her. Or Gigi would find her. Or who knew what other terrible monstrosities were lurking in the darkness, waiting to devour her. She had nowhere else to go. And while her father's name and fantastic credit would get her the best room in any establishment, she knew it wouldn't make a difference. Nowhere was safe.

And while she knew Rafe was likely just as dangerous as the monsters outside his walls, she was pretty sure she would rather die with his handsome face over her, not the melting, bloated wax skeleton that she had seen.

Did I really just rank my potential murderers by sex appeal?
Why, yes. I think I did.

Rolling her eyes at herself, she stepped inside Rafe's home and shut the door behind her with a click.

His home was precisely as she would have expected. Richly decorated in dark wood tones and saturated colors. It was a bit dated, perhaps, by modern standards. It still reflected the decadence and extravagance of decades prior, with the furniture and design searching to reflect its opulence in detail, not geometric simplicity. It reminded her a bit of her own home up north.

She squinted against the blaringly bright electric lights. It would take her eyes a minute to adjust after walking the streets with him, even with his lantern on. She could hear his footsteps above her, heading up the stairs to presumably turn all the lights to full on the third floor. And then likely the fourth and fifth. The home was narrow, but it was tall.

Why turn every light on, though? I understand the lantern in the dark but...his utility bill must be ridiculous. That felt like a rock she, despite all her best impulses to pester him with questions until he told her some dark and terrible secret, should leave right where it was for the time being.

Maybe in the morning, once she had some decent rest. Oh, sleep sounded fantastic after the trying experience she had just endured. Perhaps she could ask the professor for some alcohol before she slept wherever he put her. She waited at the bottom of the stairs, not wanting to be rude by prowling around his home uninvited.

She might have rebelled against most of the rules of society, but there was no sense in not being polite. He *was* saving her from a monster, after all.

"Merrrrk."

She blinked and looked over to the room to her right, the parlor in the single-wide brownstone home. There, sitting on a table, glaring at her, was quite simply the fattest, fluffiest cat she had ever seen. And oh, it was *glaring*. She had never seen a cat with such a perfect example of contempt on its face. It was a calico, spotted in sections of white, black, and cream. Its ruff of fur around its neck made her think of royalty.

Emma laughed, smiling. "Oh, hello. Aren't you the grumpiest ball of fur?" *Like owner, like animal, or so they say.* She walked into the room—politeness only counted when there wasn't an animal in need of being petted—and reached out to touch the cat.

Its ears folded back in perfect relationship to her nearness to the animal. *"Rrrrrrrr..."*

She chuckled again. Very much like Rafe, indeed. She lowered her hand, and half-bowed to the cat. "Forgive me, your highness."

"That is Hector."

She turned to see Rafe standing in the doorway, watching her with a faintly amused, faintly beleaguered expression. She smiled brightly, having no shame in having been caught bowing to the animal. She turned back to it. "Well, it is an absolute honor to meet you, Sir Hector. What a lovely abode you have. Your manservant Raphael was simply letting me stay in the servant's quarters for the evening. I promise I will do as little as I can to disturb Your Lordship."

Rafe chuckled quietly before turning to go up the stairs to the second floor. He gestured for her to follow. "Hector is a female cat."

"O—oh." She blinked and headed up the stairs after him. "Why did you name your female cat Hector?"

"I found her behind a trash can a few years ago, crying. I assumed, poorly, that it was a male cat. By the time I learned otherwise, I was too accustomed to calling her Hector. I fear the name stuck." He headed down the hall toward what appeared to be a large galley kitchen. At some point, he had shed his heavy overcoat and jacket, and was in a shirt and vest. His tie was also gone.

By god, he almost looked *casual*. For shame. But he also looked tired, as if something had taken the wind out of his sails as well. He was, thankfully, pouring them both a bottle of something amber that was likely alcohol, judging by the decanter. "How scandalous, you having alcohol," she teased. Nobody she knew of had ever been arrested for having alcohol in their own homes. It was really the bars and public establishments the prohibition laws were after.

He shrugged but didn't answer.

"Are you a fan of pets?" What a charming thought. She smiled.

"I enjoy cats."

"I can see why. You resemble them a bit."

That earned her the arch of an eyebrow. "Oh?"

She leaned on the wood block counter in the center of the room. "Cats are generally aloof, arrogant creatures, who have a penchant for glaring at people and knocking things off shelves. You've only not done the latter by my estimation, although to be fair—" Emma grabbed a saltshaker from the center island and placed it on the very edge of the countertop. "I haven't given you an opportunity."

It looked like he couldn't decide between being insulted or amused. Instead, he downed the contents of his drink and poured himself another as he held her glass out to her. It was the first time she noticed his rings. He had a few, each one unique, as if it were a collection from different areas, and not a fashion choice. But he *was* lacking a wedding ring. At least there was that.

She took the glass and sipped it. Whiskey. "Oh, thank you," she said through a groan of relief. When he only nodded in reply and seemed set on finishing his second glass only half the speed of the first, she frowned. "Are you all right, Rafe?"

"No." He cringed. "Never mind. Not your concern." He waved dismissively.

She caught his wrist and moved closer to his side. He watched her, with that same studious and exacting expression, like he was trying to unravel whatever kind of puzzle she was. "Rafe. You can tell me what's wrong. I owe you for saving me."

"Saving you is precisely the problem." He gently pulled his wrist from her hand and took off his glasses, rubbing his palm over his face. "It takes immense effort to dispel a creature of that magnitude. I fear it's taking its toll. The Idol sent one of their most powerful after you, and—"

"Wait." She felt that chill roll down her spine again. "What did you say—the Idol?"

"Yes, sorry. I am explaining this entirely out of order." He downed the rest of his second glass and poured himself a third. "And I kindly request to explain it correctly when I have slept this off."

She shook her head. She remembered a conversation with Gigi. Mention of an Idol. Or the Idol. Her hand was trembling as she downed her own glass of whiskey and placed the empty glass next to him.

For a moment, he looked mildly impressed as he poured her a second. She downed that without a flinch and asked for a third with a gesture. He huffed a laugh and poured her a third.

"I once got into a drinking match with a man in the Serbian north. If I lost, our only remaining working truck would be his." She smirked into her glass, suddenly missing her father. Her father would know what to do. She could call him, she supposed...but she was both deeply ashamed of her to-date failure to find Elliot, and worried about involving him in a mess that was so very dangerous.

"And you won?"

She snorted. "Shit, no. He beat me hands down. Have you seen the size of me?" She gestured down her body. "He was three times my size and a fat bastard to boot. No, but I made it far enough that he took pity on us and let us keep the damn truck."

He laughed quietly and shook his head. He put the cork back in the decanter—smiling thinly as she whined in protest—and walked from the kitchen toward the stairs. "Let me show you to your room."

"Oh, a room?" She followed him with a devious smile. "Is it yours?"

He shook his head but said nothing.

"Damn." They walked up the stairs with her trailing him, as he led her to the fourth floor.

He pushed open the door, revealing a smallish, but hardly sparsely decorated room. It was clear he didn't get many visitors, however. "My suite is just below you. If you have any issues, I should be able to hear you."

She would ask what kind of 'issues' he could possibly mean, but she knew. She sighed and, reaching out, took hold of his arm. "Rafe, I mean it—thank you. For everything. I know you don't really care, and I know you're only putting yourself in danger, but…thank you."

He sighed. "Don't remind me of the stupidity of my kindness."

"I know it's not just kindness." She grinned.

"Do tell." He did look genuinely confused.

She smiled and stepped into him. His eyes widened at her brash movement as she backed him into the jamb. She slowly, ensuring he felt every second of it, pressed her body against his, and went up on her tiptoes to kiss his cheek just at the corner of his mouth. She held it.

She slipped a hand down his stomach between them, trailing lower, until her fingers lingered just at his belt, threatening to go lower. Images of him clutching her roughly to his body before throwing her to the bed and making violent, wonderful love to her flashed through her mind. The thought of it sent a rush of liquid fire through her veins. She certainly wouldn't stop him.

But sadly, it seemed he was not so inclined, though she wouldn't go to bed emptyhanded. Rafe crooked a finger beneath her chin and tilted her head to his. He studied her with those dark, fathomless eyes for a moment before capturing her lips in a kiss.

Each time before, the kiss had been as furious as the man who wielded it. And this time was only a step milder. He wrapped an arm around behind her back. She moaned against him as he deepened the embrace.

When he ended the kiss, she was breathless, the fear of the creature in the alley nearly driven from her mind by the man before her, who seemed to fill her senses each time they embraced. He placed another kiss to her forehead. "Goodnight, Emma."

"Damn." She sighed. "I'll blame the monster."

"Indeed." He chuckled and gently pushed her a step away. He walked away from her and headed for the stairs, although not before she took some mild pride in what she had felt pressing to her body, growing more eager by the second she had spent there. She could take pride in the fact that she wasn't going to be the only one left disappointed.

"Ah. One last thing." It was as he took two steps down the stairs that he paused. "I sincerely insist you leave the lights in your room on, even after I leave." His tone left no doubt. He was serious. "That is, if you wish to see the dawn. Sleep well."

And with that, he left her to her own devices, standing in the doorway of his guest bedroom, wondering what the hell was happening. Shaking her head in confusion, she walked into the room and shut the door behind her. She didn't bother to lock it. He absolutely had a key. Shrugging out of her clothing, deciding to sleep naked since she had nothing else with her, she slipped under the covers.

With the electric lights blazing.

She sighed.

Sleep well.

Yeah, right.

CHAPTER THIRTEEN

Emma was having a miserable night.

She wasn't a light sleeper, by any means. She was notorious for being able to nod off on trains, in automobiles, in the back of wagons, it didn't matter. But she discovered, to her misery, that there was one thing that was able to keep her up.

Sleeping with all the damnable lights on.

She tossed and turned for a few hours, trying to find a way to sleep so the glaring electric lights didn't bother her, but it was seemingly hopeless. She shoved a pillow over her head, but then the air was too moist and too close to her face from her breath.

With a growl, she threw off the sheets and stormed—naked and not caring since she was on the fourth floor—over to the light switch. Pressing the little button, she sighed in relief as the bright white lights died down.

Darkness.

Muttering to herself about how eccentric and annoying Professor Raphael Saltonstall had turned out to be, she climbed back under the sheets and lay down on her side.

There was also a good chance he had "insisted" she sleep with the lights on only to annoy her. That it was some kind of bizarre revenge for bothering him. Or an attempt simply to scare her.

Or maybe he was serious, and some evil creature was going to come lurking out of the shadows to devour her. He had warned her, in a way that still sent shivers up her spine, that she should not, under any circumstances, scream in his presence.

Strange man.

No, strange city.

Stranger man.

It didn't matter. Now she could sleep. And it came for her fast, her exhaustion catching up with her.

She just wished her dreams hadn't been so...visceral.

RAFE WAS HAVING A MISERABLE NIGHT.

After leaving Emma to her room—though he was sorely tempted simply to throw her over the edge of the bed and have her, right then and there—he went to the bathroom attached to his bedroom and attempted, without any avail, to relieve himself of the boiling lust that she had triggered in him.

But he was denied. It seemed the *Things* that shared him would not allow it. No, he knew what they wanted. They wanted him to do what Rafe had imagined, and they would not let him settle for less. They would not let him sleep, either.

The whispers he heard as he lay down, desperately trying to ignore the fire that still ran through his veins, were nonsensical as always. There were never words within the Things that had found their way inside him so many years ago. The disease he tried so hard to keep from coming to the surface.

Most times, he could control it.

Most times.

This was not one of those times.

He sensed it before he heard her. The floors in his home weren't terribly thick. But even if they were, he knew he would have felt the tremors within him even if he couldn't hear her quiet whimper from the room above.

Damn it.

Damn it all to the hells.

You turned off the lights, didn't you, Miss Mather?

Throwing off the sheets, he let out a long, shuddering breath. He felt electric. Power and need were coursing through him like his veins were copper wiring. The darkness in him wanted to feed. Wanted to consume.

Emma was about to die.

He supposed he might as well be there to witness it. Besides, perhaps then he might be given some relief from the desperate need that still lurked, tight as piano wire, low in his body. He pulled on a robe, cinching the middle, hoping it did *something* to obscure his current state of being, and walked up the stairs. Not that anyone was going to see him, mind you. But decorum was decorum.

The sound of her quiet cry from the other side of her door sent a shiver through him. He was going to be driven out of his mind by her if he were not careful.

Reaching for the knob, he carefully turned it, wondering if Emma had locked the door. She hadn't, either not caring, or rightly assuming he had the key, regardless. Without a click, he pushed the door open and stepped inside.

Yes. She had turned off the lights, after all.

He expected to see the Things that lived within his darkness pulling her limb from limb. Or perhaps keeping her in a trance as they ate her flesh, devouring her body before her very eyes. Sometimes they enjoyed torturing their victims. Sometimes he enjoyed watching it.

What he saw confused him, even as much as it knocked the breath from his lungs.

Emma lay beneath the sheets on her back, illuminated by the pale glow of the moon outside. Her chin length dark hair sat in tousled waves and curls around her on the pillow. Her hand was beside her cheek, fingers curled. Her lips were parted, and she let out another small, overwrought sound.

Tangled around her, sliding over her skin, weaving between her fingers...were the Things that infested him. Seeming to be nothing more than shadows cast by some unseen source, they wound around her throat, slithering over her cheek, the thin, pointed tip caressing her lower lip.

Beneath the sheets he could see more of them, as they had mass, even if they only appeared as shadows. They curled over her like snakes as she writhed. He did not know how deep their exploration of her went.

A noise left him without intending to, and he found himself leaning against the wall, unable to tear his gaze away. Unable to turn on the lights to end what he saw before him. He pressed his palms to the surface behind him, knowing that if he did not, he would attempt to relieve himself once more.

The noises she made were not ones of pleasure. Not entirely. They were marred by fear. Whatever They were doing to her, it was not entirely pleasant. They must have come to feed upon her nightmares.

But as he stared, she arched her back, and the sheets slid down her body. Emma was sleeping naked. Her skin was pale in the moonlight, perfect and smooth. He could see the outline of her pert nipples, as the Things within his darkness curled around her breasts, exploring her in the way he so desperately wanted to do with his own hands.

She let out another gasping sound. Pleasure and fear, muddled together as one. He had never known it was possible. They were feeding on her nightmare, but their touch seemed to warp and change whatever lingered in her dream into something decidedly *other*.

By the Great Beast…what was he to do? He was unable to stop staring as his infestation wormed over her, feeling their ecstasy, feeling their sated hunger as if it were his own.

The moment was over when his back began to burn like fire ants were crawling over it, biting at him, and he swore quietly beneath his breath. *No, no, no!* He reached for his shoulder and hissed through his teeth in pain as he felt the sensation of a thousand worms wriggling beneath his skin, desperately begging to be free.

He hit the light switch with his fist.

The lights immediately clicked on.

EMMA WAS LOST within what must have been the most terrifying and yet somehow the most explicit nightmare she had ever had in her life. She was running for her life through the hallways of her childhood home, screaming as dark shadows chased her, snapping at her heels.

It was a monster. A monster who wanted to destroy her. She couldn't even waste a moment to glance over her shoulder to see what it looked like, if it even looked like anything at all.

It was chasing her. It wanted to kill her. She had to *run.* But she knew, deep in the pit of her stomach, that she was going to lose. The thing was going to catch her. And there was the strangest, darkest thrill in her soul at the notion. The fear coursing through her veins set her heart racing, set her hair on end, made some primal part of her come rushing up to the surface.

She turned right when she should have turned left and found herself in a dead end she knew wasn't really part of her home. Her sleeping mind had decided this was where she died.

Something wrapped around her ankle, yanking her backward. She fell to the floor painfully with an *"unf!"* as it dragged her backward over the wood floor. She dug her nails in, screaming, trying to claw herself back to safety.

But it was too late.

It had her.

The world around her began to grow dark, as if it was swallowing the light itself. She rolled onto her back, intending on kicking the monster, punching it, clawing it, doing anything she could to free herself.

Something snapped around her throat like a rope, and she let out gasping yelp as it squeezed. It was alive, like a boa constrictor. She tried to grab it, but her hands touched nothing, only her own skin. But it was there—she knew it was there.

Dark shadows filled the hallway around her. A million writhing, shadowy tendrils that snaked and curled around each other like a pit of worms. Whatever had her by her ankle pulled her closer, until she was underneath it, watching in horror, unable to stop it.

They looked like they were made of nothing but shadows. And now they were going to devour her. She went to scream, but another one snapped around her mouth like a gag, silencing her. She tried to pull it away. Tried to do anything. But her hands touched only herself.

More wrapped around her wrists, pinning them painfully

to the floor over her head. She winced and let out a terrified whimper.

Now it was going to kill her. She was going to watch herself die in her dream. Rent apart by these strange, not-quite-there monstrous tendrils.

That was not *exactly* what happened.

Her dream took a decidedly strange...and altogether not unwelcome left turn.

The tendrils crawled over her, wrapping around her legs, her thighs, her waist, squeezing, sliding, touching...caressing. Each moment she waited for them to tighten and pull, to rip her legs off, or to tear her clean in two.

But they never did.

Her whimpers of terror were not quite terror anymore. Not entirely.

And just when it threatened to get *really* good...the dream shattered.

Light blared into her eyes.

She sat up with a groan.

"Miss Mather?"

She squinted at Rafe blearily. He was leaning against the wall by the switch, a pained expression on his face. She sat up and rubbed at her face. "What, Rafe?"

"Please cover yourself."

"Huh?" She looked down. "Oh!" She laughed and pulled the sheets up to cover her breasts. The blankets had fallen low as she had sat up. "Sorry. Although I suppose that's what you get, coming in here and staring at me while I was sleeping."

"I was worried you were being attacked from the sounds you were making."

"No, no." She sighed. "Just a nightmare." *A pretty tasty one, to be honest. I suppose it was just a strange combination of being horrified by "Jim" and then making out with you, Rafe.* "I'm all right. Sorry about the surprise tits." She chuckled. "I don't have anything to sleep in."

"Quite all right." Rafe headed for the door, stiffly. Seeing her naked really bothered him. She grinned to herself. "Sleep with the lights on, please, Emma."

"I'll try." She paused. "You could join me. That might help. You know...keep the nightmares away."

Rafe's steps hitched and he hesitated, before he shut his eyes. He cringed, as if something very painful had just stabbed through him, and for a moment she wondered if he was going to collapse to the ground.

"Rafe?" She moved to climb out of bed, but he lifted a hand to stop her. "Are you all right?"

"I am fine. I simply need rest. Good night, Emma. Sleep... as well as you can, I suppose." He shut the door behind him.

Strange man. Very strange man.

She lay back down in the bed with a sigh. Shutting her eyes, she threw an arm over them to blot out the light, and slowly felt sleep creep back up on her. She wondered if her strange nightmare would come back.

She wasn't sure why she was disappointed when it didn't.

CHAPTER FOURTEEN

Emma awoke feeling like absolute garbage. Well, awoke was a strong word. As she slung her legs out from under the sheets and rubbed a hand over her face, she wondered if she had actually been asleep at all. Or maybe she had just been stuck in an exhausted in-between place, too tired to get up, but unable to really sleep.

Because of the *fucking lights.*

It was early morning now, or so said the quietly-ticking clock by the wall and the gray light streaming in from the windows. She wanted to flick off the lights a second time and crawl back into bed for a few hours, but she had no clue if Rafe's strange rule applied only during the night hours, or always.

And she smelled coffee.

Tugging on her clothes from the previous day, she ran her hands through her hair to tidy her curls and walked down to the kitchen on the second floor and toward the smell that also included food. Eggs, maybe.

Standing at the stove in simply a button-down shirt tucked into black pants, was Rafe. He was frowning down at the skillet in front of him, his expression telling her that she wasn't the only miserable, sleep-deprived person in the building.

Her annoyance at his stupid rule faltered a bit, seeing him with such a dour expression. "Hello."

He grunted.

She had to laugh. "Not much of a morning person, I take it?"

"No." He gestured toward the coffee carafe on the counter. "Help yourself."

"Thanks." She went to his refrigerator and, opening it... found it almost empty. She shook her head. What was it with single men having empty pantries? But she did find a container of cream, though she did sniff it for freshness. He seemed like a fastidious man, but you could never tell. It seemed fine.

Pouring some into a mug he had put by the carafe, she poured herself a cup of the glorious substance, and replaced the cream. He was still cooking whatever it was that he was making. She peered closer and smiled. "Eggie in a basket? I don't think I've had that in years."

"It's simple."

Oh, he really, really wasn't a morning person. She leaned against the counter and sipped her coffee. "Didn't sleep either?"

"No."

If she didn't feel like abject hell, she would have walked up to him, wrapped her arms around his waist, and done everything in her power to make him more of a morning person. But she hardly felt like being frisky. Besides...last night, she had seen a monster. She shuddered at the memory of "Jim." She could almost still smell the rotting flesh.

"What was that thing that attacked me in the alley?" She

felt cold all of a sudden and curled tighter around the warm mug of liquid.

Rafe sighed. His shoulders slumped a little. "Can we please wait until after we've eaten?"

How polite. She smiled. "Yeah. That's fine." She paused. "If...if I can't stay in my hotel room, and I'm not leaving without Elliot, I...uh..." *I'll barge into a lot of places unannounced, but inviting myself into his home for who knows how long is a whole different thing.*

Rafe picked up a spatula and slipped it under the piece of bread with the hole in the center where the egg had been placed. He put it onto a plate and held it out to her silently. He didn't even look at her. He was still staring down at the skillet, watching the second piece of bread and egg as it continued to cook.

If she had the energy, she would have laughed again at how perfectly grumpy he was. As it was, she was just happy for the food. "Thank you." She took the plate from him and sat at one of the stools. He plated his own breakfast, fished out a pair of forks and knives for them, and handed her a set. He sat and began to drink his own coffee.

"We will need to fetch your things," he muttered as he stared down at the plate. He was cutting his breakfast up into perfect squares. "I will go with you this afternoon."

"Probably a good plan. We don't want a repeat of last night." She chuckled. "Not that I think you really minded the view."

His neck went a little red, but he said nothing. He simply began eating his perfectly-cut-up squares of egg and bread. He had cooked his breakfast a bit longer, she noticed, so it didn't even run when he cut up the yolk. *Perfectionist. Orderly. I bet he has his books organized into subcategories.*

She wanted to break him. She wanted to provoke him until he snapped. Until he just couldn't take it any longer.

And I don't think I'm that far away. She grinned to herself. One thing at a time, she supposed.

They ate in silence, and she was honestly all right for that. He seemed to be in a terrible mood, and she was exhausted. Finally, a thought did occur to her. "Oh. Can I borrow one of your ties?"

The look he gave her was so wonderfully perplexed, his fork hovering in mid-air. "Why?"

"For a blindfold." She smiled, proud of her pragmatism in solving the problem.

She didn't know how a person could both blush and go pale at the same time. He stared at her over the thin rim of his glasses. "Pardon?"

She laughed. "Oh, you dirty boy. No, so I can sleep, silly." She poked his hand with her fork, and he jolted as if she had electrocuted him.

He cleared his throat. "Yes. Well. About that."

She arched an eyebrow at him and shifted closer to the counter. "I thought you'd never ask..."

That time he sighed in exasperation. "Emma."

"Sorry." She smiled playfully. "I can't help it."

"Apparently not." He sipped his coffee for a moment, and then studied the mug, running a finger along the edge of the porcelain lip. "I suppose I should explain why *precisely* you must always be in the light in my presence."

"And not scream," she dutifully added.

"And not scream." His jaw ticked, and it was clear he was very uncomfortable speaking about this. He sighed. "I will beg you one last time, Emma. I am pleading with you—go home." Those midnight eyes of his bored into hers, once more seeing through her. *"Please,* Emma. Save yourself from this nightmare."

She felt arrested to the spot. The sudden switch from playfully teasing him over breakfast to this intensity was jarring at best, unsettling at worst. He was very serious, and she had no doubt that he meant every word. He wasn't just trying to send her away—he was trying to save her.

But she couldn't do as he asked.

She simply couldn't.

"I...I'm sorry," she whispered. "I can't abandon my brother. Even if it means I—I join him, in whatever terrible fate that's befallen him." She fought back the impulse to cry. The idea of leaving him alone in the dark, or even in death, was just too much for her. "We're twins. We came into this world together. If we go out together, so be it."

She hadn't realized she was trembling until he placed his hand over hers. His touch was warm, and strong, and certain. She shut her eyes, and the tears she was battling and losing threatened to spill down her cheeks. But she sniffled and bit them back. "I'm sorry."

"It is all right, Emma." He stood from the counter and picked up a piece of the cooked egg that he hadn't eaten. She couldn't figure out what he was going to do with it, but...all right. To each their own. "This is your point of no return. I will explain it all to you, but after this...there is no turning back. Do you understand?"

Nodding weakly, she swallowed the lump in her throat.

"Very well." He walked away, heading out of the kitchen and toward the stairs.

She followed him, curious and wary at the same moment. She wanted to see whatever terrible thing he was about to show her—and what strange secrets he was going to reveal.

He rounded the corner into his library, and she pulled in a breath. It was beautiful—the bookcases stretched from floor to ceiling and were absolutely stocked full with volumes of every shape and size. The electric lights were blazing like they were everywhere else in his home, even though there was enough sunlight to not need them. There wasn't a shadow or scrap of darkness anywhere in the room.

The room was tastefully decorated, and she stopped to read some of the titles in Rafe's possession. Poppa would be jealous, and his collection was one of the best in the region. But one thing struck her as odd. Everything looked remarkably *normal.* Books on the history or geography of the world. Maps. Religious texts from all over the planet. But nothing she suspected he really studied—if he really was in one of the "Dark Societies" as he and others claimed. She walked up to a large globe in its stand and spun it idly, watching the carefully-painted countries whirl by. "Is this your whole library?"

He eyed her thoughtfully and then gave her a thin smile. "No. The rest is…not for public display."

"I didn't figure you for hosting frequent guests."

"I don't. But the Church has barged into my home before in search of…well." He grimaced in instant frustration then shook his head. "I am getting ahead of myself. Allow me to start at the beginning without interruptions, yes?"

"Yes, Professor." She sat in one of the chairs by the center desk. The disbelief in his expression made her chuckle. "I promise."

"We shall see." He sat at the desk across from her and placed the piece of cooked egg white on the table. She still had no idea what it was for. But before she could ask, he pulled a piece of paper out in front of him and lifted his fountain pen. "Tell me…what do you know of the Great Beast of Arnsmouth?"

"That three hundred years ago, when this city was just a settlement, there was a great evil that descended over the people. It corrupted them, and from the Great Beast came the Dark Societies—people who worshiped the monster. The Church of the Benevolent God fought them back and destroyed them." She watched him keenly. "But it's just a legend to scare people into donating money to the Church, and a reason to keep the Investigators around." She paused. "Isn't it?"

His expression was mournful, regretting his words even as he smiled gently at her. "No, Miss Mather. It is not a legend, or a children's story. The Dark Societies are very real —and they have never been driven out as the Church would have you believe, though they still hunt us with great dedication."

"Us?" She knew. She did. But she wanted to hear it confirmed.

He took the pen to the piece of paper and drew a single line, vertically down the page, about two inches long. "The Key." A triangle bisected the line, the point converging at the bottom. "The Blade." A square, point to point, came next. "The Candle." A pentagon. "The Idol." And then a hexagon, shaped like a gem, that touched both sides of the original line. "The Mirror."

It was the symbol she had shown Rafe in his office. The one he had burned. The one she had found in Elliot's apartment, scrawled in blood. She shivered, a feeling like ice settling over her, and she shifted back in her chair.

"Five societies—each tapping into the Great Beast in their own way. Each one dedicated to one aspect of the monster, seeking to control it. To wield it." Rafe was teaching her, and he sounded no more in his element than he did right now. Even slightly disheveled and exhausted, he fell into the pattern with practiced ease. "This...this is the symbol of the monster that dwells within Arnsmouth. It is both a lock and a key. A gateway, and a guard."

"And which one are you...?" Her voice sounded small and afraid. That was precisely how she felt. "Which cult is yours?"

"The Mirror." He tapped the hexagon. "I wield secrets. I see things that should not be seen. I know what is, and will be, and has been. I control all that is known. And in that knowledge, I exert my power over this world." Dark eyes met hers.

"Gigi seems to have the same gift." She glanced away, unable to take his stare. "She knows more than she should."

"She has spies, both human and not, who follow you wherever you go. She is...cheating. What I do is very different." There was an undeniable level of disdain in his voice. He took the symbol he had just drawn and, folding it into pieces, set it into a bowl on his desk. Fetching a lighter from a drawer, it met the same fate as the first time. The smell of burning paper filled the air. She watched the flames as they charred the parchment and turned it to dust.

"She's the one who sent, uh, Jim?"

"Jim?" He blinked then narrowed his eyes. "You named it *Jim?*"

"I—" Oh, here came the moment she dreaded. She hated this. Letting out a sigh, she went into the speech she had given people more times than she cared to count. "My brother and I suffer from shadows, like I told you. I see things that aren't real. Monsters. People. Sometimes just a figure that I can't describe. I hear voices that don't exist. My memories are visceral, sometimes overwhelming. I can see places I've been, like I'm there." She felt her shoulders slump. She wasn't ashamed of her illness, but she hated how people stared at her once they knew the truth.

She was broken. Damaged. Things in her brain weren't *right,* and no one knew how to fix her. "I started naming the creatures, or the people who appeared. Naming them made them less terrifying. Especially if they're jarringly mismatched." She smirked but didn't look up from the table. "It makes it funny, y'know? To see something that big and terrifying, and to name it *Jim.* Takes the wind out of its sails."

"You suffer from psychosis, like Elliot."

She nodded.

"His—ah—shadows, seemed to torment him. He was a shell of a man when I met him. Dependent on drugs and alcohol to get through his days. How is it that you are more balanced?" His tone was even, but she still didn't want to see what she knew probably lingered in his eyes. Disgust, or the thing she hated above all—pity.

She *hated* the pity.

It took her a moment to figure out how to answer him. "I went with Poppa and his fellow explorers to Africa when I was young. Maybe eleven or twelve. Deep in the dark continent, where there were no maps. We met a tribe, and our guide who could speak their language introduced us. There was an old man there, and he took one look at me and called me over. The guide said he was the tribe's shaman."

She fidgeted, picking at the sleeve of her blouse. "The man said I was touched. That I was a Seer, like him. That he saw shadows and heard the voices as well. He said they were gifts from the ancestors, and that I should embrace my power." She huffed a laugh.

"You didn't believe him." It was a statement, not a question. Still, she refused to meet his gaze.

"No. The things I see aren't *real*. They don't exist. You know how I know? Elliot and I never saw the same things at the same time. Maybe if we did, I'd have believed the shaman's story. But talking to him still helped me. I didn't feel so alone, I suppose. I realized people like Elliot and me are everywhere. That it's not…it's not something to be ashamed of." She shrugged. "That's why I was happy that Jim was real. I was afraid my shadows were turning into the things that Elliot saw. Awful things that could rip him to pieces, eat him alive, but leave him unharmed. I didn't want to see things like that. I'm sick, but I don't want to be *that* sick."

"Emma."

Finally, she looked up at him, and she was surprised at what she saw. There was no disgust. Thankfully, there was no pity. Not even a flicker of concern. His dark eyes flicked between hers, studying her. He didn't deny her illness. Didn't tell her that her psychosis was *secretly* some sort of magical power. She knew it wasn't, and she was very glad he didn't try to explain it away like so many people had in her life.

"I am impressed how you have learned to cope with your illness." He smirked. "Even if naming a creature of the dark 'Jim' is vaguely offensive to me on many levels."

She chuckled. She was all right with that. She shrugged. "I am who I am."

"And to answer your question, no. Gigi did not send that monster after you." Rafe sighed, his expression turning darker than usual. "You have two Societies hunting you. Gigi, the Blade…and the Idol. It is the Idol who I believe your brother fell in with."

"Two societies are hunting me, and you belong to a third?" She let out a weak laugh. "Oh, joy. I really have dug myself a grave, haven't I? Figures."

"Indeed, you have." He looked amused at her reaction. "I had rather hoped you would have run screaming."

"Still time for that. You haven't told me what the issue is with you and darkness, or why you have a piece of egg sitting on your desk." She pointed at it. "Unless we're both insane."

"Perhaps. It's hard to say." He glanced at the bit of egg, and she watched his posture change. He went tense and sat back in his leather and wood desk chair, the upholstery creaking. "But we do have something in common." He picked up the piece of cooked egg.

"Oh?"

"I remind you—do not scream."

With no further warning, he reached out and pulled the

chain on the desk lamp with a *click*. The bulb went out, and for the first time, there wasn't the constant and overwhelming flood of light within his home. Darkness lingered around the edges of the objects on his desk—the bowl, the lamp, his pen holder. Stacks of books.

The darkness moved.

Things came from them. Tendrils of blackness, squirming, wriggling, reaching. One went near her hand, and she pulled away before it could touch her. Her heart was pounding in her ears, her pulse instantly racing.

He picked up the piece of egg and held it out over the darkness cast by the shape of the lamp and the other lights in the room. Ensuring that she was watching, he dropped it. The moment it touched the seemingly innocuous spot on his desk…it vanished.

Gone.

Consumed.

She went rigid.

He smirked at her wide-eyed, terrified expression. There was a knowing kind of defiance in his eyes. As though he were fully expecting whatever response she might have to what she had just seen. "In this way, we are similar. We both suffer from shadows, Emma Mather."

CHAPTER FIFTEEN

Rafe waited for Emma to run away. He waited for her to tear out of the room as fast as she could, and for her to never look back. That would be the best outcome for everyone. Or alternatively...he waited for her to scream.

And for her to end her life.

She would be dead very soon anyway. She might as well end it now. Indeed, he had brought her here with the intention of killing her. Of leading her down into his basement and letting his infestation feed upon her and be done with her.

But he found himself suddenly unable to do so. Not because he wasn't carrying his switchblade in his pocket, and not because he wasn't perfectly capable of slitting her throat. No, perhaps the word wasn't *unable*, but *unwilling*.

There was no point in denying that he was oddly captivated by her. If he had not been about to lose control of the Things that dwelled within him, he would have eagerly taken her up on her invitation and crawled into bed with her last night.

He wanted her quite badly. But she was more than just a pretty face—if that were the case, he could ignore her as he did all the pretty faces he saw during his life. No. She was witty, clever, brash, and there was a wildness about her that was enthralling. She had traveled the world, seen places he could not imagine. There was a kind of wisdom in her, even with her playful, youthful demeanor.

There were shadows in her eyes. There was a darkness in her that wanted to consume her, much the same as her brother. But where Elliot surrendered to the whispers of his illness, Emma fought back against them with her own blazing light.

And sarcasm, apparently.

He still would not forgive her for giving a Crawling Terror the moniker of "Jim." It was as insulting as it was amusing. But it would have to go down on record as one of the oddest reactions to one of the creatures of the Great Beast that he had ever seen. It was endearing in its own odd way.

But Emma did not run away. Nor did she scream.

She simply sat there and stared at the Things that infested the shadows around them. Her eyes were wide, and the color had drained from her cheeks. She watched them as they writhed, reaching for her, straining to get closer. The light from the bulbs and the sunlight from the window kept them from obtaining their goal, however.

For better or worse.

"I am a monster, Miss Mather. Make no mistake." He held his hand over the desk, casting a shadow, and watched as the Things wriggled around the darkness, like tapered worms from a bloated corpse. "I am no better than...eh...*Jim.*" It hurt to say the moniker. "Indeed, I may be worse. I wear the face of a man in the daylight."

She swallowed thickly. She didn't take her eyes off the

wriggling darkness. Finally, after a long pause, she spoke. "And—and what do you—what do you wear in the dark?"

The smile he let spread over his features was a wry one. "Why do you think I abandoned you last night? Certainly not because I didn't enjoy the view."

That finally made her look up from the sight of the Things on the table. She somehow looked more shocked than before. Poor thing. He was impressed she didn't faint. Then she did the most surprising thing she had done to date.

She laughed.

It wasn't a loud laugh. It wasn't a mirthful one. It was the kind of laugh someone did when they were at the bottom of a hole with no way out, and it began to rain. It was the laugh of someone who had nothing else to do but find humor in their situation.

Leaning back in her chair, she watched the creatures that continued to wriggle along the table for a moment, before her expression turned into one of confusion and a little bit of disgust. "I had a dream last night…"

"Where you were beset by them?" He felt his jaw tick. "I told you to keep the lights on."

"Oh, my god." She put her hand over her eyes. "Rafe, they—"

"I know."

"I thought it was a dream!"

"It wasn't."

"But they—"

"I know." He wondered if she would be mortified. If she would accuse him of accosting her. In a way, it had been his fault. Indeed, he had never seen his infestation react in such a way as they did with her. Perhaps it was his own latent lust for the young woman that changed their behavior.

It made the idea of making love to her a challenging one. But if she didn't survive, it would probably be for the best.

Besides, with what little he knew of Emma, that would be preferable to when he would have to slit her throat and end her anyway.

He would not let the Idol have her. He would not let the Blade take her. And by the pits, if the Candle got involved, the chaos that would ensue would be catastrophic. No, better he end her life quickly.

But...

His thoughts were thankfully derailed as she lowered her hand from her face. She let out a weak, quiet chuckle. "This is simply getting stranger and stranger. What *are* they?"

"An infestation. The result of my tapping into the power of the Great Beast. There is a price for such things. I have methods by which I control them, and dampen their effects, but they are pernicious. And sometimes they make their displeasure of my caging them rather well known."

Emma was not a fool. "Like last night."

"Indeed."

She hesitated. "Are they going to hurt me?"

"Yesterday morning, I would have said without a doubt. That you would be devoured by them like that scrap of food." There wasn't any point in lying to her. "But after what I saw last night, I'm no longer sure. They seemed to have been feeding not on your body, but on your fear. I've never witnessed it before."

"Maybe they're attracted to me, too." She smirked at him, her first return to humor since his revelations.

"The thought has crossed my mind."

Her smile faded, and she went back to staring at the Things on his desk. "That's why you said not to scream. They eat things that are afraid?"

"Yes, precisely. That would most certainly guarantee your death."

She paused for a long moment, before she did the

damnedest thing. The young woman let out a long, tired sigh. "Well, best get this over with." She reached out a hand toward them.

He snatched her wrist before she could touch them. "What do you think you're doing?"

She met his gaze with an unflinching certainty. "I'm skipping to the end. If they're going to kill me, they can do it now."

It was astonishing how frequently bravery and stupidity could be considered the same thing. He slowly let go of her wrist. If she wanted to lose her hand today, he could hardly stop her. Especially since she could easily flick off the lights wherever she went in his house.

She reached out a pointer finger and placed it near one of his shadows. Like a creature being lured out from a den with the promise of food, a single black tendril wormed from the shade. It was jagged, with sharp edges and pointed, curling spirals. They were eldritch and strange, and not entirely organic-looking things, for all their animalistic behavior.

When it touched her, Emma pulled in a breath and held it. She watched, waiting perhaps to see if it would rip her finger off, or devour her whole hand. He wondered the same.

It curled around her finger like a sea creature, exploring her. But not harming her.

"Huh." He blinked.

"You don't need to sound so surprised." Her voice was wary and strained, her focus on watching the monster that was now winding around her other fingers, prying open her hand and moving around her palm. "Maybe it's like a constrictor…just getting into a better position to maim me."

"It's fully possible." It was fascinating to watch. Fascinating and more than a little arousing, as she turned over her hand to lay it palm up on the table, inviting the tendril to continue its slow exploration of her. This was nothing if not deeply interesting. He would have to take notes on this in the future.

Perhaps she would be amenable to experimenting with them. She seemed curious enough. Curious, and perhaps the owner of a death wish. As the tendril reached her wrist and pressed against her pulse, her cheeks went pink.

Ah.

He was not the only one finding himself agitated by what was happening. He studied her reaction. She was breathing faster than before, her body tense, and he had no doubt that her pulse was racing.

She was afraid. But as she parted her lips to breathe, there was a lust in her eyes, darkening the amber to an orange-brown that reminded him of the trees in the fall.

"Is there something you wish to tell me, Miss Mather? Something that might be useful to know, regarding our current…predicament?"

She swallowed before licking her lower lip and chewing on it. He was distracted by the movement. He fought the urge to drag her over the desk in that moment and kiss her as he had before. He wanted to be the one biting her lip, not her.

"I—well—um." She shifted in her chair. "I have a rather peculiar reaction to being afraid, I suppose."

"Not as much as you may think. Adrenaline, when it floods the system, can have a myriad of effects on the body. It allows us to fight or flee the things that wish to eat us. It quickens the pulse, releases chemicals into the body that give us bursts of strength or speed. And some, in your case, find themselves thrill seekers. Living for the sensation of standing upon the edge. Is that accurate?" He wanted to take notes. It would likely be rude.

"Very. I…oh—oh—" She looked down at the floor. "Hey! Do *not* get frisky with me. I see you down there. I have not agreed to a word of this, do you hear me? You cannot simply go about accosting people."

She was lecturing the eldritch abominations that had infested the darkness around him.

He put his face in his palm.

Emma Mather was going to mean trouble.

SHE SHOOK her ankle free from the shadow-thing that had wrapped around it. It let her go, surprisingly. She twisted to ensure she kept herself in the light of the electric bulbs and the sunlight. She gently pulled free of the one that had been wrapped around her hand.

Her heart was still racing, and she let out a wavering breath. If it weren't still before noon, she would ask for a stiff drink. But as it was, she felt it was probably best not to hit the bottle. Because there was a portion of her that wanted to get herself well and truly drunk, then find herself a shadowy corner of the house, and…flip the lights off.

Just to see what might happen.

Just to see what they might *do.*

And the intensity of Rafe's expression wasn't making her feel any less nervous. She shifted in her chair and cursed her brokenness. Taking a deep breath, she held it for a long moment and let it out in a rush. Fear certainly got her engine roaring, and she didn't need to be sitting here wondering just how personal those monstrous things might want to get with her.

Or what kind of a hand Rafe would want to play in it.

Oh, goodness. She blinked. If he had been losing control last night, she wondered if she wasn't playing with a bigger lion than she had anticipated. He was dangerous, no doubt. His monsters were dangerous.

And they *both* wanted her. Likely very much at the same time. Her cheeks went hot, and she knew she was blushing as she imagined what that might be like. Images flashed through her mind, and she tried to stomp them down into the gutter from whence they came.

Magic was real. The Dark Societies weren't simply legends. One of them had her twin brother. Two of them were after her. And she was sitting there, getting all riled up at the thought of being thoroughly ruined by Professor Saltonstall and his shadowy *Things*.

To say that she had further proof of her mental instability would be to put it mildly. She chewed her lip again. She wanted to save her brother. She wanted to save her brother *and* have a wild time with the man sitting across from her. The man and all he came along with.

Her mouth felt dry. She swallowed. "What happens next?"

He paused as he considered his answer. He likely had a list to choose from. "I would highly recommend we go fetch your things from the hotel before we have another incident."

"No, we wouldn't want one of those, would we?" *Why am I just a little disappointed?*

The twist to his lips was a sarcastic one. "We shall see. I have a feeling you will find yourself in a great many incidents soon enough. Best to avoid the ones we can."

Emma couldn't tell if he was making an insinuation or not. He stood from his desk, cracked his back audibly, and then groaned. "I am going to take a shower, dress, and then we will go."

"A lovely walk through the park. What a charming date. Perhaps we can get dinner. Then your monsters will devour me like a chicken bone. Or they'll—" She made a rude gesture.

It looked like he wasn't sure if he was insulted or amused. It seemed they rather canceled themselves out. "A dinner sounds lovely. Let us leave it at that for now." He headed for the door of his library, abandoning her there.

What an odd man. "I'll go...sit in the sun or something." She shook her head and went to do just that.

Not that she wasn't tempted to sit beneath a tree and see just how far his darkness stretched.

CHAPTER SIXTEEN

The gray clouds had been burned away by the sun, and for once—a rarity in gloomy Arnsmouth—it was a rather cheerful day. There were birds in the trees, the flowers were beginning to bloom, and it was by all accounts a wonderful early afternoon.

Save for the simple fact that Emma was walking next to a man who was "infested" with monsters who wanted to do *things* to her. The full breadth of which was likely going to end her life. It just remained to be determined precisely in what order, and involving what topics, the actions were going to entail.

Or how active of a hand the man beside her was going to play in any and all of it. Tucking her hands into her coat pockets, she strolled beside Rafe. He seemed fully content to walk in silence. She expected he probably preferred it. Well, she'd had enough of that. "So, are you going to kill me?"

"Hum?" He sounded startled by the abrupt question.

"Are you going to kill me?" She smirked. "Intentionally, I mean. Yourself. Not your—whatever-they-are." She gestured at him. "Your friends. What're they named?"

"I do not think they have a name. And if they did, they are likely fully unpronounceable by mortals."

"Have you ever asked?"

"Asked?" That earned her an arched eyebrow. "Asked what?"

"Asked *them*." She wriggled her fingers at him. "Who do you think?"

"Ask them what?"

"If they have names, silly!" She laughed.

He shook his head as if she were the strangest creature alive. And that was something, considering. "I have never attempted to speak to them, except perhaps to yell at them out of frustration."

"Well, there's your problem." She huffed in affected indignity, pretending to be offended on the wriggly things' behalf. "Do you think they are one individual, or many?" She pondered. "How many names will I need to come up with?"

"No. You are *not* naming my infestation. I will not allow this." He glared at her in warning. "I will not have you wandering about calling those eldritch blights upon my person any of your insultingly mundane monikers."

"Fine, then I won't make them insultingly mundane." When he groaned in dismay, she cackled in joy. "You're too much fun to tease!" She shoved his arm playfully. "Calm down. I won't name them."

"Thank you."

"Yet."

He groaned a second time.

She smiled, proud of herself, though she supposed she had no real reason to be anything of the sort. Professor Raphael Saltonstall seemed to go through his life in various stages of being annoyed, angry, frustrated, or some combination of all three. *Oh, lust is in there too, I suppose.* But that was beside the point. He was an easy target.

"You didn't answer my question," she prompted after they fell silent for a minute or so.

"We discussed the topic of my infestation's lack of names."

"No, no." She laughed. "Not that one. The one about you killing me."

"Ah." He cleared his throat. He went very quiet again, and the look on his face was cast ahead of them down the path in the Arnsmouth Common, and he didn't look at her.

"Oh, you *bastard,* you are!" She shoved him again, harder than before. It knocked him out of step, and he staggered for a moment.

He stopped and turned to her. "I said nothing."

"I know! That's precisely the problem. You didn't deny it." She placed her hands on her hips and glared up at him.

"I am still considering all my options." He turned and began to walk again.

With a heavy sigh, she jogged a few steps to catch up with him. "Considering all your options? And what options are those? Killing me, or not killing me?"

"Yes."

It was her turn to make a noise, this time a growl of frustration. She glowered at him, and then realized it was pointless. He was still refusing to look at her. "And why?"

"Why what?" He sighed. "Please be more specific with your questions. You're jumping all around."

"I am not jump—" She paused to take a breather before she picked up a branch from the ground nearby and beat him senseless with it. "I am asking you why you want to kill me."

"Now you're jumping to conclusions, Miss Mather. I have never once stated that I wished to do anything of the sort. In fact, all to the opposite, I have expressed my unwavering desire for you to *leave.*" His dark eyes flicked to her briefly before returning studiously ahead. "Yet you remain. So, the inevitability that I may have to be the one to put you out of your misery lies before me as a possibility that I cannot deny."

"I suppose I should thank you for being honest. Though I distinctly wish to hit you right now, so I think I won't." She folded her arms across her chest, pouting. She didn't care if it was childish. The man was talking about killing her. "How would you do it?"

"Hum?"

"How would you kill me?"

He furrowed his brow. "Why on Earth are you asking me that question?"

"Because I'm asking. Because I'd like to know. Because if you're going to murder me, *Rafe,* I want to know how you'd do it." She rolled her eyes, then smirked. "Oh! Even better. Don't tell me. Let me guess."

"Guess." He was now staring at her, flabbergasted. "You wish to guess the method by which I would murder you?"

"I have to have fun somehow. I have to find some kind of light in all this misery and death. If I don't laugh at what's happening, I'll scream. And then where will I be? Nowhere. Just a hysterical, miserable mess." She let out a breath. "If I'm going to die, no matter what, I might as well smile at the reaper when he shows up to take me away."

"I…suppose." He seemed entirely confused, but he let it go without any more argument. "Very well. Guess away."

"I'll start with the obvious." She wriggled the fingers of both her hands at him.

"I thought, yes, that I would simply flip off the lights and let them destroy all trace of you. But it seems they have other…" He cleared his throat again. "Plans."

"Maybe. Or maybe they don't." She shrugged. "Maybe they're just savoring the kill."

"Indeed."

"So. All right. If it isn't with your squiggly-wrigglers—"

"Please, don't call them that, either."

She cackled. "If it isn't from your friends"—she paused to see if he'd object to that—"let's see…" She tapped her finger on her chin. "Poison? No. Too messy. Although your friends would clean that up for you. Takes too long, then. You're an impatient man."

"I am not."

"Sure." She opted not to point out to him that he was offended by being called impatient while they were discussing his preferred method of murder. "A gun is too loud. Attracts attention. A garrote or strangulation is too feisty. You look like you could overpower me, and probably quite a few men, but it isn't guaranteed. No, you want to make sure your kills don't get away."

"I am deeply unsettled by this conversation."

"You're the murderer. I'm just puzzling it all out." She imitated his tone and accent. "Now, do not interrupt, Professor Saltonstall."

He looked so wonderfully confused. He was cute when he was perplexed, she decided.

Continuing, she started listing things off on her fingers. "Faking a suicide is too situational. Not many scenarios where you can hang someone. Electrocution is too newfangled and fancy. Murder by vehicle would be both too situational *and* too fancy. No. I think you're all about efficiency. Swift, easy, guaranteed. I think you're a knife man." She dragged her thumb across her throat.

He rubbed a palm over his face. "I dislike this greatly."

"Hah!" She pointed at him. "I'm right! You *are* a knife man!"

The beleaguered sound that left him was both surrender and like he was pleading to be struck dead on the spot by the Benevolent God himself.

"How wonderfully naughty." She grinned mischievously and slid up close to him, letting her words go sultry. "Can you threaten me with it first, before you do the deed?"

"I am going to take this moment to point out to you something of which you are already quite well aware, but I feel remiss if I don't take the opportunity to do so, Miss Mather." He shook his head. "You are unwell."

Howling in laughter, she hugged his arm. She went serious for a moment, and like all the gas let out of a zeppelin, she felt her mood crash and burn. She let go of his arm and walked beside him instead. "Just…make it quick, that's all I ask." Tears stung her eyes, but she refused to let them fall.

He took her by the arm and, stopping, gently turned her to face him. "Emma."

She refused to look at him.

"Emma."

Nope. She was going to stare at his tie instead. It was a very nice tie.

A finger crooked under her chin, and he lifted her face until she had to meet his gaze. There was a surprising amount of empathy in his eyes. Not sympathy, perhaps—he didn't feel bad for her. She was in this mess of her own accord—or Elliot's, depending on how she looked at it—but he did seem to feel bad *with* her.

Leaning down, he hovered his lips over hers for a moment and hesitated, as if wondering if she would pull away from him. They had just been discussing her murder at his hands, after all. But instead, she was the one to zero the distance between them, and he slipped his hand to cradle the back of her neck, holding her in the tender embrace.

It wasn't passionate. It was affectionate.

And for some reason, that almost made her want to cry even more than before. After a moment, he parted from her and pulled her into a hug. "If I must, I will make it quick." He hesitated, and for once, he was the one with the mischievous tone. "Or if not quick...perhaps enjoyable."

She laughed and buried her head against his chest. "Well played."

"I do have my moments." He kissed the top of her head. "Now. Let us go, before we are questioned by the Investigators or the police for public affection."

"Pah." He was right. There were no laws against kissing in public. But it would draw attention they likely didn't need. As they resumed their walk, he held out his elbow to her. "Keeping up appearances, are we?"

"Yes. Of course. Appearances."

She smiled to herself and tucked her arm into his.

THE WALK back to the hotel was uneventful. For a moment, she could almost pretend they were *normal*. That they were just on a date, or that they had simply become hopeful spring lovers, like so many others. That they hadn't just been discussing the method by which he was probably plotting to kill her, or the dark monsters that had infested him, or her missing brother.

They debated where they would go for dinner, since he was a lousy cook and he refused to be responsible for making anything approaching "romantic." So, she listed their options and heard his opinion on each one, before she opted to take him somewhere that his salary would likely not have allowed him to dine at regularly. It was a lovely French establishment, well-known for being posh.

He fussed at the notion of a woman paying for dinner, until she pointed out that it was technically her father buying them the meal, so it was still a man's wallet involved in the transaction.

He called it a loophole, and she called him old-fashioned.

So, the French restaurant it was.

To his credit, he conceded the fight gracefully.

They rode the elevator up to the third-to-last floor where her hotel room was, and she found herself oddly cheerful—no, not cheerful, perhaps hopeful would be the better word—as she placed the room key into the lock and twisted it. It clicked, revealing that there had been no more break-ins by Gigi or anyone else. Good. She let out a breath of relief.

"I will wait here." Rafe leaned against the wall beside the door and glanced up at the electric overhead light in its decorative stained-glass housing, its sharp angles and dramatic patterns casting odd, indistinct shadows. Not enough for his friends to make an appearance, she supposed. "I doubt it is well-lit in your hotel, and, well…" He trailed off with a frown as he squinted up at the light.

She had to smile at how utterly cranky he looked. His condition was a unique one, but she understood what it was like to live with a burden. Even if it wasn't always inconvenient. She reached out and placed a hand on his arm, turning his attention back down to her. "I will be right out. I didn't pack much."

He smiled faintly. "A practical young woman?"

"No. Lazy." She grinned. "I hate carrying luggage."

He chuckled, shaking his head. "I should have guessed."

Happy at having slightly cheered him up, she pushed the door open. Stepping in, the smell was what hit her first.

She knew that smell.

Blood.

And a lot of it.

Blood, and the stink of entrails. She had watched a lion kill a gazelle on the plains one day on safari, and the scent of waste leaving the body unexpectedly and through undesirable means was somehow more rancid than normal, as it mixed with stomach bile and the other ichor that dwelled inside a living body.

A smear of blood ran across the carpet, staining it in shades of what would have been deep red but had turned to dark browns by now. It wasn't fresh. It had been here for a few hours, at the very least. She pulled her gun from her pocketbook and held it low at her side. Stepping into the central living area of the room, she froze.

The only thing she could think of was Rafe's warning. It was dark in her hotel, and his words played through her head like a skipping record.

Don't scream. Don't scream. Don't scream.

She didn't. She couldn't. She couldn't do anything at all except stand there, frozen solid, staring.

There was a man she did not know, crumpled on the ground in a heap by the wall. He held a knife in his hand. His head was limp, chin against his chest. And his stomach was ripped open from one side to the other, pooling around him. He had gutted himself like a fish. But that wasn't all he had done.

Scrawled on the wallpaper, in large swipes of a hand that had been wet with blood, was a message. A message for her.

"Elliot misses you."

CHAPTER SEVENTEEN

Rafe was, despite his insistence to the contrary, not a very patient man. Or perhaps that wasn't terribly accurate to the truth of it. He was patient enough, when things were worth waiting for, or when it was expected to take time. No, he simply hated *wasting* time.

And that was why he tapped his fingers against his thigh as he waited for Emma to emerge from her hotel room, bag in hand. He could just imagine her chipper "ready to go?" as she came out holding some kind of loudly patterned carpet bag or two from one of her adventures to other continents. He would naturally offer to carry them for her, as he was—despite himself, perhaps—a gentleman.

She would tease him, and dance around him like the little impish pixie that she was, and chatter at him about where she had purchased the luggage. India, perhaps. Or the islands. He would listen to her talk about the fire-spinners and the cooked pigs. Perhaps she would ask him to travel with her someday.

He found himself smiling at the notion.

And that frightened him worse than almost everything

else. *Oh, no, what have I gotten myself into now?* He groaned and shut his eyes, leaning his head against the wall, depressing the brim of his felted hat. It wasn't that he hadn't ever had romantic feelings for a woman. It was simply that he hadn't made time for it in his life. That, and with the—eh —*complications* provided by his infestation, it had become an impossibility.

Especially after the incident with a young woman a few years ago. It had been on the eve of the passing of the prohibition laws, and he had allowed himself to be tempted to enjoy public drinking for the last time for the foreseeable future. A young woman had wished to go home with him. Curse him, he had not even managed to catch her name.

They had not even made it back to his home before...

Well.

She had screamed.

The sound had been brief. So had the moment. And there had been no trace of her when all was said and done. He had regretted the moment and vowed never to let it happen again. The woman had been innocent of wrongdoing. He had no qualms with how much murder he had committed in his life, but the other lives on his hands had ended for a purpose. Not her.

After that—a night that was fairly early in his career—he had shoved aside all thoughts of romantic or physical relations and filled the holes in his schedule with research. It was likely for the best. He wasn't precisely the most graceful or elegant of gentlemen, and if he had prioritized that area of his life over his work, he would likely have found himself lacking against the competition.

But then *Emma* had to enter his life.

Damn it all.

She was a complication he did not need by any stretch of the imagination. He spent his life quietly trying to avoid all confrontations with the other Societies of Arnsmouth, and now she was sending him on a crash-course straight for them. The Blade was involved. The Idol was involved. I wouldn't be long before the Candle followed suit. They could never miss out on an opportunity for chaos and bloodshed.

Hopefully the Key remained as aloof as always. Hopefully. He sighed and shut his eyes. But with Emma, nothing was ever predictable. Most disturbingly of all, he had begun to enjoy her company—even her good-natured teasing, which was very unlike him.

This is why I like cats. The worst difficulty they bring me is they throw up on the rug.

Finally, the door to the hotel room swung open. He donned his most annoyed expression and prepared himself to scold her for taking her sweet time. "I thought perhaps you—" He stopped upon seeing her face. She was as pale as a sheet. She carried nothing in her hand, save for her small pistol.

Emma didn't look at him. Merely stood there, her eyes wide, and stared at the wall as if she weren't seeing a single thing around her. It was a moment later that the smell from inside the hotel room washed over him. Blood and gore.

Swearing under his breath, he stepped up to her and gently urged her to give him the pistol. Her hand was limp, and she did nothing to stop him from grasping it and placing it back into her purse. It didn't smell like black powder, nor had he heard a gunshot, so he assumed that whatever was dead inside her suite had been that way before they arrived.

"I will deal with this. Stay here," he murmured and helped her to lean against the wall. It looked as though she were going to collapse.

His suspicions were correct, as she slid to the floor a second later, her knees bent, her gaze now fixed on the open hotel room door.

What could have terrified her so badly? She had seen a Crawling Terror and had almost shrugged it off. She seemed fascinated by his own infestation to a rather unnerving degree. He could not imagine that a dead body would horrify her. Stepping into the room, he quickly found the source of the odor.

Reading the scrawled blood on the wall, he let out a long, heavy sigh. *"Elliot misses you."* Yes, that would explain her reaction. He pitied her, if he were forced to admit it. He had pitied her brother, and now she seemed destined to be dragged into the abyss, tethered to him by a chain that she could not, nor did she wish to, remove from her leg.

Crouching by the corpse, he picked up the man's arm by his sleeve, careful not to touch the mess. There, on the inside of his wrist, was the branded mark he suspected he might find—a pentagon. He wanted to slam his fist through the wall in frustration.

The Idol.

Fantastic.

It wasn't a new player entering the game, but this kind of overt action was unlike the Idol. They must be desperate to have her, and he could not fathom why. And he did not like things that he did not know.

Standing, he went to the light switch on the wall and pressed the off button. With a click, darkness flooded the room, only accented by the sunlight streaming in through the windows. He allowed his infestation to clean up the mess. The shadowy tendrils snatched the rotting meat without hesitation, pulling it into the shadows, devouring every last drop. Even the writing on the wall was gone in seconds.

With a shake of his head, he walked into the bedroom and began to pack up her things. It took him longer than he would have liked, as he checked every drawer. She had packed light as she had said, and he wound up with only two moderately-sized carpet bags. They were as brightly patterned and well-traveled as he had imagined.

He tried very hard to pack up her underthings with as much indifference as possible. Very hard. But he felt his neck go a bit warm, despite his attempt to be perfectly clinical about the ordeal.

Leaving the room, he shut the door. Emma was right where he had left her, staring empty-eyed and pale as a ghost into the space in front of her.

He doubted they would be going to dinner tonight. Placing the bags down, he helped her to her feet. "Come, Emma. Let us go. You should get some rest. You didn't sleep well last night, and..." He wasn't sure how to finish. "This has been a trying few days."

She nodded weakly and said nothing in reply. That troubled him more than he would have liked. Scooping up her bags again—hooking one over his shoulder—he gently took her arm with his free hand and guided her away.

Once they reached the lobby, she sat on one of the sofas while he went to close out her reservation. He eyed the man behind the counter thoughtfully for a moment, before adding to the request. "You have her father's number, do you not?"

"Yessir, the reservation is under his account."

"Good." Rafe kicked himself mentally for finding himself entangled with her. For finding himself beginning to *care.* "Phone the estate and tell him his daughter is safe. Tell him that she is coping with the grief of losing a loved one and prefers to stay with a friend." If her father was half as clever as society would claim, he would know what that meant. He hated informing her family in such a crass manner, but it was better than not knowing at all. "And would you call us a carriage? I fear the lady is unable to walk at the moment." *Nor do I really wish to walk across town carrying her luggage.*

The man nodded thinly and went to his phone, hopefully to fulfill both requests in reverse order.

A few minutes went by before the carriage arrived. They returned to his house in silence, with Emma simply doing as she was directed. It wasn't until he shut the door behind them in his home that she numbly walked into his study on the first floor, collapsed into a chair, and wept.

Placing her bags down by the stairway, he walked to her and knelt at her feet. "Emma."

"Where *is* he?" Large, tear-stained eyes turned to him desperately. "Please, Rafe. Please, tell me."

"I don't know." He stroked her tears away with his thumb, but they were quickly replaced by more. "I am sorry."

"You—you said—you *know* things—so fucking find out!" She shoved his shoulders, her grief turning to anger. She grabbed him by the lapels and shook him weakly, before resorting to punching at his chest. "I need to know what's happened to him!"

Poor, hopeless thing. He reached out and pulled her into his arms, and she went willingly. Her false anger cracked and shattered the moment he touched her. "Shush, Emma. Shush…"

She tucked her head against his shoulder and silently cried, her shoulders shaking as he stroked a hand over her dark curls. They stayed like that for a long time, though he could not guess as to the minutes. Eventually, her tears stopped, and he realized she had fallen asleep. Smiling sadly, he scooped her up in his arms and carried her up the stairs to the room she had slept in the night before.

Gently laying her down upon the sheets, he pulled a blanket over her. He would do his best to control his infestation. The overwrought, poor little thing needed to sleep. Remembering her comment about his tie, he smirked and pulled it from his throat before laying the strip of fabric on the pillow next to her.

Unable to resist, he leaned down and kissed her cheek before heading to the hallway and shutting the door behind him with a quiet click.

"Mrraaaak."

Rafe eyed Hector, raising an eyebrow at her. His portly cat was sitting by the door to the attic where she loved to prowl for mice and was glaring at him with all the annoyance that a cat could muster.

"I know, I know." He shook his head as he walked down the stairs, hearing the *thump-thump-thump* of the heavy animal following him. "I doubt she'll be staying with us long. I doubt she'll survive for long." His infestation seemed to treat her differently, but there was no telling when that would abruptly end. A bear might seem friendly right until the moment it tore open one's skull.

He headed to the kitchen to give the cat a snack. He knew he shouldn't be feeding his overweight cat nearly as much as he was, but it made her happy, and he was a sucker for when she would knead the table with her front feet and purr loud enough that she squeaked. He stroked his hand over her thick fur and let out a breath.

Emma had begged him to find out what had become of Elliot. There was always a price for such knowledge. Nothing ever came free. But...he was also deeply curious. And it might be important to know if the Idol soon came knocking on his door.

He scratched Hector between the ears as he settled on a decision.

Yes, very well, Emma. I will see what I can discover. But I wonder which of us will end up paying the piper this evening.

Heading to his library on the second floor, he opened the passage that revealed a small spiral staircase that descended deep into the ground. It was barely wide enough for a single person to walk, as it masqueraded as part of the fireplace. Closing the door behind him, it left him in pitch darkness. He did not care. He knew where he was going.

Down, and down, and down he went. Past the first floor, the basement, and even farther still. When he reached the bottom landing, he pulled his lighter from his pocket, and flicked it. The amber flame flickered off the surface of the object he had come to see. It was enormous, standing some nine feet tall, propped up on a stand in the center of the room.

A carved wood frame would have been gilded and intricate once, but was now faded and chipped, revealing only the wood and carrying a semblance of its former glory. The mirrored surface itself was obsidian, polished to be as smooth as ice.

His reflection was shattered, spiderwebbed into a billion different versions of himself. But as he approached, the lines healed and smoothed, turning into one unbroken surface.

He stared at himself, carrying the lighter. But he knew that what he saw was a lie. For the version in the mirror was grinning, where he was not. *I do despise having to do this.* But it seemed there was no way around it.

Straightening his back, he shut the lid of the lighter with a click. Yet the image before him remained. *I wonder which of us will end up paying the piper this evening, Emma. I hope for your sake, it is I.*

He commanded the darkness. "Show me Elliot Mather."

CHAPTER EIGHTEEN

When Emma woke up, she had no idea where she was.

And she had no idea what was touching her.

She jolted, startled out of her sleep, and rubbed a hand over her face. The lights in the room were on, and she blinked in an attempt to focus. She had dreamed of being in the jungle, and something about a big snake.

So she wasn't entirely surprised when she sat up and looked down to see her leg was in the shadow of the post of the footboard. And that a particularly large shadowy appendage, about as thick as her wrist, had wound itself around her ankle several times.

"O—oh." She stared at it. It was bigger than the others by a very considerable measure. It had been hard to believe that the little things could have hurt her. But this one was harder to write off. "H—hello."

It shifted, as if responding to the sound of her voice. Or maybe it was because her heart was instantly racing from fear. It coiled one more time around her, so much resembling a snake that she could now very much imagine that it could swallow her whole.

Pulling on her leg experimentally, she found she couldn't move. It had her. And very much like its real-world comparison, it was hard to argue with something that was so very strong. She tugged again, and it only cinched tighter around her.

But on the upside, it hadn't eaten her leg. Yet. "I...um. Could you please let go?"

It didn't move. Reaching out a hand, she touched it. It was strangely soft to the touch and felt like almost nothing at all. It was neither smooth nor rough. Neither cold nor warm. It wasn't scaly, or furry, or fleshy. But as she touched her fingers to the coil, it undulated beneath her, worming its way a little higher up her leg.

From nowhere, curling out from the main appendage, or perhaps appearing from its own darkness, came another jagged-tipped tendril. It caught her wrist before she could pull away. She swallowed thickly and tried to fight the urge to scream or cry for help. She was trapped now, sitting up, her wrist and ankle tangled up in the Things that infested Rafe.

When the tip of the smaller tendril curled at her pulse, the pointed spiral pressing against her pulse, she realized what it was after. It was attracted to her fear. She took in a deep breath and slowly let it out, then again, trying to calm her pounding heart. Never mind the fire that it lit in her. Never mind how tempted she was to see what they would do to her if she flicked off the lights. Never mind her sick and twisted mind, or the fact that she should *really* see a doctor about her depravities.

"I should really apologize to Rafe. I was a little out of my mind before, and I reacted inappropriately. He was a true gentleman, and I should thank him for his kindness as well.

So...you're going to need to let me go. Kindly. Please." She kept her voice low and even, trying to sound as calm as she could.

The coils loosened a little. Yes, it was definitely her fear that riled them up. She took another slow breath and shut her eyes. She pictured a tropical beach. Or sailing with her Poppa. Or how it had felt to be in Rafe's arms.

He had smelled crisp and clean, of aftershave and mint, and he had been so warm. He had held her firmly to him, letting her weep against his shoulder. The feeling of his hand tracing through her hair had been too much. It had soothed her to sleep. She had been exhausted, to be fair. It was dark outside now, and she had no idea what time it was. But she still felt tiredness tugging at the back of her mind and knew she wouldn't have a hard time sleeping until morning. Once, well, she checked on Rafe—if he was awake—and then found a way to sleep that ensured her legs weren't touching any darkness.

The coils released her, and she watched as they slithered and retreated into the darkness. "Thank you." She smiled. It never hurt to be polite. Standing, she smoothed out her clothes. Rafe had been a gentleman enough not to undress her. It looked as though he had placed a blanket over her as well, but in the night, she had kicked it off.

She wondered if she had suffered a nightmare. It felt like she had. She couldn't remember any of it, but there was still the lingering sensation of terror. That would explain why the Things had come for her.

There, sitting on her pillow, was Rafe's tie. She furrowed her brow in confusion before laughing as she remembered her teasing. Yes, right. The blindfold. It would come in handy later when she went back to sleep. She wouldn't be foolish enough to turn the lights off.

Not yet, anyway.

Her cheeks went warm at the thought. *No, focus. Focus, Emma. You damnable fool.*

Putting her shoes back on—then taking them back off, in case he was asleep, and not wanting to wake him up—she combed her fingers through her curls and left the room in search of him. All the lights were on, as per usual, so that was no help in determining where he had gone.

His bedroom door was open, and she peered inside. Empty. Huh. The clock on the wall said it was two in the morning. She knew he had classes the next day, so it was unlikely that he would be staying up all night before having to go to work, though she couldn't say that for certain.

Another floor down, and she couldn't find him. "Rafe?" Nothing. He wasn't in his library, or his study. "Rafe?" she called louder. "Rafe!"

"Mrroooooooooowwlll."

She almost laughed at the sound of the cat meowing from the first floor. It was a long, throaty howl more than it was a meow. She headed down to find Hector, the fat, fluffy, angry creature, sitting on a table by the glass doors that led out the back of the home into a small walled garden that served as the back yard.

"You summoned me?" She smirked at the cat.

"Mmroooooooooowwlll." The cat howled again, hoarsely. Her thick tail looked stumpy on the chubby thing, and she flicked it back and forth on the table annoyedly.

"You really must stop smoking so much, you know. It's ruined your voice." She reached out to pet Hector and found once more that the closer she reached her hand, the farther back the cat's ears went. It was a perfect one-to-one ratio. She'd move her hand back, the ears would relax. Move closer, and they'd fold again. "And you must cheer up."

"Mrrrraaacck."

That time she laughed and shook her head. "Yes, yes. Well,

tell me what you—" Then she saw it. There, on the other side of the glass doors, just out of the light of the room that cast out into the night, was a body slumped on the brick patio. It was a man, lying on his side, his back to the glass door.

"Rafe!" She had the door thrown open in a second, the bricks cold and jagged on her bare feet. She didn't care. Not only was he seemingly unconscious, but he was only wearing a white linen shirt, and his back was soaked through in blood. "Oh, by the Benevolent—" She knelt beside him. She was afraid to turn him over because of the wound. She touched his arm and bit back a yelp in surprise as something beneath his shirt *moved.*

She watched the outline of one of those pointed-spiraled tendrils slither beneath the cotton surface like a parasitic worm beneath the flesh of a wild animal. She had seen some truly terrifying creatures of the natural world in her short years. But these were decidedly worse.

"Rafe?" She stroked his hair. It was almost chin-length when it wasn't smoothed back, and it was tousled and loose around his face. It was shockingly soft. She found herself distracted by how much she wanted to continue petting him. His glasses were missing, and his features were pinched tight from pain, even while unconscious. She shook his shoulder gently. "Rafe, please, please, wake up."

He groaned.

She let out a sigh of relief that was instantly ruined as he shifted, trying to sit up. "Oh! Easy, now. You're hurt—" She tried to help him as best she could.

He wound up leaning heavily on her, his head lowered. He ran a shaking hand over his face. "I am fine."

"You're bleeding."

"It's not unexpected. It will heal." He sounded terrible, as if he had been through the wringer. He tried to push up from the bricks but fell back against her with a grunt.

"Don't be stubborn." She frowned.

"Pot, kettle."

That made her laugh, though perhaps it shouldn't have. He was obviously in a great deal of pain. "What happened to you?" She sighed in frustration as he made it clear he was going to get to his feet, one way or another. So she helped him up, and though he grumbled about it, she put his arm over her shoulder and did her best to support his weight without touching the blood on his back.

"I...did as you asked." He sounded almost a little delirious as they went inside his home.

She nudged the door shut with her foot, not wanting to leave it open. "Oh?"

Hector the cat was purring loudly, lifting each front foot in succession, kneading the table. Rafe reached out and stroked the cat's head, and she watched a tender smile cross his face, unlike anything she had seen him wear before. He loved that cat. So, she supposed he couldn't be *that* bad, even if he was a murderer.

"I went looking for your brother." He hissed in pain and nearly fell to the ground. She had to scramble to catch him. He leaned on her again, his eyes shut, as he seemingly struggled to stay conscious. "Power comes with a price."

"Did—did you—"

"He is *gone*, Emma. I saw nothing. Only the void. And one does not summon the void without paying a piece of yourself in return."

She wanted to argue with him. She wanted to accuse him of lying. That no, he must have seen something—he must know something—to prove that Elliot wasn't truly gone. But his tone left her no room to protest. He had hurt himself badly in search of information on her behalf, and she couldn't throw that back in his face.

She helped him sit on the coffee table in the lounge, and she began to unbutton his shirt.

He eyed her narrowly. "What are you doing?"

"Tending to your wound, you nit." She cringed as she saw how soaked through his shirt was.

"No." He tried to push her away, but his efforts were weak. "Don't."

She frowned at him, trying to understand. "You don't want me to see it."

"No, because I'm fine." He shook his head. Those sharp lines of his face were still creased in agony, and he hung his head. His eyes were shut. But mixed in with the pain he clearly suffered was...shame. He didn't like her seeing him like this.

Men.

"Hey, stupid." She poked him in the shoulder. That was enough to get him to lift his head and peer up at her in confusion. "This is my fault." She sighed. "I made you do this. Let me help you. Whatever this is, it's fine. I promise. I've seen worse."

"I..." He trailed off, still hesitant.

"Look. This can't be worse than when I was in India with my Poppa. He fell in a thorn bush, and I had to pull a thorn out of his naked ass. I will repeat that so it might sink in. I had to pull a thorn. Out of my father's. Naked. Ass."

Rafe's lips twinged in a smile.

"So, this is not so embarrassing. I promise." She went back to unbuttoning his shirt. "You did this to help me. Let me help you."

"Very well." He shut his eyes again, his head drooping.

She pulled his soaked shirt off and cringed as she saw the state of his back. But it wasn't simply because his undershirt was soaked through like the top layer, but the...pattern that it made.

She knew it. The multi-pointed, geometric symbol she had seen in Elliot's apartment. The one that represented all of the Dark Societies. It was huge, all across his back, as if it had been carved there with a knife. And all around it wormed those Things of his, like an infested wound. "O—oh. Did—did it do this to you?"

"No. I did that." He began to pull his undershirt off, and she quickly went to help him. "If I had not, I would be lost by now."

"I don't understand." She cringed in sympathetic pain as she pulled the cotton from the wound. He growled, his body twitching as she carefully peeled the fabric away. As the light from the electric bulbs touched his back, the Things vanished. Which was probably for the best.

"Each time we command the darkness, we lose a piece of ourselves in exchange. Every action has an equal and opposite reaction. Take power from it, and it takes from us." He sounded like the most exhausted professor in the world. She was impressed he could still lecture, even as he was. "Until we are no longer ourselves at all. I wear this symbol to hold back the darkness. To lock it away with a piece of itself."

His shirt was off, and she had two thoughts at once. First, the mark on his back was just as she had thought, but as she examined it further, it looked as though it was an old wound. The blood seeped not from a cut, but as though old scars had been reopened, the skin puffy around the knife-thin lines. This was not the first time this had happened.

Second was that he was *absolutely* gorgeous without his shirt on. He was no slouch, and his suits did nothing to belie the muscles that rippled his back as he shifted. She had the sudden urge to caress him.

Not the time, idiot.

She focused on the matter at hand. "Do you have supplies? I should clean this. Wrap it."

"It won't—"

"Rafe."

He sighed at her tone. "Under the sink." He pointed in the direction of the bathroom.

She fetched the rolls of gauze, cotton, and the glass bottle of hydrogen peroxide—how fancy and new! It would sting him like crazy, but it would keep the wound clean. When she returned, she set the things beside him and began to go to work.

Sure enough, he snarled as the damp cotton touched his back.

"Sorry..." She felt terrible.

"It is doing its job. You're being as gentle as you can be."

"No. I mean. I'm sorry. This is my fault. If I hadn't shouted at you...you shouldn't have done this. Thank you, I'm grateful, but...I didn't know." She dabbed at the wound. "I didn't know this would be the result."

"If you had, would you have still asked?"

"No, of course not." She winced as she touched a sensitive spot by his side, and he jerked in pain. "You did nothing to deserve this."

"I've done much to deserve this. Trust me." He sighed. "But I appreciate that."

"What did you mean when you said that 'you' did this? I still don't understand."

"The mark bleeds because beneath my skin is a thin gold sigil that matches it. It is the sigil that is bleeding. My infection is attempting to push it from my body." He was beginning to shake, so she paused in her cleaning for him to take a breath or two. When he was ready again, he nodded once. "The darkness should have claimed me long ago. But I found ways to suppress it."

"Oh..." She had nothing to say to that. What was a person supposed to do with that information? She felt like she had to say *something*, however. "I'm sorry."

"It isn't your fault I chose to walk this path." He chuckled weakly. "But I appreciate the sympathy."

"How did you do this to yourself?" She cringed at the mental image. "Putting a gold thing this big beneath your skin on your back sounds impossible to do by yourself, and it's on perfectly straight, so—"

He laughed again, a little louder than before. He smiled at her over his shoulder. He clearly thought her comment was adorable. "I am not the only member of the Mirror."

Right. He had others in his Dark Society. She pouted. Now she felt stupid.

His smile grew. "Thank you for tending to the wound, Emma."

"It's still my fault. So, it's the least I could do." She picked up the gauze as she finished cleaning it and began wrapping it. The mark was simply seeping now, not actively bleeding, so it should be all right. She hoped, anyway. He seemed unconcerned. "Let's get you to bed."

He let out a rush of air. "Yes. I think that sounds like a phenomenal idea."

She helped him up to his feet. She couldn't help but enjoy the feeling of his body against hers. It wasn't the time to be distracted by her burgeoning attraction to him. She helped him carefully up the stairs to his room and sat him on the edge of his bed. He was clearly beyond the point of exhaustion, so she crouched and unlaced his shoes for him.

Rafe let out a quiet chuckle.

"What?" She glanced up at him between taking his shoes off.

"I had thought myself the valorous one for attempting to help you. And here I am, with you playing nursemaid."

"If you want me to play nurse, or maid, you simply have to ask." She flashed him a grin as she stood. "But maybe tomorrow night. After our nice dinner." She stroked a hand through his hair. She did love how it felt.

Humming, he shut his eyes from her touch, so she did it again. "That sounds...tempting."

"I'm not going to give up on Elliot."

"I know you aren't."

"Good." She leaned down and kissed him gently. "Your pants are all you, unless you *really* want me to play nurse tonight."

He laughed and shooed her away. "Get some rest, Emma. I can manage."

"Damn." She went to the door and smiled back at him. "Lights on or off?"

"Off. Kindly." He lay down on his back with a groan.

She clicked the switch and shut the door behind her. As she climbed the stairs to her own room, she found herself wondering what was to become of them. He was strange. Dangerous. By his own admission, he had planned to murder her. Perhaps he still was. Let alone the dark magic he wielded, and the Things that infested his shadows.

But he made her smile.

And damn if he didn't make her happy.

As she tied the blindfold around her eyes to lie down in bed, she realized something. Elliot might have been the one to get her into this mess...but Rafe was going to be the one to end it. One way or another. For better or worse. *Somehow.*

And she didn't know if she could bring herself to walk away before she found out.

CHAPTER NINETEEN

Emma woke up to the sound of someone shouting in fury. She groaned and rolled onto her side, pulling off the blindfold that had done its job, even if it had been strange to fall asleep in. She rubbed her eyes, blearily trying to clear the sleep from them.

A man was hollering at someone, and whoever was answering them was far quieter. She suspected it was Rafe, and if there was a problem, the odds that it involved her were higher than zero. Far higher than zero.

It was a good five seconds after waking up that she realized not only was she probably the source of the problem, but Rafe might be in danger. They both might be. Throwing on her clothes as fast as possible—and opting for her riding pants—she didn't bother to straighten out her unruly hair before running out of the room barefoot.

"Get *out* of my home!" Rafe shouted at someone. A quieter voice answered him, but she couldn't make out what they were saying.

Emma scooped up a candelabra on the way down, intending to use the heavy brass object as a weapon. She should have grabbed her gun, but she had no clue where her purse was. Probably where she had left it after falling asleep crying in Rafe's arms. She skipped half the stairs as she raced toward the sound of the shouting. As she rounded the corner to his first floor study, she skidded to a halt.

And then snarled in anger at who she saw. "Gigi!"

"My, don't you look...well loved." The blonde woman smirked and took a drag from her cigarette which sat in its holder. She was flanked by two men, one of whom she recognized as Mykel.

The man flashed her a toothy, very white grin. His greeting left him in a purr that left nothing to the imagination. "Hello, kitten-baby."

"That's redundant." She glared at him and gripped the candelabra tighter. "What're you doing here, Gigi?"

"Why, to see *you*, of course." She frowned. "I was worried about you. I heard about the Crawling Terror, and then you moving out of your hotel and coming here. I wanted to make sure you were safe. That our dear professor here hadn't done anything..." She smirked. "Unsavory."

"You *drugged* me, Gigi." She shifted her grip on the candelabra, fully ready to bash one of them in the skull if she needed to.

"And left you safe and sound! I could've taken you to the Flesh & Bone, but I didn't, now, did I?" She huffed. "I could have you in shackles by now if I wanted to. Even with his unique *talents,* the professor isn't a match for me."

"Oh, please." Mykel chuckled darkly. "I want to see that. Please, Momma G, can we?"

Emma stormed toward him, not caring a lick about their size difference. "I will knock your teeth out of your head, you—"

Rafe put an arm out, stopping her, and pushed her half behind him. "Calm down, Emma. The Blade provokes. That's their way. They can't do a thing to touch you in my home. They can only annoy us."

Gigi smiled. "Ooh, this all makes so much more sense now. I was wondering why you hadn't killed her yet, dear Raphael. You've gone sweet on her, haven't you?" She chuckled and held her cigarette holder close to her lips before finishing the sentence. "I wonder, have you fucked her yet?" She took a drag off the cigarette.

Rafe's jaw ticked, and everything in his posture was locked rigid, as if he was barely resisting the urge to fly at the woman in a rage. "Get. Out."

"That would be a no." Gigi laughed through a cloud of smoke. "Oh, poor boy. Still afraid of what happened last time. I expect you probably were picturing that it'd kill two birds, huh? Vent your *immense* sexual frustration and get rid of the Mather problem once and for all. But here she stands, right as rain, and entirely herself as ever."

"What the hell're you talking about?" Emma shook her head. She hated being talked about like she wasn't in the room. It was probably one of her biggest pet peeves. Being talked down to was one of the easiest ways to get her riled up.

"Oh, he didn't tell you?" Gigi looked absolutely beyond pleased with herself. She looked back to Rafe and tsked. "My, my. For shame, Professor. For shame. You didn't warn her about your disease? Such bad form."

"He warned me. I know." Emma stepped beside Rafe. She wouldn't cower behind him. He didn't look at her, but didn't stop her, either.

"Did he tell you about what happened to the last young lady he, eh…courted?" Gigi snickered. "I bet he didn't. I'm surprised you're still here, Emma, and that you haven't run screaming like the sweet little know-nothing you are."

Now it was Emma's turn to get angry. Plonking the

candelabra down on an end table with a heavy *thump*, she stormed over to the windows. Drawing the curtains with a loud scrape of metal rings on rods, she ensured that there was not a scrap of sunlight filtering into the room. Gigi was watching her, absolutely confused. Rafe eyed her with a similar expression, before a flicker of understanding crossed over his dark eyes, and the faintest of smiles fought through his anger.

Emma walked up to the light switch that controlled the chandelier overhead, blazing brightly with its electric bulbs. Reaching out for the switch, she shot a glare over to Gigi.

The woman and her two compatriots were now watching her with wide eyes. "You wouldn't." The beautiful blonde didn't seem so certain of herself.

"I've met them. How about you?" She smiled, donning her best sinister expression. She placed her finger over the little mother-of-pearl off button. "Because I'm betting you haven't."

"Wait!" Gigi cringed. "Fine. *Fine.* I apologize. This conversation has gone entirely sideways." She gestured dismissively with her cigarette. "Lower your hand, Miss Mather, please."

Emma did as she was asked but leaned her back against the wall and folded her arms over her chest, ensuring that the other woman knew she had no intention of backing down if pressed again. She wasn't entirely sure if Rafe's Things would let her wield them like a cannon, but she wasn't above giving it a try.

"I honestly came here with the kindest of intentions, I promise." Gigi sighed. "I really did want to come and see if you were all right, Emma. I did so very much love our conversation the other day. I don't trust our dear professor, and neither should you."

"I don't. I don't trust a single fucking one of you." Emma shook her head.

"Good." The jazz singer smiled. "Then you're as smart as I hoped. Keep it that way. No matter how entangled"—Gigi huffed a laugh—"you get with him, or any of us, never trust anyone except yourself. And even then, think twice." Gigi turned her attention to Rafe. "We'll be going now, Professor. But consider my proposition. It might be wise, given our situation. And given what we both know the Idol is truly after."

Rafe pointed at the door. "Show yourself out, Gage."

The blonde shrugged. "As you wish." She snapped her fingers. "Boys. Let's go."

Emma didn't move from her place by the light switch until the three interlopers had gone. It was only after Rafe threw the deadbolt with a furious click that she even let herself breathe. "I don't know what to make of her."

"Don't make anything of her at all." Rafe walked back into the study and ran a hand over his dark hair. It was still tousled. He had clearly also been woken up out of bed, as he was only dressed half as nicely as usual. "I am not sure how she managed to break in."

"Locks only keep out the honest." She said it in time with the disembodied voice of her Poppa that played in the air next to her like the clearest record player.

"Yes, but my locks are more than simply physical." He took off his glasses to rub his eyes before replacing them. "But your point is taken."

"Coffee?" Emma started past him to go upstairs to the kitchen, but he caught her wrist. She frowned. "Look, I'm sorry I threatened to use you like a tennis racket, but—"

"No." He smiled briefly, before it faded again. "That was quite clever. I likely would have murdered all four of you, but she had no way of knowing that. Were you bluffing?"

Emma shrugged. "I'm not sure. I think I would've done it.

I don't like being pushed around, and that's all it seems she knows how to do."

"Indeed." He released her wrist. "It's about what she said."

"It's not hard to figure out what probably happened to your last girlfriend, Rafe." Emma wriggled her fingers at him. "I'm betting she screamed, and they made a snack out of her. Do you expect me to be surprised? They ate the corpse that was in my hotel room, didn't they?"

He furrowed his brow. "Yes. How did you know?"

"Because the cops haven't come looking for us, that's how."

Rafe straightened his back. "I didn't give the desk my name. They have no idea where you're staying."

"That's cute. The city is small, Professor. You're already under the nose of the Investigators. They know I'm here, sure as Gigi does. And if they found proof of a murder in my hotel room?" She combed a hand through her hair, wincing as she hit a snag. "Doesn't take a genius."

He looked almost disappointed that she had put it all together. He sighed. "You're right."

"About all of it?"

His expression shifted to a darker one, as if remembering the details. "All of it."

Emma let out a breath. "Guess you weren't kidding about not screaming, huh?" She turned toward the stairs. "Coffee."

"You learn about the gruesome murder of a previous potential lover, and that is your response?" He sounded utterly bemused as he followed her.

"Yeah. It is." She paused on the stairs and turned back to look at him. "You said it yourself. I passed the point of no return. I'm going to find out what happened to my brother—even if it's too late. And you're the closest thing I have to an ally in this."

"Gigi has offered you her help."

Emma decided she almost liked being a step taller than him. He was still intense as always, with that shadowy, brooding expression of his. But it let her see him in another way. Reaching down, she picked up his tie and used it to pull him an inch closer to her as she leaned down to whisper to him. "You're much nicer on the eyes. Okay, that's a lie, but she's not my type."

The look he gave her was equal parts lustful and abjectly perplexed. It made her laugh. "Coffee, Professor. Coffee." She went back to her mission.

He could only grunt as he followed her up the stairs.

It just made her laugh harder.

By the Great Beast, Emma was going to drive Rafe to distraction. No, that was not true. She had already successfully done that. To be more accurate, she was going to drive him positively *insane*.

He decided that men's clothing suited her, as she looked perfectly natural in her riding trousers and messily-tucked-in blouse. The trousers accentuated her figure in a way the boxy dresses of the era certainly did not. It showed off her waist and the hips he so desperately wished to grab hold of with both hands.

Never mind the fact that the pale green blouse she was wearing was thin enough to reveal that she was not wearing any undergarments. She likely had been woken up by his shouting and had come down in a hurry. Her unkempt dark curls and grumpy expression made him want to throw her over the kitchen island and be done with it.

She was leaning against the wood surface on her elbows, her head lowered as she clearly tried to gather her thoughts.

It meant she was already almost bent over the surface,

and he was forced to adjust himself in his own trousers lest he make things exceedingly awkward. Though, to be honest, he highly doubted she would mind in the slightest.

He wasn't quite sure why he still fought the impulses he felt around the young woman. It was more than clear that their attraction was mutual. And the foolish thing wasn't afraid of his infestation, the fallout of which she was aware was inevitable. Therefore, it wasn't any of his concern.

But that wasn't true, was it?

It was his concern.

Because *blast it all*, he had begun to care about her. He didn't want to hurt her. He didn't want her blood to be on his hands. There was likely no avoiding it, but he found himself no longer accepting it with a passing shrug and a cavalier disregard.

Damn, damn, damn.

"Where is he, Rafe? Where's my brother?"

"I don't know." It wasn't a lie.

"What *do* you know?" She lifted her head to cast him a slightly irritated glance. It made him only want her more.

"I commanded the darkness to show me Elliot Mather. It showed me, as I said, nothing but the void."

"But what does that mean?"

"It means that your brother is gone."

"No, I mean what does that *mean*, Rafe? Does it mean he's dead?" She was irritable this morning. "No more half-answers and partial-truths. If he's dead, why didn't it show you his corpse?"

"Because we are not the flesh we wear, Emma. I am no more this body than I am this coffee mug." He sipped from the vessel in question. "Elliot Mather, more specifically his soul, is outside of the reach of the Great Beast of Arnsmouth. It is out of the reach of the darkness itself."

"You're lying." But her tone held no punch. She pulled a

stool out from under the kitchen island and sat on it, her shoulders curled and her face a perfect mask of despair. "I'd...I'd know."

"Would you?"

"I thought I would." She frowned into her own coffee, twisting the mug between her fingers. "He's my twin. I love him more than anything in this world. I always knew when he was in trouble. That's why I came back from Japan as fast as I could. I knew something was wrong."

"Then perhaps that was the moment of his passing."

She shook her head. "I had a letter from him that was dated after I left. The handwriting was messy, and not like him at all. He said he loved me, and he..." She choked off.

"What, Emma?"

"He said goodbye." She shook her head. "He's said it before. He's always been the melodramatic one of the two of us." Her hands tightened and then loosened. "I need to know where he is. I need to find him. Bring him home. Whatever's left. Poppa deserves some closure, too."

"There may be nothing to return."

"Then I need to bring the head of the person who killed him." She grimaced in rage, and for a moment, Rafe found himself distinctly concerned that she might be just as much of a murderer as he was, even if she did not know it yet. But it faded a moment later, and she sighed. "Who'm I kidding? I'm not the type for revenge."

He walked around the counter to sit beside her and stroked a hand up and down her back, trying very hard not to be distracted by the feeling of her otherwise naked body beneath it.

Now is not the time, Raphael.

Reaching out, he tucked a strand of hair behind her ear. "We will discover what precisely befell your brother. I can't command the darkness again for some time without taking undue risks, but when I can, I will ask it to show me what happened to him."

"You would? I—I saw what it did to you, and I don't..."

"It's fine." He smiled faintly. "It won't be the first or last time." Leaning over, he kissed her cheek. "I have to prepare for my classes. When I return, we will go have that nice dinner."

She smiled back at him, though it was clear her heart wasn't in it. "I promise to explore the entire house and look through absolutely everything you own while you're gone."

"From you, I would expect nothing less." He stood and grunted, cracking his back audibly. "Don't unlock the door for visitors. I'll ensure you have no other intruders before I leave."

She caught his hand before he walked away, and he looked at her with an arched eyebrow. She didn't meet his gaze. "Thank you, Rafe. Really."

"You are welcome."

As he walked away, he found himself wondering the same thing he had been asking himself since the moment he met her.

What am I doing?

CHAPTER TWENTY

Emma made good on her threat.

Professor Raphael Saltonstall had left her alone in the house for hours with absolutely nothing to do, and a chubby cat who wanted nothing to do with her. So, she was going to loot through every single scrap of personal belongings the man owned.

She warned him, after all!

Hardly her fault that he still left for work after that.

"Goodness, Doctor Saltonstall." She stared at his closet. It was entirely in monochrome. White, black, gray, more black, more gray, darker gray, and even more black. She laughed. "You certainly do know how to stick with a theme." She rooted through all his drawers, finding his socks, his suspenders, his belts, his ties, his underthings—all just as boring as the rest.

She had hoped to find that he wore pink boxer shorts. But sadly, no such luck. She hummed a song to herself as she went through his watches and cufflinks, finding them all perfectly tasteful and precisely what one would expect a professor to wear.

"Boring, boring, boring." Then again, what was she expecting? He had warned her that all his more interesting items were hidden far from where any Investigators with a warrant might find them. And she was certain his house had been searched more than once.

"Not even any pornography!" She huffed. "If you're half as pent up as Gigi made it seem, I'm sure you must have some stashed away *somewhere*." She even looked under his mattress. Nothing.

How much of a laugh would that have been? Presenting him with his naughty collection when he returned from his classes? She chuckled at the notion. Sadly, she'd be empty-handed when he returned, it seemed.

"I wonder where all your hidden passages are. Oh! I bet there's a bookcase. It's always a bookcase, isn't it? Poppa's are. Well, the two I know about, anyway." She stopped halfway down a hallway to see that Hector was sitting there, staring at her, blocking her path. "Hello there, fluff."

"Mmrrr-*aack*."

"I'll make a deal with you." Emma put her hands on her hips. "Show me where the professor is hiding all his secrets, and I'll find something tasty in the refrigerator for you."

A swish of a tail was all she received in reply.

"Well. Let me know if you change your mind." She stepped around the cat as she went to the study on the first floor to find a secret passage. She checked every book and light sconce, checked by the edges of the fireplace—everything. It took her the better part of an hour. Sitting down on the sofa, she let out a sigh. He was more clever than she had paid him credit.

"Mrrr-*aaack*."

"That really isn't a normal noise for a kitty to make." She eyed the rotund animal that was now sitting on a table, staring at her, tail still swishing away. "And he said I could be here, and he basically gave me permission to search the house." Placing her elbow on her knee, she put her chin in her hand. "He said it wasn't for public display. But I've looked everywhere, even the basement. And if he has a second basement, it certainly isn't..."

Oh.

Huh.

She stood. "If I wanted to hide a sub-basement, I certainly wouldn't make it accessible from the normal basement, now, would I? No. That's right where I'd look for a secret door. Same with the first floor. But the *second* floor? Who would look there? Certainly not me."

That was precisely where she was going to look, then. Heading up to the second-floor library, she began poking around.

"Mrooooowl."

"Now I know I'm on to something, Hector." She chuckled as the cat scrambled up onto the sofa, a noise that sounded rather brutally painful for the upholstery. It was further proof the cat needed to lose some weight. Oh, well. To each their own. "I think you're beautiful, just the way you are, Hector."

"Mmmrrrraaack."

"You're welcome. Although I worry about your health, with—ah-hah!" She jumped up and down a few times as she found a tiny button hidden behind the front face of one of the bookshelves by the fireplace. She cackled with glee as she pressed it. She always did love a good button.

Poppa said it'd be the death of her someday.

"Here I go, proving you right." She took a step back as the bookcase in question swung out into the room. It was narrow, far smaller than she would expect a secret door to be. But perhaps that was also part of the ploy. If she hadn't been intent on searching literally *everywhere,* she probably would have skipped it. The passageway beyond was little more than the size of a broom closet, and pitch black. Leaning closer, she could see a teeny little set of stairs that led down into the darkness at a rather alarming angle.

Muttering to herself, she shut the door before Hector could go exploring, and went about finding some candles and matches. It took her another five minutes before she found what she needed.

She could see the latch on the back of the door, and she could only hope that it worked. She knew she should leave it open and not risk the danger of closing it behind her. But putting her own stupid self at risk was one thing. She didn't know how she could live with herself if something happened to Rafe's cat while she was off spelunking through his house.

What if it's a torture chamber down there? She tried to keep her mind out of the gutter but failed spectacularly. She could picture him ordering her around in that no-nonsense tone of his, with that heated and intense stare in his dark eyes.

She shivered at the thought. "Maybe tonight, if I'm lucky." She stared down the tiny set of stairs. "If I'm not dead."

Letting out a puff of air, she went inside the tiny passage. She had to go down to steps to even be able to turn around enough to shut the door behind her. And there was Hector, sitting ten paces away, glowering and swishing her tail.

"Oh, don't look at me like that." She took hold of the handle. "I'll be right back. I promise I won't break anything."

Hector's ears went back.

Emma shut the door with a click. She unlatched it again and let out a sigh of relief as it opened an inch. Good. She latched it again and swiveled in place carefully, not wanting to slip off the stair and go crashing down into the abyss.

There wasn't a railing, which made matters even worse.

"Why would there be a railing, Emma? You're in a secret passageway. That's just called security." She put her hand against the brick wall, glad for the texture, and began making her way very slowly down the harrowing set of stairs. Up would be easier and something to look forward to. She debated going down backward, but she liked to be able to see where she was going.

Just in case there was another Crawling Terror down there, waiting for her. Or some other terrible and unspeakable monster. No, face-forward it was going to be. The stairs descended an abnormally long way. She figured she had to have been past the first floor and very likely the basement at that point. And still it went on.

"I wonder if this goes on forever. Or if it goes straight to hell." She grunted. "It would figure Rafe would have an endless stairway to—" And right in the middle of her complaining, her foot touched packed dirt instead of wood. The stairs ended just as abruptly as they began. Holding up her candelabra, she nearly fell backward at what she saw.

The room was almost empty. The walls were circular and made of brick. She had expected a secret library or laboratory, filled with stacks of paper and books, or jars with squishy bits of various previously living—or currently living —monstrosities and victims. But there wasn't anything in the room save for the largest mirror she had ever seen in her life.

It towered over her, some fourteen feet or more. It was shaped for all the world like a typical mirror that one might hang on the wall, save for its size. It was an oval, with a wooden frame that was carved in elegant swirls and acanthus leaf patterns. Atop it was the wooden carving of a hooded figure, looming over the room. She couldn't see if there was a face within its shadows. She honestly was happier not knowing.

It looked as though the mirror had once been gilded, but

the gold leaf had long since flaked away to reveal the worn and weathered surface beneath.

The glass looked like polished onyx, darker than any glass should be, just as reflective. It was shattered into a billion pieces, spider-webbing away from the center and casting her own image back at herself, distorted and twisted, in a dizzying array.

It was suspended from the ceiling by two enormous iron chains.

How long she stood there, staring at it agog like an idiot, she had no idea. Finally, she shut her mouth. "I have so many questions."

Tilting her head, she addressed the mirror for lack of anybody better to talk to. "First, how in the blazes did he get you down here?" She scratched the back of her neck. "Maybe you were here first, I don't know. He said he has friends—or cohorts. But this seems like a bit of a lift, no pun intended."

As she stepped forward to examine the enormous mirror more closely, she pulled in a sharp breath. The glass—or onyx, or whatever it was—*healed.* It stopped the moment she froze. But as she took another step toward it, much like Hector's ears, the motion began again.

Piece by piece, fracture line by fracture line, the blackened surface mended itself. A billion versions of Emma became a million, a million a thousand, a thousand ten, and then she was staring back at herself.

But something seemed off.

More than a healing mirror? She rolled her eyes at herself. *More than shadow monsters who eat people? Get your priorities straight.* There was no point in being afraid of her reflection when she had seen what truly lurked in the shadows. She took another step forward, and the image matched her movements.

"Oh. Goodness." She looked down at her chest and realized that she could absolutely see her nipples through the thin fabric of her blouse. Chuckling, she shook her head. "I owe Rafe an apology. Or perhaps he owes me a thank you."

Something whispered from the edges of the room, something that might have been laughter. She turned her head but saw nothing. It was likely just the memory of laughter finding the moment to interject itself into her life. Ignoring it, she looked back at her reflection.

It did still seem off, but she couldn't place how. Narrowing her eyes, she leaned in closer. It was her face. It was like it was reversed, maybe? *Or not reversed, as the case may be.* But the image followed her movements perfectly.

Leaning in closer, she studied her face.

Her reflection grinned. *"Boo!"*

With a loud yelp, she fell back and landed hard on her ass, dropping her candelabra. The flames went out, and the darkness that surrounded her was total. The kind of nothingness that existed when light had never touched a place in its entire existence.

Something laughed at her. It was her own voice.

But nothing touched her. Nothing killed her or maimed her. Her heart was racing a thousand miles a minute. "Are you real?"

"You wouldn't rightly know, would you?" The voice hummed thoughtfully. *"I suppose that's part of the fun."*

"Who are you?"

"Part of the whole of nothing."

That was about as clear as mud. But she decided to move on. "Are you going to hurt me?"

"Haven't yet."

"Doesn't answer my question."

"Mmmm...not today."

Fine. That was good enough for now. She pulled her legs closer to herself, though, just in case. There was no point in standing, she would probably just trip and fall over again a second later, stumbling around in the darkness.

It was still her voice talking to her. *"Pretty little Emma. Lost little Emma. People think you're brave, but it's simply because the fear arouses you. Nothing makes you feel more of a lust for life than this, hmm?"*

Something brushed against her cheek. It felt sharp and pointed, and for some reason she had the mental image of a bony finger. She pulled in a gasp and shut her eyes—though she didn't know why she bothered. Not like it was any brighter or darker either way.

"Or a lust for our dear professor..." The voice was sing-songy now, and she could almost imagine that she heard other voices talking in unison with it. Some high, some low, all together and all slightly awry at once.

"I hope you don't mind sharing him."

The voice howled in laughter, sounding genuinely pleased. There wasn't an ounce of malice in it. She wasn't sure if that made her more or less uncomfortable.

"Such a quick one, you are. No, no...don't you worry about that." Three of those pointed nails traced through her hair. They were too large to be human, and so sharp that they stung. They traveled down the back of her neck, and she let out another cry as they hooked over her shoulders from behind and yanked her to the ground. Somehow, they kept her there, both inside the dirt that she could feel, and *not* at the same time. *"Though you might have to be concerned with the opposite."*

"Don't scream, don't scream, don't scream—" She repeated the words to herself as a mantra. Something else was touching her then. A tendril, wrapping around her ankle, slithering up inside her trouser leg. "Don't-scream-don't-scream-don't—"

"Sshhh...now, now. You needn't worry." The tendril around

her ankle tightened. *"The professor isn't here...you can scream all you like."*

She did.

CHAPTER TWENTY-ONE

Raphael came home rather eager for the evening, which was unlike him. But he was going to an expensive dinner—on Emma's father's money, which he was still annoyed about but couldn't do anything to stop—with a beautiful young woman. A beautiful young woman who would more than likely join him in bed if he asked. Although he did not much plan on speaking about the matter. It wasn't necessary when she seemed just as eager for the act as he was.

Wandering thoughts threatened to make his walk home extremely unfortunate for both himself and anyone he happened across. He did his best to shove them from his mind. When he finally reached his house, he found Emma asleep on the sofa, one of his books on her chest, splayed open where she had dropped it. He frowned. That was from his bedroom. She had looted his bedroom. *She did warn you, after all.*

The poor thing was caught in another nightmare, her breath coming in short gasps and her body covered in sweat.

With a shake of his head, he sat on the edge of the sofa beside her and shook her shoulder gently. "Emma."

She sat up.

Then punched him straight in the jaw.

Yanking his head back in surprise, he knocked himself off the edge of the sofa and wound up sitting rather quickly on the ground instead. He grunted, pressing his hand to the offending spot on his face. "Good afternoon."

"Rafe! Oh!" Her hands were on his head then. "Oh, I'm so sorry—I was having a nightmare." She laughed, belying her true lack of concern over having hurt him.

"That is how you react when woken up from a nightmare?" He checked his lip. No, it wasn't split. She was a feisty thing but packed very little weight behind her blows. "Note taken."

She threw her arms around him, hugging him to her chest, still laughing. "Come on. I punch, as you now know, entirely too much like a girl." She kissed the spot where she had punched him. "All better."

He tried to stop himself from smiling. It got the better of him. Triumphant, she sat back, and then let out a shudder. He arched a brow at her.

"That wasn't a fun nightmare," she answered his silent question. She wrinkled her nose, as if remembering a detail that was unpleasant and unexpected. "Not a fun nightmare at all." Falling back onto the cushions, he was once more distracted by how thin her blouse was. "How was class?"

He blinked away from staring at her body, and her knowing little smile told him that she had caught him red-handed. He wouldn't admit it, so he dutifully ignored the moment. Save for the part of his anatomy that insisted on defying him. "Quite fine. None of the students spoke to me, which is an improvement over most days."

She chuckled. "You don't like them much?"

"I like them fine, when they operate as normal intelligent individuals and not as though their brains had been boiled." He was glad for a change of subject. Its mundanity was oddly refreshing. Although he did enjoy that he needn't hide his true research from her, even though he had enough other secrets to hide.

"I'm starving!" She slapped her hands on her thighs.

He jolted in surprise at her proclamation, and then chuckled at how perky she could be. "You may want to change, first."

"What, you think they would have a problem with my tits showing?" She picked up the front of her blouse, pinching it between her fingers, and held it up like points. When he pinched his nose and sighed, she laughed harder and shoved his shoulder playfully. "You are so dour. I love it." She sat up and climbed from the sofa, heading up the stairs toward her room. "Fine, fine, fine. I suppose I do like that restaurant and would like to continue to be welcome there."

Rafe won over the urge to follow her upstairs, throw her to the bed, and skip the preamble. But as his stomach growled, need overcame want. He had to admit to the fact that he was only human.

Mostly.

EMMA DESCENDED the stairs and lingered at the second floor. She had woken up from a nightmare that she could have sworn was real. It had been so visceral. Staring at the bookcase that she had dreamt was a door, she didn't know what to do.

If it was real, then that hadn't been a dream.

And if it hadn't been a dream…she couldn't remember what it had done to her. Only that it told her she could scream, and she had, and then Rafe had woken her up. She didn't feel violated—not physically, anyway.

But something had happened.

She knew it.

She just didn't know *what.*

But was it real? Had any of it actually occurred? If that bookcase really was a door, then she'd know for certain. *I imagine it would ruin dinner plans.* She glanced down the stairs at where she knew Rafe was waiting.

But that enormous, unknowable Thing had done—

"Emma?"

She blinked. Rafe was standing at the bottom of the stairs, looking up at her curiously. She stared at him, and then grinned wide. "Professor Saltonstall, are you wearing a *tuxedo?*"

"I believe that's what this is called, yes."

She didn't laugh, though she was tempted to. Not because he looked silly, or even out of place. It wouldn't have been a teasing laugh, but a happy one. He had dressed up for dinner with her, and by the Benevolent God, he looked *incredible.*

"Now I feel underdressed." She descended the stairs to stand beside him, looking up at the stern expression of a man who was simply delicious in a tuxedo. She wasn't underdressed—she always packed a fancy dress—but she knew he would turn more heads than she would tonight.

"You look lovely." He reached up and cupped her cheek. "Are you certain about this?"

She knew what he was asking her. It wasn't about dinner, and it certainly wasn't about the clothes. It was the fate of his previous lover that he was asking her about. *Do you want to risk it?*

Looking him over again, she made her decision. Yes, Yes, she did wish to risk it.

The terrible mirror would have to wait.

OF VISIONS & SECRETS

MARLIAVE WAS BUSTLING THAT NIGHT, the glassware tinkling and quiet laughter of friends and lovers, hopeful or otherwise, filled the air as Emma smiled over the table at her date.

A date who seemed nervous about the quantity of shadows in the room. She had wondered if it was the presence of so many strangers that had set him on edge. What gave it away was that he kept moving the tealight on the table closer to him, until she was worried he would singe his cuffs.

"Are you all right?" She frowned.

"It takes focus, that is all. I am fine." He smiled at her thinly. "But if they all are dead before the morning, I will not be held to blame."

"Noted." She chuckled and folded her arms on the table, shifting her chair and herself a nudge closer. They were still waiting for the first course, and he had been very quiet. "If this is making you too uncomfortable, we can go. You look like you're about to explode."

"That has shockingly little to do with the lack of light in this room." He sipped his water and set the glass back down, spinning it in his fingers. "But it can't be helped at the moment. Distract me, Miss Mather, as you are wont to do. Tell me about your life."

She blinked. Whatever was bothering him was clearly not going to be a topic of conversation. With a shrug, she decided she'd probably get it out of him sooner rather than later, so it wasn't worth fighting over. "Well, you know most of it, I think. The rich daughter of a rich family who has spent more of her life overseas than home. Unless you want to hear ridiculous stories of my escapades in Egypt or Iceland, I'm not sure what you want to know." She sipped her own water. "But I don't know a damnable thing about you, Professor."

"Nothing much to tell. My family was firmly middle class. I did not live in a workhouse when I was a child, nor did I live in…" He stopped himself from saying a particular word as he looked at her over the rim of his glasses.

"Say it." She chuckled. "I promise I've heard worse."

"Excess."

"I have heard worse. Continue."

He smiled thinly. "I was away at University when my childhood home was broken into, and my family murdered."

"O—oh." Her smile fell from her face like a lead paperweight. "I'm so sorry."

If he appreciated her condolences, he didn't show it. He kept talking as if she hadn't said anything at all. "On the wall, in their combined blood, was a symbol. I needn't draw it for you again." He was staring into the reflections in his water glass. "I vowed to uncover the truth of the motives involved. It led me to where I am now."

"Oh." She didn't know what else to say.

"I understand your need to know the answers, Emma. Believe you me, no one in this damned city understands you better than I." The undercurrent of fury in those words clung to the air around them like a thick and heavy fog.

She sat there in silence for a long moment. "Well…here's an upside."

He shot her a raised eyebrow.

"You don't have to worry about introducing me to your mother." She smiled nervously at him, knowing her joke was entirely out of line.

To his credit, he laughed. Tired and low, but a laugh, nonetheless. "She would have adored you. I was entirely too serious for her taste." He sipped the water. "I wish this was stronger."

"Hear, hear."

Conversation paused as he measured his words. "Go home, Emma."

"No." Reaching out, she brushed the backs of her fingers against his. "But thank you for trying."

The smile that touched him was tender and warm. It almost dulled how sharp his features were. Almost.

"I say we eat quickly," she murmured to him. "And go back to your home, find that bottle of yours…"

His expression darkened again, his eyes somehow growing even more black. "I think that sounds like a wonderful plan."

THE REST of dinner had been as brief as they could make it, while still enjoying the wonderful food that had been put in front of them. But as tasty as everything was, they were both clearly eager for something else.

"I'm going to change out of this nonsense." Emma smiled at Rafe as she headed up the stairs, her heels already in her hand. "Pour us a couple glasses, I'll be right back."

"For once, I won't argue." He headed into his parlor.

She smiled as she went up the first flight of stairs. Everything in her was already anticipating what was about to follow. They would come back, share a drink or two, things would become heated. There were only a few questions left.

What room would it happen in?

How drunk would they be?

And would the lights be on or off?

Her steps once more hesitated on the second floor. That small bookshelf to the left of the fireplace drew her attention like a moth to a flame. She shouldn't. She should go change, and she should stick to the plan. *It's my plan!*

But…

The button.

She had to know if it was there or not. She couldn't go the rest of the night knowing she had a chance and she didn't take it. Crossing quietly into the study, glad she had already taken her heels off, she walked up to the tiny bookshelf.

It was with her hand stretched out to find if the switch was there that a hand came from behind her and pressed a blade of a knife against her throat.

Someone had broken in! She pulled in a hiss, grabbing the wrist as the arm yanked her back against someone that smelled like crisp cologne and mint.

Rafe.

She didn't know if that made this better…or worse.

He pressed the blade against her skin, forcing her to tilt her head back against his chest as he threatened to slice her throat. The voice that left him was a rumble. "What am I to do with you, Emma Mather?"

CHAPTER TWENTY-TWO

Emma didn't dare move. She didn't dare pull at the arm that held the knife to her throat. If she did, he'd press harder, and he'd slit her throat. She pressed her back to his chest, desperate to gain any extra space. "Please—I—"

"Are you working with Gigi? Did she send you here?" His voice had lost all the tender emotion of before. It was cold, it was dark, and it was terrifying. "Or was it the Idol, using you as *bait?*"

"I—no—Rafe—I—"

"How did you find it?" He snarled. "Tell me!"

"I was just—I was just bored, I looked—I looked everywhere. I'm not working for anyone, please, calm down—" She was shaking. She clung to his arm, desperate for something to hold on to. Was this really how she died? His Things would eat all evidence of the crime. She wouldn't ever exist again. Her father would have no children to bury.

"Stop lying to me, you little spoiled brat."

"No, please—I—" She shut her eyes, trying in a foolish way to hide from what was happening. But she really was a fool, wasn't she? He had warned her that he was plotting to kill her. He had warned her that he was deadly—that he was a murderer—but she had just blithely gone along as though it had all been a game.

Spoiled brat. He wasn't wrong. She couldn't deny it. Nothing *bad* had ever happened to her, even through all her dangerous misadventures. Murder wasn't real. Even the man in her hotel she had been able to write off, in some childish way, as theatrical. She hadn't known him, so he hadn't been truly substantial.

It wasn't until he held the knife to her throat that it all came crashing down around her. The monsters she had seen had every intention of killing her. Including him. "I already saw the mirror," she whispered. "I was already down there. I...saw something, it—" She yelped as he spun her around, slamming her against the wall, the knife returning to her throat a second later.

He towered over her, his eyes as dark as the onyx glass of that terrible thing he kept hidden away. "What did you see?" When she hesitated, he pressed the knife harder, forcing her to tilt her head back. His words were a furious hiss. "What did you see, Emma?"

"M—myself. But not me. It laughed at me, and then... something touched me, I screamed, and it all went dark. I—I woke up on the sofa, where you found me, and—"

He swore. His other hand now joined the knife at her throat. It seemed he wanted to choke the life out of her *and* slit her open at the same time. "Do you understand what you've done?"

"N—"

"Of course, you don't!" He tightened his grasp. "You just blunder into things with a smile and a laugh, uncaring for the seriousness of it all. Can you even fathom how many people will die now, because of what you've done?"

"I—don't—I don't underst—"

"No. You don't." His gaze moved to her lips and stayed there. "I should kill you now. I should just end it all."

She said nothing, afraid to move, afraid to do anything at all. Her life was in his hands. Her fate, wherever it went after this, would be because he either decided to kill her, or not. She had never felt so very small in her life as she did in that exact moment.

His voice dropped from its fury and turned into a base rumble, sounding like a thunderstorm in the distance. "You trifle with forces you cannot comprehend, Emma."

"Then…do it." She let go of his arm, and rested her hands on his chest, holding lightly to the lapels of the tuxedo vest he still wore. She tried to accept her fate, letting her muscles go lax, and tilted her head back, inviting whatever fate he was going to pay her. "Just make it quick, like we talked about. Save yourself the trouble."

His dark eyes flicked between hers, as if searching for something. His expression never changed.

"I—" She never got to finish her thought. It was fine. She had no idea what she was about to say, anyway. Maybe that she was sorry. Maybe that she was just starting to really understand. Maybe another pointless plea for him to spare her life. It didn't matter.

He kissed her.

It was harsh. It was possessive. It was just as violent as the knife he still held to her throat or the hand wrapped around it. It was as angry as the rest of him. It was bruising and left no room for argument.

And she moaned. By the Benevolent God, she moaned at the force of it all. The fear that rampaged through her system was only the kindling, and he was the gasoline. The fire roared to life. He was threatening to kill her…and she wanted him.

I have very, very serious problems.

The world whirled around her suddenly as he took hold of her shoulder and threw her from the wall, sending her staggering toward his desk. She had to catch herself on the edge of it to keep from collapsing. He snatched her by the hair and yanked her head back, the knife only leaving her throat for a split second.

She was shivering. Only mostly from terror, though the other half of her was quickly winning. "Rafe…"

"Undress."

The single command threatened to knock her knees out from under her. Threatened to undo her, right then and there. The sharp blade against her throat made it very hard to catch her breath. She made the mistake of hesitating.

He pulled on her hair harder, arching her back, and slid the knife closer toward her jaw. *"Now."*

Emma never thought herself the kind of woman who would deeply enjoy being bossed about by a man. In fact, she had lived her entire life toward the opposite. But perhaps it was just a matter of the who, not the what. She went about taking off her expensive dress, undoing the zipper on the side, and slipping the straps from her shoulders until the beaded fabric fell to the ground about her ankles. It was a harrowing experience with a knife against her throat.

It made it all the more intense. The fire that roared in her rid her of all her common sense. The idea of asking him to stop, to wait, to please not do this—it was out of the question. Not because she thought he would hurt her. No… because she didn't want him to stop at all. What she wanted from him was entirely the opposite.

I have very, very, very serious problems.

He removed the knife from her throat and placed it—rather pointedly within her reach—on the desk beside her. "Is this what you want?"

"That is a hell of a question, after you—" She yelped as he yanked on her hair again. He pressed his palm to her abdomen, over her stays and chemise, and pressed her body against his. She moaned at the feeling of him there. The strength in his frame, the power of it all. And the presence of his need pressing against her rear, with nothing but a few layers of fabric between them.

"Is this what you want, Emma?" He lowered his head to her ear, his breath hot against her skin. "This is your choice. Not mine."

Of course, he'd make her say it. Of course, the insufferable bastard was going to make her *say* it. He couldn't have just had the kindness to make it—

He growled at her. *"Emma."*

The sound of his anger knocked the floor out from under her. She felt like she might melt into a puddle at his feet if he weren't careful. She could barely breathe, even with the knife no longer pressed to her throat. "Yes—I —please—"

He threw her forward toward the desk, and she caught herself on her hands. It left her half bent over the wood surface, and entirely at his mercy. "Keep your hands flat against my desk. Do not move."

She shivered as he picked up the knife, and she decided it was a very good idea to listen to him, as he began to run the knife over her, trailing the point up her bare arm, sending her breaking out in goosebumps.

Why did that do terrible things to her? Absolutely awful, rotten, wonderful, blissful things? The sensation made her head spin, and she hadn't even gotten a sip of alcohol that night. She pulled in a sharp breath as he slipped the knife beneath the straps of her chemise and sliced them off, one after the other. It was trapped beneath her stays, which was the next victim of his blade. She felt the laces pop one by one as he cut them. The straps that attached to her garters followed.

It was almost a blur as he sliced her clothes from her, piece by piece, until she was standing before him naked, save for the silk stockings that ran up to her thighs. It seemed he had every intention of leaving those where they were.

He had yet to even *touch* her. Not even a stray hand or a graze of fingers anywhere. And by all the angels, demons, gods, and monsters in this world or any other, she had never been left so wanting by anyone or anything.

She wasn't a virgin. She wasn't some blushing bride. She knew what it meant to be with a man. But a passionate, if brief, foray with a stranger in Marrakech was a far cry away from where she was now.

Would he take her like this? Bent over his desk, unable to see him or touch him? Would he just walk away, leaving her like this, humiliated and exposed? The options were endless. When the tip of his knife ran down her spine, she hissed and arched her back. It didn't cut her. It was only there to remind her that it could. Sharp, and threatening, and sending shivers like electricity through her. "Rafe—" His name left her in a needy gasp.

She heard him place the knife back down on the desk with a click. And only then did she let herself breathe. It was a moment later that he touched her for the first time, his palms gliding over her back, tracing what must be a slight scratch from his blade.

When he kissed her between her shoulder blades, slow and sensual, she let out a small, helpless whimper. His palms slid down her body until they grasped her ass, squeezing the globes roughly, turning her whimper into a cry. She tried to squirm away from him, but there was no helping it. He had her trapped.

When one of his hands slid to cup her core, it was his

turn to moan, a deep and desperate sound behind her. It was clear just how very much she was enjoying their situation, and how very mutual their desire really was.

His fingers stroked over her, strong and certain, knowing precisely how to play her as if she were a musical instrument. And she tried to bite back the notes but couldn't help it. When he pressed a finger inside her, delving into her body, she wailed.

Rafe moaned her name quietly into her skin as he kissed her back again, his other hand now pressed to the wood surface beside hers. She could feel the scrape of his clothes against her, feeling horribly out of place with how naked and exposed she was. But the distraction didn't last long as he explored her in earnest, a second finger joining the first, sinking as deep as they could go before slowly withdrawing.

It wasn't enough. She needed more. Pressing back against his hand, her need was becoming desperation. But he was cruel, slowing his pace in response, or removing his fingers entirely to stroke over her. She whined, and her exasperation only made him chuckle.

"You deserve this." He straightened, and she should have suspected trouble. His hand came down on her ass cheek with a *crack*.

Yelping, she bit her lower lip, glaring back at him in annoyance. She barely resisted the urge to make some sort of scathing comment.

He only chuckled again at her expression. "Careful. I think I've discovered I quite like you when you're frustrated." A second slap had her dropping down to her elbows, unable to stay on her hands any longer. It only exposed her to him farther. He hummed thoughtfully as he pressed two fingers back into her body, stretching her, but not enough. Not nearly enough. "Frustrated and eager."

Everything upended again as he dragged her up by the

hair, turned her about to face him, and half-threw, half-placed her onto his desk. She found herself quickly on her back, staring up at him as he stood between her knees.

What a sight he made. Angry and victorious, smug and on the edge of losing control, all at once. Superior but nearly frantic as he undid the buttons of his vest and shrugged out of the fabric.

She watched as he stripped for her, and was sorely tempted to touch herself as he did. She couldn't take her eyes away. He slipped the suspenders from his shoulders, leaving them on, before turning to his bowtie. But he didn't toss the fabric aside as she expected. Instead, he pressed a palm to the wood of his desk by her head and leaned over her. "Open your mouth, Emma."

"Wh—" She clamped her lips shut. What was he thinking?

His expression was one of equal parts lust and malice. She would have shrunk away from him if she could. His dark hair had fallen from its careful placement and cut stark black lines against his pale face. She felt like a butterfly in a collection, pinned right to the spot.

One word left him, sinful and bottomless as the abyss. "Open."

Shivering, she obeyed.

He shoved the fabric of his bowtie into her mouth. "No screaming." He sneered. The man who straightened in front of her was no longer reserved. It was like a dam had burst. She could see things moving beneath his shirt, his infestation rising to the surface with his lack of control. But the lights blazed bright in the room, and hopefully—*hopefully*—that would keep her safe from them.

Rafe undid his buttons so quickly, he ended up ripping the last few off, as he tossed his shirt aside. His undershirt went into the pile. It seemed he was planning on leaving his pants on for the moment. *Damn.* But she could take in the wonderful sight of his muscles as he reached down to stroke his palms over her body, all temperance having left him.

He grabbed her breasts, squeezing them hard enough that she cried out against the makeshift gag in her mouth, arching her back as she tried to search for relief from—and more of—his violent touch. When he pinched her nipples, she was suddenly glad for the bowtie he had stuffed into her mouth. She didn't scream, but the noise that left her wasn't any more dignified.

He bent down, resting on his elbow, and replaced his fingers with his teeth. He bit down upon her tender flesh without mercy, before rolling his tongue over the tortured spot as if to soothe the damage he'd just done.

She could pull at his hair. She could rip the gag from her mouth and toss it aside. She could kick him or grab the pocketknife that sat beside her. She could do a great many things to stop what was happening. But instead, she clung to him, her hands resting on his shoulders, and whimpered and wailed, muffled as it was. If she could speak, the only things that would have left her mouth would be cries for *more, please, more!*

His other hand traveled south, returning to her, and didn't even pause before he rammed two fingers back into her, causing her to jolt on the desk, the sudden invasion causing her head to reel in pleasure. When his thumb stroked over the sensitive ball of nerves at her core, that was it. It was over. That was all it took. Just a glancing blow, and she was sent crashing over the cliff into abject bliss. Her body clenched around his fingers, wishing that they were something else.

He lifted his head from tormenting her breast to watch her as she unraveled around his fingers, taking in the sight of her as he left her panting, gagged, naked, and ready to beg him to fuck her, if only she could speak. Not that she was fully confident of her ability to form words at the moment.

He cupped her jaw with one hand, studying her. "I expect that if you survive until the morning, you will likely have bruises." He straightened, and she watched as he undid his fly and freed himself from his trousers.

She swallowed. *Oh. Goodness.*

She suspected that he was right. Yes. Yes, she was going to have bruises. Not only from the sheer mass of him—not that she was complaining—but she had the distinct sensation that he was not going to be gentle on her.

He picked up her knees and yanked her toward him until her hips were just at the edge of his desk. He bent her legs until they were hooked over his elbows and leaned forward to cage her in. The action…bent her in half. There was no stopping him. She was exposed. Vulnerable. And entirely at his mercy.

And she loved every second of it.

He shifted her leg so he could line himself up at her core, rubbing the head of his length over her entrance, teasing her. He watched her, eyes as black as pitch and smoldering with his own desperate need. This was not going to be gentle.

Good.

In one movement, in one fell stroke, he plunged into her with a violent snap of his hips. He sank himself to the hilt in that one movement. And with that action, ecstasy overwhelmed her. It hit her with such force that she thought she saw stars. But what she knew she did…was scream.

RAFE CLAMPED a hand over her mouth, muffling her further, stifling the sound that left her as the young woman beneath him—this imp, this scandalous little thing—clamped around him in such a violent release that he was almost dragged down with her.

He snarled in anger, his frustration with her building again. She had almost ruined everything. Everything. Their night had been going so well. This wasn't how he wanted it to end. But the feeling of her around his fingers, tight and volcanic, and the feeling of her needy whimpers, was too much.

It was all too much.

The beast in him needed to be fed. And feed, it would. He let loose the reins, come what may. He would face the aftermath in the morning. Either his infestation would consume her, or he would owe her an apology for what he had done.

But the die was cast. The choice was made. And he was going to have her with all the vicious and overwhelming desperation that had built in him.

He pinned her in place, holding her firm, as he began to unleash himself on her, moaning her name against her shoulder. He would make a place for himself inside her with each stroke, each impact of his body into hers. She was gasping and moaning, her hands holding on to his arms as he crudely bent her in half and used the leverage to seek out a way to somehow, someway, go deeper inside her.

He wanted her. He needed her. The idea of having to kill her, never having tasted what was being so willingly offered had shattered what little control he still had left in her presence.

The Blade would not have her. The Idol would not have her. *You are mine, Emma Mather. You are mine!*

And those thoughts scared him. But not nearly enough to stop him.

THE MAN over her that was questioning the very nature of her reality was a far cry from what she had expected from the professor. She could barely think. She could barely breathe. He was loving her with all the tenderness of the pistons of an automobile engine, driving everything but *him* out of her and leaving her with nothing but the overwhelming stretch and the ecstasy of it all.

She had to hold on to the edge of the desk to keep his thrusts from pushing her away. She did all she could to greet his body with her own. This was simple. This was right. This was bliss. Again and again she unraveled until she had gone nearly limp beneath him.

How long it went on, she had no clue. But it seemed he couldn't take any more either, as his thrusts became stuttering and erratic, somehow even stronger than before. The action sent her once more into ecstasy, unable to do much more than let out a whimpering, muffled whine as her body spasmed again in release.

He rammed himself to the hilt, let out a loud snarl, and then pulled himself from her. She felt him spend himself on her stomach. Caught up as they were, the conversation around a condom or a cervical cap certainly hadn't happened.

It seemed that even when Rafe was entirely out of his mind, he somehow managed to be a gentleman. Who had threatened her with a knife. A gentleman of sorts.

She pulled the bowtie from her mouth and tossed it aside, glad to be able to move her jaw. And breathe. Rafe was still over her, shuddering in the throes of his own release. She reached up and gently tilted his head to hers.

The expression he wore was stormy, like the open sea during the worst of gales. She lifted her head and kissed him. Slowly, gently, and as tenderly as she could when she felt as shaky as a leaf. When she parted, he looked so confused that she had to laugh. That only made matters worse for him.

"Could you kindly put my legs down?" She needed a cup of water. Her throat was hoarse. "It's…a bit uncomfortable."

"Oh—" He let go of her, as if the thought hadn't occurred to him. "Yes, of…of course." He straightened. "I…should get you a towel." He tucked himself back into his pants, cringing as he did. "Stay there."

And with that, he walked away.

She chuckled and threw an arm over her eyes. He was a gentleman of sorts, indeed. She didn't know what was going to happen with them. She didn't know if what they had just done had made their lives more or less complicated, longer or shorter.

But as feeling was slowly returning to her legs, she realized that even if she knew the answer, it wouldn't have changed her choice.

That had been entirely worth it.

CHAPTER TWENTY-THREE

Rafe was not quite certain what to do with himself.

It wasn't that he felt ashamed for what he had done—she had been a willing participant, after all—but the aftermath of it was…strange. She was sitting beside him on his sofa, having gone upstairs to put on some nightclothes, and was nursing a drink he had made her.

He did not know what to say.

He had ravaged the girl, and she had taken it with a smile. So, there he sat, rigid and upright, while she leaned idly against his arm and sipped her drink, her head occasionally resting on his shoulder.

She should be dead for several reasons. She should not have survived looking into the mirror. She should not have survived screaming in his presence—though perhaps because it had not precisely been out of fear, that provided an explanation. And she should be dead because if he had a single functional brain cell left in his head, he should have killed her.

But there she was. Leaning against him.

And there he was.

Not knowing what to do.

He sipped his drink. Hopefully, the alcohol might dull his awareness of his awkward situation, even if it wouldn't provide him any answers to his current predicament.

"How did you get that thing into that hole in the basement?"

Her question caught him so distinctly off guard that he stared at her dumbly for a long moment. "Excuse me?" The young woman was wearing nothing more than a dressing gown, drinking alcohol, after they had brutally made love, after she had been terrorized by the Great Beast of Arnsmouth, and *that* was the first thing she asked him? A *logistics* question? "How did I get it down there?"

"Yeah. I mean. It's certainly larger than the stairs." She snickered before a thought occurred to her and she snapped her fingers. "Did you bring it down in pieces? I bet you took it down in pieces."

"I—"

"Did you?" She grinned, very pleased with herself. "Tell me I'm right."

"Well—"

"C'mon." She nudged his arm.

"It's hardly the point!" He didn't mean to snap at her. But that was what happened, regardless. Her joy at her brief victory over having solved the mystery of the large-thing-through-small-hole shattered and fell from her face. For a second, there was doubt in those amber eyes. Doubt, and hurt. Why was she…?

He frowned. He had already known that most of her carelessness was a facade. But it seemed he was now keenly able to break through it. He reached out and gently tucked a strand of her dark brown hair behind her ear. It was as unruly as the rest of her. Her short bob of curls suited her perfectly. "I'm sorry, Emma."

She shook her head and looked away, hiding the vulnerability she had shown him. Sighing, he shifted his arm and pulled her against his side. She went willingly, curling up against him, and rested her head on his chest. Whatever they were, whatever they were to become, what had just passed between them wasn't strictly casual.

It might be a death wish. But it wasn't strictly casual.

He kissed the top of her head. He was still at a loss for words. But admitting that he wished to hold her was not going to do either of them any more harm. They were well past that point.

They sat there in silence, and after a while, he wondered if she had fallen asleep.

"But I'm right, right?" She looked up at him.

He leaned his head back on the sofa and said the word through a groan of defeat. *"Yes."*

"I knew it!" She laughed.

I have made a very terrible mistake, haven't I?

EMMA POUTED UP AT RAFE. "You're kidding me."

The professor chuckled and leaned his head down to kiss her forehead. "I don't want to risk it."

"But—" She started to argue. It was silly to not sleep in the same bed, and damn it all, she wanted to cuddle. But his expression had a finality to it that was impressive. She had never seen something like that from her own father, although Poppa was notoriously soft on her. With a long sigh, she wrapped her arms around his waist and hugged him. "Fine. But I think it's stupid."

"We still don't know what my infestation will do with you, if left unchecked. I don't want to be asleep and wake up to find you gone." He stroked a hand over her hair.

She shut her eyes, basking in the sensation. She nuzzled into his chest for a moment, squeezing him a little tighter. He finally wrapped his other arm around her and returned the gesture. He was a little awkward and unsure of what to do in this kind of situation. His lack of charm was, oddly, somehow charming anyway. "I get it."

"Good."

"I don't like it, but I get it."

"I will issue a complaint with management." He kissed the top of her head before stifling a yawn. It was the early hours of the morning, and to say they had an eventful night would be putting it mildly. She finally got that drink.

She smiled up at him. "See that you do." Going up on her tiptoes, she kissed him and went toward her borrowed bedroom. "Goodnight, Professor. Or good morning, however you want to look at it."

"Have a restful sleep." He walked halfway down the stairs to the floor below before he hesitated. "Oh. Emma? Do not go near the mirror again."

She frowned at him. "I—"

"Emma." Again, his tone dropped her name like a gavel. There was no arguing.

"Okay, *Dad*." She rolled her eyes. "I won't go near the mirror again."

He wrinkled his nose. "Please don't ever call me that again. I have suddenly learned I find it rather revolting."

Laughing, she shook her head and walked into the room. "Can't say I'm a fan of it myself. Goodnight, Rafe."

"Goodnight, Emma."

She shut the door and stretched her arms over her head, yawning and enjoying the wonderful dull ache that she felt pretty much everywhere. She was already in her nightclothes, so she draped her dressing gown over the end of her bed and slipped under the covers. She still had to leave the blasted lights on and sleep with a damnable blindfold.

But the other option was...

No, I don't think I'm in the mood. Best let myself rest up from the man, before I let the monsters do whatever it is they're going to do to me. Not that the idea of it didn't curl low in her stomach anyway.

No. Not right now. She smiled as she slipped the makeshift blindfold over her eyes. *Maybe tomorrow.*

And I will not go near the mirror again. I won't.

She yawned, snuggling into the pillow. *Although...I didn't promise.*

RAFE DESCENDED the narrow staircase toward the secret chamber beneath his home. He did it without the need of his lighter in his pocket. He didn't need to see where he was going. The steps were familiar to him. As he reached the bottom, he leaned against the brick wall next to the only entrance or exit from the space and waited.

Waited for Emma.

He had asked her not to return here. And he knew precisely what that would do—ensure that she *did*. Part of him hoped she would listen to him and stay away. And part of him hoped she would defy him and force his hand.

It was clear he could not rid himself of her on his own. He lacked the gumption. He was—

"Lonely."

He cringed at the sound of his own voice in the small space. "I am not lonely."

"*Oh, yes, you are, Professor. Painfully, achingly lonely. Don't lie to yourself, it's childish.*"

With a sigh, he shut his eyes. Not that it much mattered in

OF VISIONS & SECRETS

the pitch-black space. He knew that if he carried his lantern, the image of himself in the onyx surface would be sneering at him. "Very well. I am lonely."

"And she is so very sweet, isn't she? Sweet and tart, like a summer berry." The voice hummed.

A surge of jealousy welled in him with such viciousness that it alarmed him. She wasn't his property, no matter what had run through his mind in the moment they had made love. But the idea that the darkness had— "You let her live."

"How could I not? She is so much more fun when she's alive. Not like her simpering brother. No, this one whimpers and moans with such abandon! What a wonderful toy. When we touch her, she—"

"Don't! Don't." He put his hand over his face, resisting the urge to fly at the mirror and attempt to shatter it again. But it would do no good. "I have to get rid of her."

"Spoilsport. Well." The voice sighed dramatically. *"Then you know what we need to do, don't you?"*

"Yes." His jaw ticked, and he finally snarled in frustration. He did know what he had to do. He knew how to solve his Emma Mather problem. But it didn't mean he wanted to do it. He liked the young girl. He saw so much of his own insatiable curiosity in her that it spurred some strange protective instinct in him. He wanted to teach her. Guide her. Maybe even initiate her into the Mirror.

That would have been lovely, if she wasn't being pursued by not one, but *two* of the other Societies. He could deal with the Blade, perhaps. Gigi was a tough negotiator, but there could be a trade to ensure Emma's safety. But the Idol? There was no dealing with the Idol.

"For shame. Such a wonderful plaything."

"Please stop talking."

The darkness chuckled. *"Here she comes..."*

Dread welled in him as he heard the door to the stairwell

click open, then shut once more. He waited. The light from her candles came first, casting odd shadows as she rounded the corner into the room. She didn't see him at first, holding up her candelabra to take in the enormous, looming, shattered mirror.

He reached out and took the candelabra from her, knowing she would drop it. "I told you to stay away."

She clamped her hands over her mouth, muting the shriek of fear as she jumped away from him. She was so startled that she staggered over her own feet—she had gotten dressed, but not put on shoes—and fell to the packed dirt. But her startled expression never faded from fear.

She believed he was going to kill her.

Perhaps he was.

Perhaps that would be a kinder fate.

Oh, no. Oh, no.

She was such an idiot! Emma flew back up to her feet, trying to keep some distance between her and Rafe. But the professor was blocking her path back up the stairs. It left her trapped between him and the enormous mirror, whose surface was reflecting the scene back to them in a billion distorted fragments.

"I—I—"

"Don't bother making excuses. I understand." Rafe sighed. "And part of me shares your compulsions, trust me." He peered up at the broken mirror. "How do you think I wound up the way that I am, Emma? Simply because I, like you, cannot leave a box unopened. No matter the cost of it."

"So…you're not mad?" She still kept her distance.

"Mad? No. Disappointed? Hm. Perhaps." He shrugged. "But I'm certainly not surprised." He took a step toward the mirror, and she watched as the pieces of it began to slowly heal back together into one smooth surface. "And yes. I brought this here shard by shard, fragment by fragment, twisted piece of wood by twisted piece of wood. Some of it was given to me by my fellow associates. Others, I had to track down. Others, I paid a steep price for." His expression darkened. "A price I continue to pay."

The Things that lived in his shadow. She fidgeted with the sleeve of her nightgown. "So..."

"My Society deals in knowledge, Miss Mather." The reflection of Rafe in the mirror was now whole as he stood a few feet from it, the light of the candles in the image seemingly brighter than the ones he held. "Things that should be known, and things that should stay unknown. There are some secrets that should remain such, no matter how much we regret it."

She didn't understand. When he held his hand out to her, beckoning her closer, she knew whatever was about to happen next wasn't going to be good. But it was Rafe. They had just—they were lovers now. He clearly had a soft spot for her. Maybe it would be fine?

No.

No, it was not going to be fine.

But what was her other option? She could turn tail and run up the stairs. She might be able to squeak around him. Might. But then what? Finally abandon her mission of finding her brother and retreat home, writing this all off as a bad dream? Or be eaten by that Crawling Terror or whatever Gigi wanted to do to her.

"Are you about to kill me?" She needed to ask, even if she didn't really want to know.

He chuckled sadly. "No, Emma. We have passed that point."

Swallowing the lump in her throat, she slowly walked

over to him, placing her hand in his, and let him draw her closer to his side. He held her hand, almost sweetly, as they watched their reflections on the dark surface in front of them.

"Some knowledge is best known, and some best unknown. And it is the purview of the Mirror to decide what remains seen, and what unseen. Do you understand?" He was ever the teacher, even when it was grossly inappropriate.

"In theory." She was shivering. It was cold down in this place, and fear was still gripping her spine, keeping her rigid and waiting for something terrible to happen. "But I fail to see what you will do about it in practice."

His smile was faint as he turned to her. He released her hand to gently cup her cheek in his palm, running his thumb slowly over her skin. "You would be a phenomenal student. If this had all played out differently, I would have taken you as my protege. Sadly..."

She searched his eyes for something, but they were just as unfathomable as the onyx beside them. "Sadly?"

Rafe leaned down and kissed her, slipping his hand to cup the back of her neck. The kiss was slow and passionate, and she melted into it, forgetting for a moment that he was likely about to do something terrible to her.

When he parted, he rested his forehead against hers. "Believe it or not, Miss Mather, I am trying to protect you."

She wanted to speak. Wanted to ask him not to do whatever it was he was about to do. But her words were failing her. All she could think of to say, quietly, was, "I'm sorry."

He smiled. "Don't be sorry, Emma. For all the annoyance you've brought to me the past week or so, I...oddly enjoyed every second of it." He lifted his head and kissed her forehead.

This felt like goodbye. It sounded like goodbye. Her eyes

were beginning to sting with tears. "Please, don't..." She didn't even know what she was asking him not to do.

"I must. For my sake, and yours." He sighed, the hand on the back of her neck tightening just a little. "It is the only way you make it out of this alive. This is...for your own good, Emma Mather. Goodbye."

"No, I—"

She never got to finish her sentence. He threw her toward the mirror. She squeaked, putting out her hands to stop herself against the blackened surface. But the reflection of herself was not there.

There was nothing there.

Her legs hit the edge of the frame, the wood reaching just above her knees. And instead of smacking into the hard onyx?

Her hands hit nothing at all. She pitched forward, losing her balance. Flailing her arms about, trying to catch the edge of the mirror, she struggled to keep upright. But nothing worked.

She fell.

She tried to scream. But she wasn't sure if anything came out. She supposed it didn't matter anyway. Nothing mattered.

Darkness took her.

CHAPTER TWENTY-FOUR

Bishop Patrick Caner sat at his desk, whittling a small lump of wood in his hands. He was carving a new figurine to add to his collection. A collection that served a purpose, but a collection all the same. It was a hobby that helped him think in more ways than one.

The other carved statues with their blocky features and sharp angles sat on his desk next to the small pile of shavings that he was creating as he worked on carving them a new companion. A new player had entered the game, and she needed a figurine to go with the others.

He hummed as he worked. He wasn't a particularly good woodcarver, but that wasn't really the point. He wasn't going to sell these at a fair, or pretend it was anything more than a way to keep his hands busy while he reasoned through his next actions.

"Now, I wonder where you're going to wind up," he murmured to the little figurine. "Seems like everybody wants a piece of you. Literally." He sighed. He felt bad for the woman the lump of wood was meant to represent. It seemed she had fallen into the mess that was Arnsmouth with truly benign motives.

There were a few kinds of fools who fell in with the so-called "Dark Societies" that he had dedicated his life to eradicating. The ones who thought themselves able to control the corruption and wield it for power. The ones who thought they had no other options. The ones who didn't care for the death and chaos they caused, as long as they got ahead. The ones who simply wanted to hurt others. And then there were the ones who didn't *mean* to. The ones who meant well.

And she seemed to mean well.

But what was the phrase? The road to hell? He pitied them all. But he felt for the ones who had good intentions.

A quiet knock on the door interrupted his thoughts, if not his hands. He knew who it was by the sound of it. "Come in, Father Lombardi."

"Bishop, there's been a bit of an incident." The man who entered was older than he was, maybe twice his age, despite the fact that Patrick outranked him in the Church of the Benevolent God. Some souls preferred to stay where they were. Lombardi was a good priest—a great priest, actually—but had no desire to climb the ladder.

Neither did Patrick, really. But he was very good at his job, and the Church saw fit to promote him. Actually, he was extremely good at his job in one area and rather miserable everywhere else. But the Church wanted the Dark Societies gone, so here he was as a glorified exterminator wearing the moniker of Bishop. He was a relative newcomer to the city, and he hated every minute of it. Arnsmouth had a chill in the air that never left, even on the brightest summer day. A chill that was felt in the soul.

Patrick waited for Lombardi to continue. When he didn't, he resisted the urge to roll his eyes. "An incident, Father Lombardi?"

"A woman collapsed on our doorstep. We found her unconscious there at first light. None of the Investigators saw her approach, she just...seemed to appear."

"Women don't appear out of thin air, Father." Patrick smirked. *Unfortunately,* he added silently in his head, deciding to keep his sinful comments to himself. "They simply failed to see her walk up. She collapsed, and? I assume alcohol or drugs were to blame?"

"We don't believe so. She doesn't seem inebriated. She just seems...Bishop, she's forgotten herself. Her memory is gone." The man frowned, his thick white brow furrowing. "I think she might be insane."

"Or." He hated how some people could jump to the worst conclusions. "She had a traumatic event." Setting his whittling knife down on his desk, he placed the unfinished figurine in front of him. He wasn't quite done with the details of the hair. "It's probably best if she goes over the river anyway." He hated the sanitarium that sat on the hill just northwest of the city. He hated it with every ounce of his being.

Nowhere had he ever found a place that stank of death, rot, fear, and sadness quite like Arnsmouth Asylum. Nor had he ever seen a place that tried to make itself look exactly like its contents, as if the architecture itself was a warning.

He shook his head. "Where is she now?"

"She's resting in one of the visiting quarters at the parish house, for the moment. We thought it best, since...well..." Lombardi fidgeted.

"Since, well, what?" Patrick rubbed a hand over his face. Lombardi was a good priest. But irritatingly slow. He looked over at the old man and carefully laced his fingers together and placed them on the desk in a careful show of patience. He smiled as warmly as he could. "You look like you're going to crawl out of your skin. What aren't you telling me?"

"She might not know who she is anymore, but the Investigators know her. It's...it's Miss Mather."

Mather.

He stared down at the figurine he had just been carving, wondering if he hadn't accidentally managed to summon her. But that kind of magic wasn't part of his gifts. He had other ways of protecting the city. But she was here, and with no memory? How—no, not how, *why?* Picking up the figurine, he held it tight in his palm as he stood from his desk and headed quickly for the door, not waiting for the old priest to get out of his way.

What have you done, Saltonstall?

"We called her father, Doctor Mather. He's on his way down to collect her." Lombardi was jogging after him, puffing from the exertion.

"Good." Patrick almost felt bad, except that he was now very much in a rush. It wasn't his fault he had longer, younger legs. He had somewhere to be, and somewhere to be immediately. *Her father will take her home away from all this mess, and hopefully the rumblings will calm down once she goes.*

There had been whispers in the dark. Whispers of creatures summoned from the below to hunt her down. The Societies were chasing her like she was a prize. Almost every single one of them were tripping over each other to get to her. And the ones that were quiet were likely just quiet*er* in their actions.

Getting this new piece off the board was the best possible outcome for everybody involved.

And I think you knew that, Saltonstall. It almost made him smile. He would like to think that the professor's actions were out of kindness. But he knew better. Saltonstall knew he was left holding the baton in a game of capture the flag. It was an act of self-preservation. The infested bastard could hold his own in a fight, but not against the Blade *and* the Idol, who were both making overt attempts to take her for their own interests.

Turning the figurine over in his palm, running his thumb over the fresh woodcuts, he made his way through the winding hallways of the church to the guest rooms in the back. They were meant for traveling priests, visitors, and the like. He wasn't sure as he could remember a time that they housed someone like Emma Mather.

Or whatever was left of Emma Mather.

That made him frown. He was hardly an expert in the magic wielded by the Mirror, but there was no telling how deep the damage ran. It might be difficult to tell how much damage Saltonstall had done to the poor girl. It was easy to tell which of the guest rooms she occupied—there were two Investigators flanking the door, their hands folded in front of them in an identical pose.

Their pure white masks were just as unnerving to him as they likely were to everyone else, though he just had more practice ignoring them. And he knew they would never come knocking on his door—he would never be dragged off into the depths of the church and questioned. He was "above reproach."

The idea made him want to laugh.

Approaching the door, he jerked his head to the side, motioning for the two Investigators to leave. They bowed their heads and wandered away in their monk-like silence. *Creepy bastards. Useful, but creepy bastards.*

Raising his fist, he knocked on the door quietly. "Miss?"

There was silence for a long moment before he heard someone reply. "Come in."

He opened the door cautiously, frowning at the figure he saw standing by the window. She was dressed in a white robe, as it was probably all that they had to give her. Her arms were wrapped around herself as if trying to console herself. He instantly wanted to hug her, to tell her it was all going to be okay—that now she was safe. But considering what she might have permanently lost, it seemed gloriously inappropriate.

She turned her attention to him. Her large, amber eyes were tired and full of dismay. She leaned against the windowsill. "I'm afraid I—I don't know you. Should I?"

He smiled sadly. "No, dear. No, you don't know me." He walked into the room and took a seat at the small desk by the wall. The tiny wooden chair creaked under his weight. He always tried to make himself seem smaller than he was—his height and his general size could easily frighten people.

It came in handy sometimes. Like when he was getting his face bloodied in a brawl or a boxing match. Other times, like now, he didn't want to further spook the poor thing. Nobody ever expected a Bishop to be a belt-holding champion boxer, but here he was. He'd used the skills he'd earned on the job sadly more frequently than not, it seemed. "My name is Bishop Patrick Caner." He kept his voice gentle and friendly. "Please, call me Patrick. You've...had a terrible accident."

"The old guy said I was crazy." She cringed and looked away. "I might be. I think I am. But not—not like this." She shook her head. "I'm sorry, everything is just a jumble. It's like butterflies. I reach for them, but they just"—she was clearly getting more anxious as she spoke, struggling to remember anything—"just keep escaping me."

"It's all right, dear. I promise you. What's happened to you isn't your fault." *We know who did it to you. We just don't know exactly why.* He kept those thoughts to himself. If Saltonstall was trying to get Miss Mather off the board and out of reach, he was fully on board with that agenda. "This can happen to people when they've had a mighty shock."

"Do you know what caused it?" She finally left where she

was standing to move over to the edge of the small bed. She sat on it, not bothering to put much distance between them. Her instant trust of him made him smile. "I feel like...I was searching for something. Or someone."

He pulled in a deep breath, held it for a second, and let it out in a long rush. Leaning out, he reached for her hands, and she let him take them in his grasp. He held them together and squeezed, attempting to console her. "You lost someone very dear to you. Your name is Emma Mather, and you were here trying to find your twin brother Elliot."

Emma's eyes lit up for a moment in recognition. It flashed over her briefly before it died again, as if someone—or some*thing*—had snuffed a candle. That something had taken that brief flash of remembering and snatched it away from her and devoured it.

Damn. He kept the dread and frustration off his face. Saltonstall hadn't simply removed her memory. He had corrupted her. *Shit, damn, fuck!* Now Patrick was at a crossroads himself. Go left and put her back in danger. Go right, and...leave the corruption inside her. Where it could fester, rot, and turn into something even more dangerous down the line.

This wasn't going to go well. None of it was going to go well.

Emma shook her head dumbly. "I don't...what you're saying doesn't feel wrong. But I can't—I just—" Her eyes began to shine, and soon a second later, she was crying. Embarrassed, she tried to wipe them away and hide them, but they were coming too quickly for that to do any good. "I'm scared. I feel like—like somebody hurt me—and I just don't remember—and what if they come back?"

He shushed her and, standing from the chair, sat down on the bed beside her. He pulled her into a hug, tucking her

OF VISIONS & SECRETS

head underneath his chin. "It's all right. You're safe. No one is going to hurt you."

When another knock sounded on the door, she stood from the bed and wiped her eyes, trying valiantly to make herself look as presentable as she could. She smoothed out the white robe she was wearing. "Come in."

The door creaked open as Patrick stood as well, ready to greet whoever had arrived. He smiled sadly, happy to see the man but sad for the circumstances, as if they were at a funeral. And in many ways, they were. Patrick knew the man who entered, if only from social situations. But there was also no mistaking the short, mostly round, white-haired older man who stepped into the room. Patrick was well over six feet and towered over everyone and everything. Because of that, the other man felt like he only came up to Patrick's waist, even though he was likely just a little shorter than usual. But the newcomer had enough personality to command the room under most normal circumstances.

But at the moment, Dr. Eustis Mather's expression was drawn tight in concern, all his usual charm and charisma broken down by one simple thing—concern for his daughter. "Emma, sweetheart, are you all right?"

Emma cringed as if she had been struck. "I—I'm sorry, no, I don't think I am." She wiped her eyes again. "I'm not even sure if that's really my name."

"Oh, my poor girl. My poor, sweet girl." Eustis walked up to her and reached out his arms, offering a hug. "It's going to all be all right, now. I'm your father."

Emma stepped into the hug. Eustis only reached her shoulder. She hugged the smaller, rounder, older man, and a sob shook her shoulders. She might not remember her father, but Patrick could tell by the way her shoulders sagged that she still *knew* her father.

Eustis tutted and rubbed her back gently. After Emma

had calmed her tears, he led his daughter over to sit on the edge of the bed. He stood beside her, a hand on her shoulder. Eustis turned to Patrick. "Thank you for not sending her over the river."

"Of course." Patrick shook his head and stationed himself by the wall. The room was small, and he was large, and he didn't want to crowd the poor girl. "First, I know about her… uh…" He scratched at his beard. He wasn't ever a fan of these sensitive situations. He was more of a *punch it in the face* kind of priest. Gentle platitudes, he was fine with. But political maneuvering, or sensitive conversations? No. Not his style.

"Her condition." Eustis supplied firmly. "One that is entirely under control and has nothing to do with this incident. Or…the loss of her brother." Grief soured his defensiveness.

"Who told you?" Patrick was rather glad the news had been spoiled. That was one part of his job he was fully capable of—telling people their loved ones had died—but he hated every second of it. Sadly, he had plenty of practice.

"A 'friend' of hers had the desk at the hotel she was staying at call me. Said that she had suffered a 'great loss' and was staying with him. The description given to me offered me no clue as to who the man was." Eustis sighed. "I'm not surprised this is how she reacted. Blocking out the memory of her brother. I cannot properly describe how close they were."

"Of course." Patrick folded his arms.

Emma stayed silent, watching the conversation as if numb to the world around her, or as if it wasn't about her at all.

And if he didn't do something, that was how she was going to stay. He braced himself for what he knew was coming. "But I don't think her current condition is natural. Nor, if left unabated, will it ever go away."

Emma looked up at him at that, curious and concerned in equal measures. Eustis, meanwhile, had an expression of a man who knew he was about to get into an argument. He was simply waiting for the other shoe to drop.

Straightening his back, mostly because he was instinctually crouching like he always was, Patrick did the same. And then promptly dropped the shoe. "She is in need of an exorcism."

And lo, the shouting began.

CHAPTER TWENTY-FIVE

Emma—that was her name, or so they told her—stood from the bed and moved back over to the window. She let the two men in the room shout at each other. They were talking about her, but it felt so distant and remote that she couldn't quite be bothered to follow along.

It wasn't really about her. It was about someone they knew she had been, until...something had happened. It itched at the back of her mind, like a mosquito bite in the middle of her spine where she couldn't reach it. No matter how hard she tried, no matter how she focused, she just *couldn't get there.*

Something had happened to her. Something had been done to her. And now she couldn't even remember what. And there was a strange part of her that found that even more insulting. That this "Emma" they were talking about had her entire life taken away from her, only to have "Emma" left on the doorstep of the Church like an abandoned and unwanted pet.

She glared out the window down into the street, halfheartedly catching snippets of what the little old man and the enormous Bishop were bickering about.

"—I figured that on all your global travels, you would have seen all sorts of miracles—"

"—seen piles of dung of every shape and size to know that this is a steaming heap of *bullsh—*"

She tuned back out, trying not to laugh.

The little man seemed familiar, even if she couldn't place his face or voice. He said he was her father, and while there wasn't anything she could think of that would make that untrue, she also had nothing to back it up other than a gut feeling. But that was all she'd been left with. Feelings. Instincts.

Whoever did this was going to pay.

She didn't know how. And she didn't know if it was ever even going to be possible, or if it was just some kind of shield she was using to protect herself. Revenge was a decent thing to live for, she supposed. Revenge, and a mystery. Who was she, what had happened to her, and did she truly have a missing twin?

The little man was screaming something to the effect that the loss of her brother had simply triggered some sort of emotional break. That this was all just too much strain, and her mind had decided to ignore all of it, instead of facing the truth of her grief.

The Bishop—who was a *mountain* of a man and would be absolutely terrifying for his size if he didn't have such a kind face—was arguing that the Great Beast of Arnsmouth was corrupting her mind.

She knew about the Great Beast of Arnsmouth. She knew about the town, the history of it, the mysterious and entirely fictional Dark Societies. She knew about the world. She knew what year it was. Who was mayor of the town, president of the country, and what day and month it was—though she had been a few days off, to be fair, as some of that time was truly missing.

She just didn't know anything about her place in all of it.

All she wanted to do was stare out the window at the people passing by and watch them live their little *known* lives, while she tried her best to dig up whatever she could out of her fragmented mind.

But she couldn't do that when the two idiots in the room with her were so very loud.

"—backwater, superstitious—"

"—there are more things in this world—"

Finally, she couldn't take it anymore. Placing her hands over her eyes, she screamed, *"Stop it!"*

They both went silent. She turned to them to find both men staring at her, wide-eyed in surprise. It was a pretty comically identical expression, considering the fact that the two men couldn't be farther apart in size and nature.

The little old man who probably really *was* her father had tanned skin that was in sharp contrast to his white hair and large mustache that connected to his sideburns and obscured his upper lip entirely. His eyebrows were just about as bushy as his mustache. She instantly liked him. Her mind might not remember him, but her soul seemed to.

The other man was also oddly endearing in a strange way. The Bishop was well over six feet tall, and the poor bastard probably didn't even notice when he had to duck under doorways anymore. He was broad and built like an ox, his black garb doing very little to hide the fact that he could probably end her life with a punch. She didn't know exactly *why* the Church of the Benevolent God promoted a man who was a walking streetcar to the rank of Bishop, but she was suddenly very nervous about finding out.

But his smile was gentle, and his expressions came fast, and seemed genuine. When he had spoken to her, he had done so with patience and caring. Maybe he was a fantastic liar, but she wasn't so sure. He ran a large hand over his short ginger hair that was graying at the temples, leaving him looking a bit like cinnamon sugar. He was handsome in a broad, bold kind of way. *Like an ox.* The comparison came through again.

Both men were still staring at her as she tried to think through what she wanted to say. "Why not?" She shrugged.

"Excuse me?" The Bishop blinked.

"What's the harm?" She put her back to the window frame and folded her arms across her chest. "If you do this exorcism, and I'm *not* possessed by some...whatever you think I'm possessed by—"

"A demon. A shard of the Great Beast," the Bishop interjected gently.

"Whatever." She waved a hand dismissively. "A thing. If you think I'm possessed, and I'm not, and you do the exorcism, will it hurt me?"

"No. You may be at risk if we try to dispel the monster. They often do not go quietly." He frowned. "But I have never met a demon I cannot defeat. You will be all right."

"So, if you're right, I'm in danger. But if you're not, I'm fine." She sighed, and then threw up her hands. "Sure. Fine. Whatever."

"But, Emma, darling." The little old man who was apparently her father, took a step toward her. "You've been through a terrible shock, and this won't do any good."

"I agree with you." She smiled at him faintly. "I don't think it'll do any good, either. But in case you're wrong, what's the harm in trying it his way?" Turning her attention to the Bishop, she couldn't help but enjoy how hopeful he looked. "If your exorcism works, will I get my memory back?"

His expression fell. "I can't promise anything, Miss Mather. Think of the corruption like worms, burrowing through your mind. They leave holes wherever they go. If we let the worms remain, they could continue to do further damage. But if we remove them, their tracks may not heal. Or at least, not immediately."

She shuddered at the image, the description causing a visceral reaction in her that made her skin crawl.

"Eat it! C'mon, Emmie, eat it!" The voice of a young boy played out next to her, and she jolted in surprise, staring at the empty air in horror. She knew the young boy was holding a fistful of worms—or had been—and was trying to convince her to eat the pile. Letting out a frightened whine, she stepped away from where the voice had been.

"It's all right, Emma, it's all right." The little old man was there beside her now, holding her hands in both of his. "That's normal."

"Normal?" Laughing incredulously, she shook her head. "What is wrong with me?"

"Nothing, darling. Nothing at all. I suppose I mean to say that it is normal for you. You hear the voices of the past like they're right there with you. You always have. It's part of your…particularities." The old man frowned. "Elliot called them his shadows. Yours always seemed friendlier than his."

"I'm—" Her heart sank. "I'm sick, aren't I? I should be in the Asylum, and this is all just—" Tears ran down her cheeks.

"No! No. You belong nowhere like that terrible place." Her father hugged her. "I vowed after what happened to your mother's family that you and your brother would never see the inside of such a monstrous building. You aren't sick. You're unique."

Unique. Right. Uniquely broken. She kept that to herself and, taking in a deep breath, let it out slowly. "No harm in doing the exorcism." *Maybe it'll cure me of everything. Or maybe it'll do nothing at all.* "If what he says is true."

Her father nodded and took a step away from her. "It's

your choice to make. Very well. We'll go through with this inane scheme." He shot a look at the Bishop that was likely meant to be withering, but only made her smile, seeing as he was attempting to threaten a man who was three times his size. "If you hurt her…"

The Bishop nodded. "I promise, she's safe with me." He placed his palm over his heart. "I give you my word, on the Altar of the Church of the Benevolent God, I only want to help her."

Her father let out a sigh and, reaching back to her, took her hand. "The Bishop has the most stellar of reputations, darling."

"Great." She chuckled. "It's not like it matters. I don't have anything else to try, do I?"

"I love it when religion is a last resort." The Bishop shook his head, shooting her a playful smile that endeared him to her just a little bit more. "It makes me feel great about my job."

Yeah, she was starting to like the Bishop, even if she probably shouldn't. "Let's get it over with."

"Are those *strictly* necessary?"

Emma—a name that she was slowly getting more used to each time she heard it used—had to agree with her father. The older man was standing by the wall, his brow furrowed, as Bishop Caner…strapped her to a bed.

The cuffs were thick leather, buckled tight around her wrists and her ankles, and attached firmly to the bedframe. She really wanted to make a sexual joke at his expense, but she wasn't going to do anything of the sort with her father—if he was her father—standing in the room with her.

The Bishop frowned and nodded once. "You'll see. If my suspicions are right, then yes. They're needed, trust me."

"What are your suspicions, Bishop?" She watched idly, still feeling a bit removed from reality, as he shackled her ankle to the footboard. "What do you think's happened to me?"

He watched her for a second, his green eyes flicking between hers, as he debated telling her. It was clear he didn't think it was a great idea. Maybe it was honor that drove him to finally speak, or maybe it was pity. She wasn't sure which, but she supposed it didn't matter.

"I believe your brother fell in with one of the Dark Societies."

Her father snorted. "Poppycock. Outrageous superstitions. Those so-called Societies don't *exist*, Bishop."

Caner ignored her father and kept his attention trained on her. "Your brother…is likely dead and gone. You were here searching for him. My Investigators kept an eye on you as best they could, but the Societies keep their work obscured, even from us. I believe you got too close to something, or someone." He turned his focus back to the shackle on her other ankle, finishing the task of lashing her down. "That's all I feel is right to tell you."

"Do you believe in magic?" she asked her father.

The little old man frowned and folded his arms over his chest. He watched her carefully. "I have seen things I can't explain. But to think that there is an underground network of warlocks and magicians here, right under our noses, is impossible."

"I wish you were right, Dr. Mather." Caner stood and moved to a table, unrolling a leather toolkit. She lifted her head, craning to see what was inside. Nothing that looked pointed or deadly. That was a relief. Caner picked up a bottle of liquid and pulled the cork from the neck of it. "How I wish you were right."

He turned to her and, holding his finger partially over the neck of the bottle, began to recite something in a language she didn't understand. It was archaic and ancient, and as far as she knew, not even the language of the prayers spoken by the Church.

The words put her teeth on edge. She felt anxious, her heart starting to pound a faster tempo in her chest. "What—"

He flicked the bottle of water, and the liquid hit her.

She screamed.

Something held her spine in its claws. Huge, impossibly pointed nails curled around her very being. She felt it digging in, even as something was trying to pull her away. More of those terrible words were spoken, louder over the sound of her wailing. She couldn't see anymore. The world around her didn't matter.

Just that hand around her spine. With every word, it tightened. With every word, it pulled her closer.

Mine. It wasn't a word. The thought itself was unfathomable. It was too large, too inhuman, too beyond her to truly understand. But the sensation ripped through her like lightning. She was owned, and she was not for this Bishop.

"Emmie! Emmie, come here!" The voice of a young boy called to her through the chanting and the hunger. Through the cruelty and the pain, and the *pulling. "Emmie, look what I've found!"*

A boy crouched by a river, giggling as he pointed into the stream. *"Fishies!"*

She ran up to him, smiling, eager to see the little animals that darted through the water, their scales shining in the sunlight. "Oh, fun!" She knelt at the edge, the water of the mud staining her skirts. She didn't care. Mother would be furious, but Father would simply smile. "Look at them go."

"They're my pets now." The little boy nodded. *"I'll come and feed them. Oh, what do you think they eat?"*

"Worms," she said even as she pondered her answer. "I think fish eat worms, don't they? Maybe little bugs, too. Like grubs."

"Oh, good idea." The little boy sat down and tapped his finger on his chin. *"How do I make them happier? Can I bring them gifts? They're my pets now. So I should take care of them."*

She chuckled. "I don't know what fish like for gifts. I suppose you can try different things and see."

"Maybe they'd like a new rock!" The young boy scrambled away, finding the largest possible rock he could lift. He grunted under the strain as he waddled back to the shore, carrying it between his knees as if it were the heaviest thing in the world. He threw it, as best as he could, into the stream with a loud *blooosh!*

It sent water splashing everywhere. She laughed, lifting her arm to protect her face from the spray. But the little boy wasn't laughing. He was watching the water, a dire expression on his face. He turned to her, and she could see tears streaming down his chubby cheeks.

"I think I hurt them. I didn't mean to!"

That single sensation came over her again, so huge, so immense, so vast compared to how very little she was. She was insignificant. An ant. A speck. She was the grub to feed the fish that had been crushed by the rock.

Mine.

Who was she to argue?

She was nothing.

Nothing at all.

CHAPTER TWENTY-SIX

Patrick held the young woman while she wept. The exorcism was over. It had...not been an easy one. Not for anyone. She was covered in sweat, and she had retched up the meager contents of her stomach. So had her father, once he had seen the vile things that had crawled out from her mouth and eyelids.

Black, wriggling things, the color of pitch. They shone in the dim light of the room. Two of the straps of the bed had snapped as she had screamed vile obscenities at them and thrashed in violent abandon. She wasn't strong enough to break the leather—but the creatures inside her had been.

He didn't know if he had succeeded. He didn't know if the darkness had fully left Emma Mather. But he knew they were all too tired to continue. Emma was curled up in his arms, her head down, and she was mindlessly crying. Hopefully, she wouldn't remember anything that had happened. If the Benevolent God stayed true to their name, she would simply wake up in a few hours, not knowing any of what had transpired.

Kissing the top of her head, he stroked her hair, doing his

best to console the poor thing. Her father had left the room, needing fresh air. The old man looked shaken to the core. Patrick would work on feeling superior when he wasn't so exhausted himself—*Is it still outrageous superstition to you now, Doctor?*

Best not to taunt the old man when he had just witnessed his daughter undergo such agony. No, the Mather family had suffered a great tragedy. The loss of a son, and the corruption of a daughter. It was something no family should ever have to endure.

When the young girl's tears had finally stilled, he carefully scooped her up in his arms. "We have a fresh room waiting for you. You can bathe, change, and get some rest. I have two nuns who will assist you. Once you're feeling well enough to travel, your father will take you home."

"Home." The word was a whisper, barely audible, and it broke Patrick's heart for how hopeless it sounded. As though the word was something that would forever be out of reach.

He carried her to the room in question and turned her care over to the two women who were far better suited to tend to Emma than he was. When he returned to the hallway, he pulled a handkerchief from his coat pocket and ran it over his forehead before rubbing it on the back of his neck.

He needed a stiff drink. It was against the law, he knew. But at the moment, he honestly didn't care. Walking to his office, he shut and locked the door behind him, before heading to his stash of liquor he kept locked away in one of the wood cabinets that lined the walls. His hand shook as he poured himself a few drams of whiskey.

It burned his throat, and it was absolutely what he needed. He poured himself a few more, filling the glass halfway, before he sank into the leather chair of his desk. Emma had been touched by the Great Beast of Arnsmouth. Infected by the darkness that slithered through every corner of this damned city.

He couldn't say if he was successful or not. He couldn't say if the disease had fully left her. It had wormed its way deep into her, farther than Patrick had seen in a very, very long time. Why was it so intent on her? Why did it want her and her twin so very badly? He chuckled sadly at his own foolishness and sipped the alcohol.

It didn't need a reason. It didn't need intention. It was a force of nature—of pure *evil*—and only had one singular goal in mind. It merely wanted to spread and grow. To consume all that it touched. To think that there was any sort of mindful intelligence behind it was giving it too much credit.

And giving him too much hope that it could be reasoned with. A creature with a mind could be rational. But a force of nature was simply that—immutable. And it was his duty to be the bulwark against it. It was his duty as Bishop to protect the city of Arnsmouth and all those within it. It was his duty as Bishop to protect the Mather twins. He hadn't been able to save one of them, but now he would do everything he could to save the other.

Something told him his work had only just begun.

DAYS TURNED TO WEEKS. And weeks turned to months. And little by little, Emma learned to answer to the name when it was called across the house. A house she was told she had grown up in, that she had spent years laughing and playing in. That when she was a child, she had crashed through the halls with her father's fencing foil, whacking and jabbing at her twin as he shrieked and ran away.

But they were just stories told to her. They meant nothing to her. They didn't trigger any hint of remembrance.

She could only smile kindly at the people who claimed to be her family, eat dinners together, and apologize quietly when they expected something from her that she couldn't give them.

She had met an older cousin who told her a lengthy story about Emma and her mother, with such hope in her eyes that it had broken Emma's heart. Everyone wanted to be the one to *help* her. The one to *fix* her. That maybe they had the shard of information that would put together the broken pieces of Emma's mind.

But it never worked.

And what came alongside the sinking disappointment was guilt. Emma felt terrible each time she let them down. She knew it wasn't her fault. She knew it. But that didn't stop her from feeling like a burden.

It was four months after she had left Arnsmouth when the dreams began. And it was a month after that when the dreams began to spill into reality. She found herself waking up in the middle of the night, staring at a spot on the wall or the ceiling. It looked like black mold at first. But when she went to touch it, it vanished, leaving nothing beneath her fingertips.

She learned to ignore the mold that began to appear in the daylight, just as she learned to ignore the voice of a small boy calling to her. A voice she knew wasn't real.

"Emmie, come play with me!"

"Emmie, I'm so lonely."

"Emmie, what's wrong? Why're you crying?"

She didn't dare tell anyone about the little boy she could hear, but never see. The one she knew was meant to be the voice of her brother, Elliot. The twin she was told she had loved above all else, and who had tragically died, though nobody knew how.

Elliot was dead. And for all intents and purposes, so was

Emma. She saw photographs of herself wearing men's clothing and standing beside her father, a large rifle slung over her shoulder. Photos of her in Africa, New Zealand, Tibet, South America. They were all fantastical places with strange and wonderful animals—she would *love* to remember meeting a giraffe. But they were as remote and removed from her as everything else.

Stories told to her about a woman she didn't remember existing.

There was a large part of her that wondered if she shouldn't let her body join the mind of the woman who had died in Arnsmouth when the Great Beast infected her mind. If she didn't deserve to be dead, and this was just an aberration. She thought about hanging herself or rummaging through her father's pills and taking as many as she could find until she died.

But she couldn't do that to the poor old man that she had come to adore, even if she couldn't remember why. She found him crying in his study late at night when he thought he was alone. Wiping at his eyes with his handkerchief, clutching a portrait of his family who had all left him.

His wife. His son. And his daughter was a shell of what she once was.

No, she couldn't abandon him. She couldn't take away from him the only thing he had left, even if it was a terrible facsimile.

But something had to change. Something had to be done. She couldn't live like this—not herself, not someone else, but trapped in between. She had to know what had happened to her and why. She had to fix it. She had to make the bastards who did this to her *pay*. They had killed Emma Mather. They had taken her away. And she was going to fucking *find her.*

It was six months after she had lost her memory that she resolved herself to action. Her father had gone overseas, and she was left alone in the home for several months. He finally trusted her not to do anything foolish but didn't consider her well enough to travel.

He was wrong on the first count. Very wrong. Because she was about to do something extremely foolish. She stood in her bedroom, staring at a spot of black mold on the wall. Mold that seemed to shine like it was slicked with oil.

Mold that seemed to *writhe*. It moved like boiling tar, shifting slowly. It made no sense, but then again, it wasn't real. Hallucinations didn't need to make sense. The line between the psychosis she was told she suffered from and the rest of whatever dark magic corrupted her was blurry at best. Indistinguishable at worst.

Was this her own mind?

Or some dark god, toying with her?

She supposed in the end it didn't matter.

Lifting her hand, she went to place her palm against the mold, but hesitated. "Show me. Tell me where I need to go. I want to be whole again, and I know you can help me." Placing her hand against the spot on the wall, she went tense.

It didn't disappear like it did every time before. It began to surround her hand, oozing around her fingers, crawling up her wrist. The sensation of it was as cold as ice.

This was a terrible idea. This was a mistake. But it was the only thing she could do—bad idea or not. She shut her eyes… and let it take her.

Mine.

There was a pull. A draw. A feeling of sinking, of falling. Of the weight of the world atop her, of miles of dirt, of wriggling tendrils pushing, needing, stretching, reaching. There was only the lonely void and the crush of tons of earth around her. She choked, able to taste the grit in her mouth. She couldn't breathe.

Make it stop!

Cold stone was pressed to her cheek. Cold, damp stone. She shuddered. She was soaked to the bone, her clothes clinging to her. She had been out in the rain for hours. But where was she? How was she—was this real?

Sitting up, she pulled her wet coat around herself, though it didn't do any good to keep away the chill. She was on the sidewalk, tucked against the wall like a vagrant. If people noticed her, nobody had stopped to check to see if she was all right. There was honestly no telling how long she had been there.

Shivering, she tried to understand what had happened. She had a purse, in which she found some money, keys, a notebook, and a small pistol. Furrowing her brow, she opened the notebook. It was empty, save for one message scrawled in writing that she couldn't identify as her own. It simply read *Flesh & Bone.*

Pushing herself up to her feet, she felt unsteady and leaned against the wall for a long moment as she tried to focus on breathing. She had no clue how she had wound up in a dark alley in the middle of the night, soaked through in the rain. But here she was. Or wasn't. Pressing her hand to her head, she tried not to cry.

The world around her felt real enough. She had to act on it, as she had no other choice. Where was she supposed to go? What was she supposed to do? Two words weren't much of a guide. As she struck out from the alley, she took a left turn and pulled up her steps.

And laughed.

It was sad and weak. But it was a laugh.

There, blinking at her, with its bright lightbulbs and garish paint, was a sign. *Flesh & Bone.* Beneath the name was another scrawl of carefully-painted lettering. *"See the gorgeous Gigi Gage!"*

It was a nightclub.

Taking in a breath, she held it and let it out in a groan. She knew this was probably suicide. But there was only one road in front of her. There was a small crowd waiting to get inside, gathered by the entrance, each with umbrellas over their heads. They had dressed appropriately for the rain. She very much hadn't.

Not knowing what to expect, she walked up to the clump of people. The bouncer saw her, a big man with a face that looked like it had been punched a few times. He grunted and gestured to one of his cohorts, who took one look at her before ducking inside.

It seemed they knew her.

Great.

She really wished she had the details on precisely *how* they knew her. Either she was about to be shot, or molested, or murdered, or fed a nice dinner and given a dry coat. Or all of the above, in any particular order.

A man stepped out of the door. She wrinkled her nose at the sight of him. She might not remember why she didn't like him, but his impression had run deep. He grinned wide, his expression just a little too feral. "Kitten-baby."

She narrowed her eyes at him. "That's redundant."

He barked a laugh and motioned for her to come inside. "Get out of the rain, sweetheart. Lady G wants to see you. She's so happy you've finally come."

"At least that makes one of us." Wrapping her arms around herself, she stepped inside the club.

"Don't you worry," the man crooned. "We'll take good care of you."

That's exactly what I'm worried about.

OF VISIONS & SECRETS

PATRICK FELT LIKE A FOOL, standing in the rain in the shadows of an alley. But when his Investigators told him that Emma Mather had returned to town alone, he knew trouble was brewing. He held the umbrella over his head, hearing the patter of the raindrops on the fabric overhead, almost drowning out the woosh of the nearby automobiles or the late-night streetcars.

He grimaced at the sight of the nightclub. He was well aware of the Flesh & Bone, and he knew the connections it had to the Great Beast. Not enough that he could prove anything—not enough for a public trial—but enough that he kept a close eye on the jazz club and speakeasy.

The illegal alcohol was the absolute least of his concerns.

"Oh, Emma," he muttered.

She should have stayed away. She should have stayed as far away from this damnable city as she could. He had begged Dr. Mather to take her away to England, or Switzerland, or Italy. Somewhere she would be safe, if his exorcism had failed in curing her of the corruption.

Which it was clear now that he had.

The little wooden figurine sat in his pocket, finished and ready to be placed on the board. He had hoped he would never have to use it. Broken as she was, she was at least *safe.* Her soul might go on to greet the Benevolent God when the day came.

But the darkness called her home.

And it was up to him to save her—or whatever was going to be left of her when the Great Beast was done.

"Oh, Emma," he repeated woefully. "What've you done?"

RAFE REACHED out and ran a hand over Hector's fur as the overweight cat pawed about on his desk, purring loudly and leaning into his touch as she did. His nights were lonely ones, save for his fluffy companion.

It had been six months since he had sent Emma away. Six months since he had kissed her last. And for six months, she haunted him. It was as though he had taken her life and kept it in a jar on his shelf.

Her laughter echoed in his mind. Her touch, her smile, the taste of her lips. The sensation of her in his arms. He didn't regret his actions—it was all he could do. There was no way he could let her be destroyed like her brother.

What other choice did he have? In the dark of the night, he could admit to himself how much he missed her. But at least his loneliness was for a woman who was out of his reach, and not in the grave. And for all he knew, she was safe at home. Caner performed his exorcism as Rafe knew he would, and cured her.

Or so he hoped.

A hope that shattered with a single phone call.

Lifting the receiver to his ear, he said nothing. And the presence on the other side spoke no words. For the Mirror did not trade in such things, and the Church was always listening. He shut his eyes as the knowledge simply pressed into his mind and was among the rest of his thoughts as if it had always belonged there.

Foolish Emma.

You should have stayed away.

He hung up the phone and pressed a hand over his eyes. Emma had returned, no doubt drawn by the pull of what lingered inside her soul. Standing, he gathered his things. Shrugging into his coat, he grabbed his lantern and an umbrella.

And one more thing.

He slid his pocketknife into his coat and let out a long

sigh. He didn't wish to use it. He had never wished to use it. But it seemed all his efforts had only delayed the inevitable.

As he struck out into the dark, raining night, he knew what he had to do.

He had to murder Emma Mather.

To be continued in book two of Tenebris:
Of Flesh & Bone

ABOUT THE AUTHOR

Kat has always been a storyteller.

With ten years in script-writing for performances on both the stage and for tourism, she has always been writing in one form or another. When she isn't penning down fiction, she works as Creative Director for a company that designs and builds large-scale interactive adventure games. There, she is the lead concept designer, handling everything from game and set design, to audio and lighting, to illustration and script writing.

Also on her list of skills are artistic direction, scenic painting and props, special effects, and electronics. A graduate of Boston University with a BFA in Theatre Design, she has a passion for unique, creative, and unconventional experiences.

Printed in Great Britain
by Amazon